FOOL'S GOLD

Sam Harris Adventure Series

Book 1

PJ SKINNER

First published as the Frog Cypher 2016

Fourth edition
ISBN 978-1-913224-05-9

Copyright 2019 PJ Skinner

Cover design by Self Publishing Lab

For my Family

Discover other titles in the Sam Harris Series

Hitler's Finger (Book 2)

The Star of Simbako (Book 3)

The Pink Elephants (Book 4)

The Bonita Protocol (Book 5)

Digging Deeper (Book 6)

Concrete Jungle (Book 7)

Green Family Saga

Rebel Green (Book 1)

Africa Green (Book 2)

Fighting Green (Book 3 coming soon)

Go to the PJ Skinner website for more info

www.pjskinner.com

Chapter I

Lindos 1987

Mike Morton couldn't believe his luck. He gazed over the railings of the yacht into the translucent water where shoals of small fish glided by, their scales flashing in the sunlight. After his conversation with Edward Beckett the night before, he had been standing on thin ice. Despite the intense heat, he shuddered at the memory.

'So far, the whole Sierramar venture's been a complete cock-up,' said Edward. 'My money's going down the drain. You spend it faster than my wife does.'

'It's true things didn't go so well this time, but it's new ground for us. There's still plenty of opportunity to make a big discovery. We have to chalk this up to experience,' said Mike.

'Experience, eh? In my humble opinion that's exactly what we're lacking. We need a geologist.'

'Well, yes, in ideal circumstances, but we have to pay for one.'

Edward had glared at him over the lip of his glass. The conversation had become awkward. Mike looked around for a distraction. He spotted a young woman sitting alone in the corner, eating her meal with the ferocity of someone from a large family or a stint at boarding school.

'Hungry?' he said, trying to be funny.

She had coloured, a bright traffic light red. She ate the final mouthful, chewing with savage intent on the food, and then gathering her things, she had stood up to leave.

He had apologised. Despite her scarlet face, he couldn't help noticing that she was attractive, in a boyish way, not the type of woman who interested him, but there was something about her, an independent spirit, a proud bearing. Her not wanting to attract attention had only made her more intriguing.

'Are you alone?' Damn. The wrong thing to say. She folded her arms over the book she carried as if defying them to comment further.

'Yes, I'm here finishing the dissertation for my master's degree,' she said.

The two men looked at each other.

'What subject?' said Edward.

'Geology,' she said over her shoulder. Mike glanced at her to see if she was joking. She headed for the exit with the air of a startled deer and she hit the doorframe at speed.

'Are you okay?'

But she left, rubbing her shoulder as she took the stairs two at a time. An opportunity lost, but he had pretended to be sanguine. He raised an eyebrow at his companion who looked amused and raised both in reply.

'So, what were we saying about needing a geologist?' said Edward. He chortled into his whisky. Mike snorted. He was not accustomed to being upstaged. He smiled at Edward, the tension dissipating from his broad back.

'The one who got away?' asked his friend.

'No woman has ever escaped from me. When I want a geologist, I snap my fingers.'

'So, you'd employ a female geologist, then? I didn't realise you were a feminist.'

'Edward, Edward, where have you been all your life? I guarantee she's desperate. Do you imagine it's easy for her to get a job? I know it's nineteen eighty-seven, but she hasn't a hope of being taken on in the real world.'

'You may have a point. Well, it's a small town. I expect she's here on holiday so you're sure to see her again. I suppose it's worth a try.'

'She'll come cheap and accept crap conditions. It's a win-win for us.'

'Ha! You're even more of a bastard than I thought you were,' said Edward. 'Don't tell my wife. She'll start a diatribe on women's lib. Do you fancy one for the road?'

'Yes, that sounds good. Waiter?'

***

Two months earlier, Sam Harris had been reading the travel section of a newspaper in the London University library when she noticed one of the travel agents offering a cheap package holiday to Rhodes, a Greek island she had visited in the past. Her last visit had left her with unpleasant memories, but Sam needed somewhere to finish her thesis after her lease ran out, and she was a pragmatist who found it hard to resist a bargain.

She replaced the receiver after her call to the travel agent, anticipating the sun beating down on her back already. It was cheaper to go to Rhodes than stay in London, and she loved Greek food. There was a free swimming-pool on her doorstep in the form of St

Paul's Bay, the smaller of the two bays at Lindos. *Luxury.*

Despite her glee, her mixed feelings about going to an island she visited with Simon surfaced and made her wonder if she had made the right choice. *He's not ruining this holiday too, the bastard.* She pushed him out of her mind.

'You're going to Rhodes again? That's nice,' her father said, as he drove her home from the university in a car filled to the roof with her belongings.

'Yes, it's so cheap, they are almost paying me to go.'

This elicited a smile of approval. As a member of the Harris family, it was compulsory to buy cheap and get a good bargain. The make-do and mend culture of World War II still obsessed both her parents, and they frowned upon full-price goods as the territory of the squander bug.

Sam bought into this philosophy and spent her life rummaging in sales and looking for cheap offers. Sometimes she wished she could go into a shop and buy something nice in her size at full-price like her sister, Hannah, did. But she always waited for the sales.

'Going back to Rhodes, darling? Are you sure that's a good idea?' said her mother. 'You know, with the whole Simon episode?'

'Yes, Mummy, I'm sure. I can't cross half the planet off my list because I've been there with Simon. He came here, remember? Are you suggesting I stop visiting you, too?'

'Don't be silly. I'm worried that it might upset you to go back to the scene of the big breakup.'

'It's fine. I won't have time to think about Simon. I'll be far too busy.'

***

The charter flight to Rhodes was full of crying children and grumpy parents, on their way to all-inclusive family resorts. *Thank goodness Lindos was so child-unfriendly.* The steep cobbled streets and tiny beaches of Lindos didn't suit buggies. They landed with a thud at the parched concrete airport and she stepped out into the heat, blinking in the bright sunlight. Within seconds her shirt stuck to her as sweat trickled down her back.

She left the airport and found the travel agency's bus to Lindos ready to leave, its driver idling the engine and releasing black smoke into the still, hot air. She showed him her voucher, and he directed her to the rear of the bus. It was air-conditioned, and she sighed with contentment as she leaned back against her seat in the cool air.

The bus made good time and arrived at Lindos as the tourist buses were leaving the car park on the outskirts of the village. Sam jumped off, collected her luggage from the hold, and set off down the main street following the map the agency had given her. She only lost her way once before arriving at her temporary home, but her rucksack got heavy by then and the straps dug into her shoulders.

The sign above the door said Sotiris Villas. She swung her bag onto the ground in relief and rang the doorbell. The owner who had waited for her in the cobbled courtyard let her in and grabbed the bag from her grasp. His rough, dry hands felt like the branches of an olive tree.

'Welcome. You're Sam?'

'Yes, and your name?'

'I'm Sotiris, your landlord.' He winked. 'Follow me.'

Shade covered the courtyard, but it was as hot as an oven. He took her to a door off one corner and led her up a short staircase into a studio flat. He showed her the little bathroom and kitchen, and stood with her in the main room which had a bed tucked into a cool corner at the back.

'Nice, eh? I put the typewriter on the terrace for you.'

'Thank you. It's wonderful.'

'You a writer?'

'No, I need to finish a project.'

'You're working on holiday?'

'Sort of.'

'Well, have fun. I live behind the red door if you need anything.'

He left, shaking his head.

Despite the heat, the apartment felt like a little piece of heaven. The building was painted white inside and out, with a balcony running along its length. Built into the steep side of the hills encircling the bays of Lindos, it provided a view of the entire town.

She stepped out on the balcony and found a small table with an ancient typewriter sitting on it. She squinted out over the glittering sea, breathing in the dry air. A cool breeze dried her sweat-soaked shirt.

She sat on the balcony until it got dark and the mosquitos found her. She thought about her last trip to the island when she discovered that Simon was a serial cheater and they had broken up after being together throughout their time at university. Missing the chance, as her mother pointed out, of meeting someone nice.

She still missed him a year later. His charm and wicked ways combined with his handsome exterior meant that Sam was as shallow as a puddle where he was concerned. She couldn't believe she would never see him again.

She went indoors with a sigh and closed the shutters on thoughts of Simon. The double bed invited her into its grasp and she succumbed to its crisp, cool interior.

***

Sam soon settled into her small paradise on the hill. Every morning, she descended the steep stone steps that cut through the cobbled streets of white, flat-roofed houses to St. Paul's Bay for a snorkel. After her swim, she climbed the hill back to her studio for some Greek yoghurt with fresh peaches or apricots and honey for breakfast.

She followed this ritual with a morning of work on her dissertation. Inking in the diagrams and charts was a painstaking business, but one made less tedious sitting in the shade of her balcony and gazing across the low, white houses of Lindos to the Crusader Castle. The shadow of Simon lifted and flew out to sea on warm zephyrs.

Most days, she spent an hour or two on the beach after the worst of the heat had dissipated, becoming as brown as a nut. One afternoon, she struggled up the hill to the castle in the blistering heat, narrowly avoiding being knocked over by some donkeys coming down from their last shift of the day, taking fat tourists up the hill to the castle, their grey coats caked in dust. She flattened herself against the cool wall and let them clatter past, their hooves slipping on the polished cobbles, their musty smell lingering in the air.

She made her way up to the top, where she stood on a platform in the ruins and gazed out to sea. A large yacht sailed into the bay opposite her studio. Several people sunbathed on the top deck, and even from the castle she could see they were naked. As the sun went down, she walked back to the studio through the cooling streets and got ready for dinner.

Sam ate at Philomonas's restaurant, her favourite, where she ordered a small Greek salad and a portion of moussaka. She was enjoying a gin with lime cordial and soda at her habitual corner table when a party of people arrived and sat opposite her. The five men and two women, tanned to a deep mahogany, had the aloof aura of the wealthy.

Could they be the occupants of the yacht? Both women were tall and willowy. They appeared to be a mother and daughter rather than sisters. The men were also tall, except for one older and stockier than the others, but still in good shape. He seemed familiar, but she couldn't place him.

Her food arrived, and she concentrated on the delicious meal, savouring every bite. She ordered another drink. When she finished most of her food, she glanced over and saw that some members of the party had already left. Only two men remained. They spoke in a manner that suggested a row but they did not raise their voices. She asked for her bill and gobbled up the last mouthfuls of food, wanting to get back to her studio to continue reading.

The older man stared at her making her uncomfortable. She still didn't remember where she had seen him before. *A friend of her parents?* Out of the blue, he made some stupid comments to her. Unwilling to engage, she excused herself and left, bumping into the wall in her haste to leave.

The next day she descended to the bay for her morning swim. She needed to swim around the yacht, moored beside the best snorkelling area, as if someone parked in her space. Despite the yacht, she was the only person in the water, and soon her observations of the local sea life absorbed her. A shy octopus, a master of disguise, fascinated her for an hour before she turned back to shore, swimming around the prow of the boat.

Someone shouted from above her and she craned her neck upwards. The man who had greeted her the night before was leaning over the railing, waving to get her attention. She recognised him even through the fog of her goggles. There was no way to pretend that she hadn't seen him. A light bulb went on in her head as she realised who he was: Mike Morton the notorious entrepreneur. She pulled the goggles up on top of her head and tried not to look surprised.

'I thought it was you,' he said, in his broad cockney accent.

'Hello,' said Sam. 'I remember you. We ate in the same restaurant last night.'

'That's right. I'm sorry if I appeared rude. Too many whiskies.' He grinned. 'I'd like to make up for it. Can you join us for dinner tonight?'

Not the most social being, and still embarrassed about the evening before, Sam fought her prejudices. She might be shy but she would not turn down dinner with Mike Morton. Rather a coincidence and definitely something to tell her family.

The man was a celebrity. Born in the East End of London, he became a successful businessman but his unfortunate habit of abandoning get-rich-quick-schemes and leaving his investors to flounder around without him, had made him notorious in City financial circles. Her father had fallen prey to one of these schemes and they rarely mentioned the name Mike Morton in the Harris household unless it was linked to an Anglo-Saxon insult.

'That would be nice,' she said. 'Same place?'

'Yes, we're meeting up there to eat and then on to Lindos-by-Night for dancing, if you fancy.'

'What time?'

'Is eight o'clock okay?'

'Yes, I'll be there.'

She pulled her mask back down over her face and swam to shore. Once she arrived at the studio, she ate her breakfast before sitting at the table to work but she found it hard to do any drawing. A famous person had asked her to dinner. That counted as a significant event and not one that was likely to repeat itself.

Sam found it hard to believe he had an interest in her for any reason, but the chance to meet him up close was way too tempting to turn down. He was a mainstay of the gossip columns and was once profiled by *The Sunday Times* magazine. His personal life was incontinent but his long-suffering wife stayed with him despite the tabloid reports of his various dalliances.

As the day wore on, the prospect of going to dinner with a man of such notoriety loomed larger in her mind. She needed to dress to impress. When she looked at the options, her sparse wardrobe alarmed her. She had not anticipated any glamorous evenings in Lindos, nor did she frequent such events. She had nothing suitable to wear.

Not wanting the two elegant women in the party showing her up, she walked into the narrow streets and looked for something to fit the bill. Most of the shops had their dresses hanging on rails out in the street, so searching for a suitable one didn't involve much effort. Sam chose a white dress with brocade on the bust, perfect for the warm evenings in Lindos. It was cheap but stylish enough to disguise its humble origins.

She examined her reflection in the mirror and

decided that she would pass. She had tried to style her hair but ended up putting it in a messy bun as usual. Five feet six in her socks, she had an athlete's body, mousey brown hair and green eyes, and skin that had tanned to a mocha colour. Stray freckles marked her nose and cheeks, making her look even younger.

She tried to imagine why Mike Morton had invited her to dinner but couldn't find an answer. She twirled around in her dress and stood on her toes to make herself look thinner. Her only footwear was an old pair of Greek sandals, but her budget did not stretch to anything better and they would come into their own if she wanted to dance.

Sam walked to the restaurant at half past seven judging that she would be the first to arrive and choose a chair with her back to the wall at the big round table. The streets shimmered with heat, full of people sitting outside their shops and chatting on stone benches built into the walls of the street. A cat followed her along the road carrying its tail in the air and brushing against her bare legs.

When she reached the door, the cat sat on the step as if to wait for her and washed itself with meticulous tongue strokes. Sam climbed the stairs to the roof garden, patting her bun to check for stray hairs.

Heading for the table, it surprised her to see Mike Morton already there, in the shadow of the oak tree that grew up from the courtyard, expecting her. A stocky man with a handsome face, at forty-two years old he had lost most of his hair with the rest cut short. He wore baggy linen shorts and a light-blue short-sleeved shirt, which emphasised his blue eyes in his craggy face.

'Hello,' he said, 'we should do introductions. I'm Mike Morton.'

Sam smiled and held out her hand.

'Sam Harris. It's a pleasure to meet you.'

'I'm glad you came early. I hoped I'd have time to talk to you before the others arrived.'

'What about?'

'I thought a project I'm doing might interest you. Would you like a drink?'

'Yes, please. A gin, lime and soda.'

Mike ordered their drinks as Sam wondered why he thought his projects could interest her. She was wearing a cheap dress and old sandals. It didn't seem likely that he was after her money.

'A year ago, I went to a cocktail party and Sierramar came up in conversation.'

'That's in South America, isn't it?' said Sam.

'Yes, that's right. One guest told me he used to work for a large petroleum company there during the sixties. Men from local tribes used to wander into their exploration camp in the jungle and offer large gold nuggets for sale. That got my attention, and I researched the country in the British library. It turned out that there were several productive gold-mining districts there during the nineteen fifties.'

'Didn't they close because of a lack of investment?'

'There are no working mines left, but that's because of the crap mining law. The mines are still viable. I contacted the Sierramar embassy and discovered that the government was on the brink of bringing a new law to liberalise mining and encourage foreign investment in the country.'

Mike paused and took a deep slug of his whisky, the ice clinking in his glass. Beads of moisture dripped onto the tablecloth leaving deep coloured stains. Sam sipped her drink too and tried to look relaxed. Mike Morton, the famous entrepreneur, talking to her about mining. She tried not to get excited. *Why tell her this story? Maybe he wanted her opinion on something?*

'That's great detective work,' said Sam, as he waited for some encouragement to continue. 'What did you do?'

'I visited my mate, Edward Beckett; he's the man you'll meet this evening, along with his wife and daughter. He's my wingman in these ventures. I met him at the Monaco Grand Prix twenty years ago and he's been the source of finance for them ever since.'

'And he agreed to fund your search?'

'Exactly. So, at the end of last year, I packed my bag and set off for Calderon, the capital city of Sierramar. The aftermath of the national holiday week *Las Fiestas de Calderon* greeted me on arrival. They celebrate the city's liberation from the Spanish by General Vasquez. There are bullfights every day for a week, and the entire population indulges in a seven-day orgy of drunkenness. The streets were littered with cans and bottles and sleeping revellers. I'm no slouch myself, you know.'

'I've read things about you in the past,' she said, unable to prevent herself from smiling.

'Have you now?' he said.

He looked at her from under his short eyelashes and winked, making her blush. A man who liked to be the centre of attention. It was obvious why women liked him. His strong animal magnetism made her sweat, but he had 'trouble' tattooed across his forehead. Sam did not need another Simon in her life, not one as notorious as Mike Morton. She determined to steer clear.

'Undaunted that I had missed the biggest partying week of the year, I got established in Sierramar with the help of contacts at the British embassy and acquired exploration licences. I resembled a lamb to the slaughter in the beginning. My first venture did not go well. They conned me out of a large sum of money and I wasted time digging holes in a barren riverbank on the fringes of the Amazon Basin.'

'But that didn't put you off?'

'It was my fault. I stayed in the most expensive hotel in town to impress people. The locals assumed that I had lots of money and fell over themselves trying to be the first to swindle me. I consider myself to be sharp and I'm not averse to double-dealing from time to time, but I never imagined the locals could con me. I was wrong. Gringos are prime targets in Sierramar. The national hobby is relieving dumb foreigners of their cash.'

'What are you going to do now?'

'I need a geologist to sort the wheat from the chaff before I spend any more of my investor's cash.'

'Oh, I see, and here I am.'

'And there you were. This is weird karma, us meeting. I need a geologist and you appear just like that. It's kismet.'

'I don't believe in fate,' said Sam, regretting it. *Get a grip*. The hairs on her arms stood up anticipating what he would say next.

'Could you work abroad if you got the opportunity?'

'Yes. I'd jump at the chance.'

'I think we might arrange that. Do you speak Spanish?'

'I did O-level Spanish so I'm not fluent, but I should be able to manage.'

'Water off a duck's back.'

Sam wanted to ask more questions but before they could continue, the rest of the party arrived and there was a tacit agreement not to talk any more business. Mike did the introductions.

'This is Edward Beckett, and his wife Ophelia, her brother Toby and his daughter Jocasta.'

'Hallo, I'm Sam.'

'Edward's been a client of mine for many years and he invited me to stay on his yacht. Sam's a geologist, folks. Isn't that great?'

Sam blushed and mumbled something self-deprecating, pleased that someone had taken her seriously for once.

After introductions, they ate, drank and had a good time. It was a relaxed evening. Even better, Ophelia and Jocasta wore dresses from a similar factory in India to the one she bought. After dinner, the party went dancing at the disco along the road but Sam needed time to digest the events of the evening so she refused the invitation.

'Can I have your number so I can call you when I get back?' said Mike.

'I'll be staying with my aunt in London when I return in two weeks' time. I'll give you her number.'

'Okay, that's perfect. Good luck with your dissertation, and I'll see you there.'

The yacht weighed anchor the next day, and the party set off for their next port of call. Sam watched from the ramparts of the Crusader castle until it disappeared over the horizon. She tried to be realistic concerning her job prospects with Mike Morton. Not a man on whom to rely, being more infamous than famous. There should be no counting of chickens, especially those from Sierramar, before they hatched.

And yet, she hoped that he would get in touch with her. *How often would she get a similar opportunity?* It was a risk of course. Everything about the man shouted cliché but gift horses and all that. There was nothing she could do until she finished her dissertation, which now appeared superfluous and boring. It was a real grind to finish, with the bay sparkling below her studio, beckoning her into its warm crystal waters.

Chapter II

On her return to London, Sam stayed at her Aunt Charlotte's home in Chelsea, a cosy two-up, two-down, Victorian terrace house, lined in books and paintings, on a side street behind the King's road. With the encouragement of an infinite supply of coffee and cake, it didn't take her long to finish her dissertation, and she handed it in at the university.

On her return, her aunt opened the front door of the house as she struggled to get the key in the lock, almost throwing her to the floor.

'A man telephoned for you. He said his name was Morton. Is he a new boyfriend?'

Sam flushed with excitement. Mike Morton's offer had been serious. Given the option of a job in Sierramar, however badly paid, there was no chance of her turning it down. She had already decided that if he didn't ring her, she take temporary secretarial work until something better came along. Temp work paid relatively well, and she had a good typing speed after doing her dissertation. At least she would earn money instead of sitting at home moping.

'Not really, Lottie. I'm hoping he might offer me a job.'

'A job? How splendid! Do I know him?'

'I don't think so. I met him in Greece. He was on a yacht.'

'Sounds like a good boyfriend,' said Lottie.

'Too old, I'm afraid, and too married.'

'Ah, that is a problem. The job will have to do instead.'

'When did he want to meet me?'

'Tomorrow at one o'clock in that little bistro on the King's road.'

'I know the one you mean. Thank you.'

'Perhaps he'll get divorced,' said her aunt, an eternal optimist where Sam was concerned. Sam had not told her about the reasons for her breakup with Simon, and she was unaware of her niece's determination to avoid boyfriends for the foreseeable future.

'Maybe,' said Sam, who had no intention of ever getting married but had given up telling people this, as they thought it was compulsory, like being born and dying.

The next day, Sam arrived at the bistro ten minutes early. The waiter showed her to a table with a red-checked tablecloth and a candle holder made from an empty bottle of Mateus Rosé. The minutes passed with no sign of Mike. She tried not to get concerned when he was late, or to consider the possibility he might not turn up at all.

She picked at the wax running down the neck of the bottle, flicking the pieces across her plate. The waiter glared at her, so she transferred her attention to the breadsticks instead. Mike strolled in as she finished the last one. He was twenty minutes late, but he did not apologise. Sam doubted if he even noticed that she had been waiting.

'Ah, Sam, you're here. Good. How are you? Did

you have a good trip home?' said Mike

'Fine, thank you. And you?' said Sam.

'Good, thanks. Master's finished?'

'Yes, I handed in my dissertation yesterday. Well, they still have to tell me if I've passed or failed but I have no worries on that front.'

'Excellent. Shall we order?' He signalled to the waiter who, to Mike's obvious exasperation, explained the menu in great detail.

'Don't bother with that. I'll have the rack of lamb, please,' he said.

'Me too,' said Sam, thrilled to order her favourite, which was normally way beyond her budget.

Mike got down to business.

'I want you to come and work with me in Sierramar,' he said.

Well, that was cutting to the chase. Sam noticed that he did not ask her if she wanted to work for him. She wasn't keen on his assumption but playing it cool was not the right tactic. She was also a little disappointed that he had not tried to flirt with her, having taken more than usual care over her appearance. Not that she fancied him, but it hurt her ego he didn't even notice.

'That'd be fantastic,' she answered. 'What would I do there?'

'Work as my project manager, reviewing the exploration projects I get offered in Sierramar and ruling out the scams and worthless properties.'

'When would I go?'

'Straight away. As soon as I can organise you a ticket. You can go on a tourist visa for the time being. We'll see about getting you a work visa once you've settled in.'

'How much will I earn?' She would have worked

for free but she couldn't tell Mike that. He looked nonplussed for a second as if it had never occurred to him that she would expect to be paid. He fiddled with his napkin.

'Um, I can't afford to pay you a salary in cash.' He raised his head and looked her straight in the eye, his voice more confident. 'I'll give you shares in the venture, which will be worth a fortune when the company floats on the stock exchange.'

Sam had no experience of owning shares in a start-up company but she understood what it meant money wise. She didn't want to risk annoying him and changing his mind, but she had no money left after funding her master's degree.

'So how will I pay for my expenses in Sierramar?' she said.

'I'll pay your round-trip ticket to Calderon and put you up in the company apartment while you're there. I'll cover your board and lodgings and give you petty cash for the occasional trip to the disco. You won't need much money if you're working in the jungle most of the time.'

'And when are you planning on floating the company?'

'I'm not sure. Probably in a year or so. That depends on you too. If we get a good portfolio of properties together quickly, it might be sooner,' said Mike, avoiding her inquiring glance.

'That's quite a long time to work with no salary,' said Sam.

Annoyance and frustration showed on Mike's face. Sam forced herself to think rationally. *He was banking on me being desperate. I'm honest to a fault, a character trait not common in Sierramar according to him, and not one that Mike himself is overly familiar with. He needs to work with someone he can trust, someone cheap. I must call his bluff.*

And she needed this job. There was no likelihood of being offered anything else in this market. The recruitment guy at university had made that crystal clear. This was a unique opportunity, and she wanted it. She soldiered on.

'The thing is,' she said, 'I took out a loan to pay for my master's degree. I must cover the monthly repayments if I'm to accept the position.'

'How much are you repaying the bank a month?' asked Mike

'One hundred pounds.'

'I think we can manage that.' He looked relieved. Obviously, he had imagined a much bigger payment. 'Give me your bank details, and I'll organise a monthly transfer. Does that suit you?'

Sam didn't know Mike well enough to question the likelihood of him setting up a monthly payment into her bank account. From what she had read in the newspapers, she doubted the chances of a rich haul from one of his schemes but having a geology job on her CV was priceless. She had also told a white lie as she only had to pay the bank fifty pounds a month but she wanted to have some pocket money and she would not beg.

'I'd love to go to Sierramar and work with you. You won't be sorry. I'm a quick learner, and I love working in the field,' said Sam.

This was not strictly true as the only time she had been in the field was on trips at university when she had slept in a hotel or hostel. She had no idea what it would be like in a jungle or if she could cope with the limited facilities. There was only one way to find out. Besides, it was exciting to be offered a job. Getting work as a junior geologist was difficult at the best of times. This was a genuine launching pad for her career, and she could learn to speak better Spanish, too.

'Okay then,' he said, 'sort yourself out and I'll phone you when I have your ticket.'

***

Sam returned home to her parents' house to get her field gear from the loft. She crawled up the rickety ladder which wobbled and almost fell as she reached into the cobweb-filled darkness and pulled her gear toward her. She had stuffed it up into the rafters after her last field trip and some of the clothes were still dirty. She dropped it onto the floor of the landing from where her mother, Matilda, surveyed her antics with concern.

'Do be careful, darling. Those steps are lethal,' she shouted up at Sam.

'Don't worry. I've finished. I'll be down in a minute. Just shutting the hatch.'

'We're so excited you've been offered a job. Where will you be working?' said Matilda

'Sierramar.'

'That sounds rather exotic. South America, isn't it? Which company?'

'None of the companies are hiring right now because of the recession. Do you remember Mike Morton?' said Sam, biting her lip.

'How could I forget?'

'I met him on holiday in Lindos and he's offered me a job.'

'Mike Morton offered you a job?'

Her mother did not hide the disapproval in her voice. Hardly surprising under the circumstances, but Sam pretended not to notice.

'I can't believe it. I'm so excited,' she said.

'That's nice, dear,' her mother said. She picked Sam's field gear off the floor and sniffed it cautiously, wrinkling her nose in disgust.

'Ugh. These clothes smell terrible. Do you want me to wash them? I can put them in the dryer and they'll be ready before you leave if you stay the night. I've put clean sheets on your bed and we're having lamb chops for supper.'

Sam thought about refusing, but she wasn't sure how easy it would be to get anything washed in Sierramar and she needed babying before her first big trip. Also, she noticed the strategically offered bribe of lamb chops her mother considered a deal maker. She didn't know Sam had eaten the same with Mike days earlier.

'Yes please, Mummy. You're an angel.'

She hadn't expected her mother to be keen on her going to Sierramar with Mike Morton. The fact he had swindled her father was not something that Sam found comforting regarding her new employer, but she had to focus on her budding career and getting experience on her resume, whatever it took. She needed some moral support. Her sister Hannah would understand.

Hannah was the antithesis of Sam, physically similar in height and build, but in character they were poles apart. Older by a year and bossy with it, she had a confidence that eluded Sam and a conservative outlook on life. She was also girly and couldn't understand why her sister was more like a brother and couldn't be persuaded to play with dolls or steal their mother's lipstick. She could be economical with the truth and was happy to let Sam take the blame for misdemeanours when they were younger. Luckily this had not affected their deep bond, and they always agreed when it was important.

'I hear you've got a job. That's brilliant,' said Hannah.

'Yes, I'm off to the tropics,' said Sam.

'That's amazing. Who will you be working for?'

Sam hesitated.

'Mike Morton.'

'Jesus. Are you serious? Mike 'the swindler' Morton?' Hannah's eyes widened.

'Don't be like that. He's not all bad.'

'How do you know? Are you sure this is a good idea?' said Hannah.

'I have the choice between temping in tights or going off to the jungle like Indiana Jones. What would you do?'

'I work in an office.'

'I meant what would you do if you were me, silly. I hate tights, and offices. This may be my only chance to be a real geologist.'

'How much are you getting paid?'

'I'm getting paid in shares and he's paying my expenses.'

'Is this a joke? You'll never get paid anything,' said Hannah.

'It's my dream. I don't need money. I need a job on my CV so I can kick-start my career. It'll be fun and great to experience something new. I can learn more Spanish too.'

'Couldn't you go to Malaga and pick up a waiter?' said Hannah.

'Don't be silly. It will be great. Think of it as a free holiday to Sierramar with expenses paid and a boost to my CV.'

'Now you put it like that, I suppose it could be an adventure.'

'Exactly, and you know how I love an adventure,' said Sam.

They both snorted.

'And, on the positive side, Simon will be nearly six thousand miles away,' said Sam.

'Now that is positive. Okay, you've won me over. Have a fantastic time. Will you be able to call me?'

'Thanks. I will, though I don't know if I can call you. I imagine it's expensive from over there. How about a postcard?'

'A postcard? Lots of postcards would be better,' said Hannah.

'Okay, lots of postcards. See you soon.'

'See you soon, sis.'

***

Later, while Sam watched television in the sitting room, Matilda Harris cornered her husband in the kitchen.

'I'm not enthusiastic about Sam working with that man,' she said. 'Do you think it's a good idea?'

'Ah yes, the dreaded Mike Morton, scourge of the private investor,' said Bill Harris.

'Don't joke, darling, this is serious.'

'It certainly is. That man took my money and made it disappear.'

His wife looked cross, and he raised a conciliatory hand to her face.

'I know what you mean, pumpkin, but it's a job. Experience is worth its weight in gold these days.'

'But what sort of experience will it be? Will he ever pay her?' said Matilda.

'I doubt it, but I don't think that's the point. Don't worry, I'll keep an eye on her bank account and make up for any shortfall. She told me he's only paying her a hundred pounds a month. Even he should be able to manage that,' said Bill.

'How much?'

'One hundred a month.'

'But that's terrible. We should stop her going.'

'No, I don't think so. Even if she gets no money, she'll have valuable experience that will give her more chance of getting the next job, one that pays more. It may even get her past the 'women can't work in mining' thing.' He sighed. 'Poor old Sam, she's such an idealist. No one can tell her that women's lib is a pipe dream and people don't believe men and women are equal.'

'She's always wanted to be a boy, ever since she was little. She got furious when I told her it wasn't possible. I despair of her ever settling down to a normal life like her sister,' said Matilda.

'Sam will be fine, darling. You'll see. A trip to the jungle could be what she needs to work things out. She can look after herself, you know. She's tough, she's got your genes.'

'You're right. Anyway, she's so excited. Did you see the way her eyes are shining? Nothing will stop her now.'

They kept their counsel and waved Sam off the next day without giving her a lecture on the evils of Mike Morton. Her father had tried a word of caution but Sam didn't want to hear anything bad about her new boss.

'I'm a grown-up, Daddy. He's no angel but I'm not naïve. I know what I'm doing and why I'm doing it. It'll be fun.'

'Watch out for those Latino men,' quipped her father.

'I'd say Mike Morton is far more dangerous,'

muttered her mother.

***

When the doorbell rang at the house on Eaton Square, Edward Beckett and his wife, Ophelia, were in the throes of a bitter argument.

'I don't know why you tolerate him. He's a charlatan,' said Ophelia.

'Now darling, don't be a bore. We've already talked about this. It's my money and I have a right to enjoy it. I earned it.'

'But wasting it on his cockeyed schemes?'

'It's not a waste. I love the thrill of the chase. It's more than unlikely that we'll ever strike it rich, but I enjoy funding a ludicrous adventure now and again,' said Edward.

'Ludicrous. Yes, that sums it up. You make me so cross.'

'Look, it's my casino money. I don't gamble or womanise. You should be happy it's such a small indulgence. There's the doorbell. Answer it like a good girl.'

His wife turned on her heel muttering and went to answer the door.

Mike Morton stood outside composing himself. He was sweating after his trip across town on the underground train surrounded by cute French exchange students with adorable accents, nearly distracted from his mission by the lure of the ingenue. Concentrating long enough to get off at the right stop, he inhaled the scent of the long brunette hair of the nearest student as he got off. What a pity!

He steeled himself for the sarcastic comments about his latest 'sure thing' and knocked on the door again. Ophelia opened it, glaring at Mike as if he were something nasty that she had picked up on her shoe.

'He's in there,' she said, indicating the study with a flick of her head. 'He's waiting for you.' She stepped back as if to avoid being contaminated by contact with the visitor.

Mike was immune to disapproval. He had the skin of a rhinoceros, vital to any entrepreneur who relied on other people's money.

'How nice to see you again so soon after our trip,' he said and headed straight for the study, where Edward Beckett was sitting in an armchair reading the newspaper with fake concentration, his greying hair coiffed. His manicured hands grasped the pink sheets in their soft fingers. He oozed wealth and privilege. Sometimes Mike hated the bastard.

Edward Beckett was a man born with the proverbial silver spoon in his mouth. A product of Eton and Oxford, and lots of family money, he treated Mike like an exotic pet from the East End, one he could flush down the lavatory if he lost his allure.

'Edward, old mate. How are you? Back to the grindstone?'

Mike forced himself to sound as upbeat as possible. Stoney broke after his run-in with the river gravel project in Sierramar; he needed to get Edward on his side again. He was confident he could still interest him in the possibility of owning a gold mine in South America if only for the kudos he would gain down at the club.

Asking for more than he needed was the best policy, as he had experience in being bartered down in similar circumstances. Edward Beckett could afford to be generous. He loved making money, and he understood Mike's need to get rich quick. Edward looked up from his newspaper with a warm smile, a sign that it would be a good day. He smiled back.

'Let's hear it then,' Edward said, knowing his friend needed no encouragement.

'I'm, um, sorry that our first venture in Sierramar didn't go well. They did me up like a Christmas turkey on that one. I'd like to have another go. Do you remember Sam, the geologist we met in Lindos?'

'Of course,' he answered, 'we had dinner with her. She seemed like an interesting young woman.'

'I've convinced her to come over to Sierramar for a modest salary to help me select projects. It's more than I expected but she has experience. I believe she will prove her worth,' said Mike.

He felt bad lying to Edward about Sam, but he might need extra funds if he got in a tight spot. Sam needed the job more than the money, and she would profit from the shares in time, so everything would turn out all right. He went on.

'Armed with our experience of the first dud project and Sam's help, we've got a much better chance of success. We've a first mover advantage over there. There are amazing projects lurking all over the country. If you want to get involved again, I guarantee you it'll go better this time. The gold price is on the move and there's lots of money to be made. We could make millions with the right deal. Millions.'

Edward looked at his friend, who sweated with anticipation. He couldn't help feeling that frisson of excitement that kept him investing with Mike, time after time. He would not miss out on a gold mine. That was for sure.

'What's the deal?' he said.

Chapter III

'You're a geologist? Don't geologists have beards?'

The hum and chatter of the airport filled the silence that followed as Sam searched for a comeback. The man smirked at his friends. *Why did she speak to this idiot in the first place?* She should have told him she was an air hostess. There was no point in fighting back. She had learned this the hard way.

She shifted from foot to foot on the tiled floor, her face burning with shame.

'Um, well, I've tried, but it's not working.'

She rubbed her chin as if searching for bristles and tried to smile, desperate not to be labelled as a humourless feminist. That fine line again. The combined effect of faking a smile and choking back a retort resulted in more of a snarl.

Uncertainty replaced the gloating expression on the man's face. He stepped back, falling over a suitcase behind him and landing in an undignified heap at the feet of his companions. He kicked the bag and swore. She allowed a delighted grin to creep over her features and she took a photograph for future reference with her green eyes. She turned away from her aggressor and sat in a quiet corner of the airport to wait for her next flight.

Although uncomfortable, the plastic chair felt like a refuge. The encounter had unsettled her. She had minimal chance of being accepted in the mining industry even though it was nineteen eighty-seven and the supposed liberation of women had happened decades before. If she wanted easy, she had chosen the wrong career. Yet, of all the people in her master's year, she was the only one with a job.

Working with a dodgy entrepreneur who couldn't pay her in cash, and might not pay her at all, wasn't the most desirable of situations, but the key to getting better paid work was having experience on her resumé. She couldn't resist the chance of adventure that Sierramar offered. She had no idea what awaited her in the mountains and coastal jungles but she was off to Latin America, if not to make her fortune, at least to make a start on her career. A beard was optional; a brain was better.

Once she settled into her seat on the aircraft, Sam dug around in her rucksack and pulled out her new book *The Lost Treasure of the Incas*. She picked it up in a charity shop when she was looking for some second-hand clothes suitable for field gear. Her search had yielded two pairs of khaki trousers with lots of pockets, one of which was a little tight, but she was planning on losing weight.

While she was paying for the trousers, she spotted the book on a shelf behind the counter and couldn't resist buying it. She had already read several chapters, and while the style was dry, the story of the lost hoard fascinated her. Tales of El Dorado and ancient treasure troves in Latin America were old hat, but there appeared to be at least a grain of truth to this story of Inca gold. The best bit was that someone had hidden it in the mountains of Sierramar.

Sam speculated how much it would be worth. She wanted to believe that it was still there, no matter how unlikely it seemed. Geologists spend months looking for the tiniest traces of gold. Imagine finding mountains of it.

Landing at Calderon, the capital of Sierramar, was alarming and exhilarating in equal parts. The plane swooped low over the city, right over a circular stadium, so close that Sam could see the individual seats. The jet landed with a big thud on the patched runway and continued along it for miles in the thin air of Calderon before it slid to a halt.

As the aircraft pulled up at the gate, the crew swung the door open and Sam staggered down the steps, stiff from twelve hours in the small seat. She had moved to the non-smoking section of the aircraft, but she smelt as if she'd been to a pub. The bright sunlight assaulted her eyes, and she fumbled in her bag for her cheap sunglasses.

Airport security guards with large guns and small stature watched her as she joined the queue of passengers at immigration.

The process of stamping their passports took ages because of the lack of agents. The desperation on people's faces grew with each passing minute. Sam's mother would have prescribed a nice cup of tea, but then she would have done the same for someone suffering from bullet wounds. Sam hoped that Mike Morton would remember to turn up.

When Sam got to the front of the queue, the man stamped her passport with a ninety-day visa and she was waved through with a big smile before she could even explain what she was doing in Sierramar. She soon found her bags, which were already doing an endless loop on the carousel.

She threw them onto a wonky trolley, pushing it through customs, veering further and further to the left until an agent grabbed the front wheel and pulled her through. He didn't show the remotest interest in her, being far more focused on the locals arriving home from Europe with their bulging suitcases of contraband and more clothes than Liberace.

When Sam emerged from the airport building, Mike Morton was waiting for her, surrounded by the excited relatives of the other passengers on her flight. It was Sunday afternoon, and he had the air of a man only recently emerged from his bed. His face was puffy, and he looked tired and cross.

'Hi Sam. Good flight?'

'Yes, thanks. Like clockwork. We flew over a stadium as we were coming in to land. Do you know what it is? A round thing?'

'Ah yes, that's the bullfighting plaza. They have a festival once a year with matadors from all over the world. When the bullfights are boring, the aficionados shout *Õle* at the planes instead of the matadors. That your bag? Okay, let's go then.'

'How are you?' said Sam. 'You look tired.'

'Not bad. I've got a terrible chuchaqui.'

'Chuchaqui?'

'Hangover. It's a Quechua word, the most common of the indigenous dialects in Sierramar. The Spanish is bastardized here. I use the word a lot.' He grinned at her.

They got into a battered four-wheel-drive vehicle and then drove along pitted roads with rows of dangerous looking concrete bumps up the middle, lined by low-level, shabby buildings made of breeze blocks with zinc roofs. Here and there, with increasing regularity, a tall new building broke up the lines of houses. They drove along the middle of the valley as the city of Calderon rose away up steep hills on both sides. To the west, a large mountain with a skirt of conifers loomed over the city. Above the trees, a black cone covered in snow rose into a sharp peak.

'Wow. A volcano in the suburbs,' said Sam.

'Yes. And it's still active, in case you were wondering.'

'Funny place to build your capital.'

'Funny people. They live day to day here. That it could blow them to smithereens at any moment doesn't register.'

'Like Mount Etna?'

'Yup.'

It occurred to Sam that Mike was living there, too, but it didn't seem like the right time to comment. They turned up onto the eastern flank of the city and into a long avenue lined with modern blocks of flats, each one newer and taller than the last.

Mike stopped at one made of glass and chrome and pressed a button to open the security gate to the basement carpark. He drove down the ramp and parked in a numbered parking bay near the elevators. They got into the lift and rose through ten levels of luxury apartments stopping at the eleventh floor. The chrome doors opened to reveal an entrance hall with a large wooden door.

'You'll like the apartment, Sam. Since you were looking out of the window as you landed, you may have noticed that the plane swooped over an avenue of tall buildings on your way into the airport. That is the Avenida Miranda where we are now.'

'It looks wonderful.'

Mike opened the door and Sam entered what looked like a show flat. It was huge, light and airy with shiny wood floors and sparse furniture. She tried to hide her dismay but Mike saw her expression.

'We're short on furniture,' he said, 'but we've ordered more. Your bedroom is the one on the left at the back. Let me show you.'

They walked around the apartment looking into the rooms. There were three large bedrooms, all with en-suite bathrooms and built-in wardrobes. The dining area was in the central part of the apartment which was open plan. It led into a huge empty living room with a stereo system on the floor against the back wall.

There was also an area off the living room that served as an office. This held two desks and a filing cabinet. There were no carpets, rugs or curtains and the walls were bare except for a map of Sierramar with illegible scribbles all over it.

'That's the master plan,' said Mike. 'It's sketchy right now.' He gestured at the windows. 'The furnishings are sparse but you can't complain about the view.'

Sam, who mourned the lack of a comfortable sofa or chair to read in, gazed out of the apartment, first to the front and then to the back. The windows in the living room looked over most of modern Calderon and showcased the enormous volcano on the other side of the valley.

The view from the back of the apartment was even better, taking in the valley of Bella Vista and several more snow-capped volcanoes, including El Grande, which resembled an ice cream cone. Mike had given her the back bedroom with no view, and she fancied the other one looking over the valley. Best to wait until he was in a good mood and ask to move then.

She turned down offers of food and returned to her room to unpack. She opened her suitcase to find that her mother had concealed extra supplies of tea bags amongst her clothes. It made her smile. Living at home often cramped her style, but this was her mother's way of saying 'I love you'. There were also some bars of Cadbury's chocolate and some McVities chocolate digestive biscuits. *Ready for anything then I guess.*

***

Further up the Avenida Miranda, a few of the old colonial style houses still stood, squashed between the new concrete towers. In the prettiest and most decrepit of them, Alfredo Vargas, Sierramar's pre-eminent young historian, paced the room trying not to look at the bottle of whisky that sat on the table in the middle. The golden liquid changed colour as the dim light entered through a gap in the heavy velvet curtains, falling on the bottle. Vandals had broken the streetlight outside months ago so he could tell it was the sun creeping through.

Alfredo often lost track of time as he worked through the night without result. He grabbed a notebook and sat down in a tattered armchair, the smell of his unwashed body rising on the puff of air released from the cushions. It was time to have a shower. He ran his fingers through his prematurely grey salt-and-pepper-coloured hair, making flakes of dandruff fall on his battered tweed jacket.

How was it possible that, after twenty years, he still couldn't figure out where a tribe of primitive people had put a hoard of treasure in a tiny country like Sierramar? There must be something he had missed. He was a failure.

Something hidden in those piles of paper and books spilling all over the floor like an explosion in a library. *Could someone have already found it and* taken it out of the country, piece by piece, undetected? What if they had melted it down to disguise its origin?

To make things worse, his dear friend, and the financier of his adventures, Jorge Vasquez, had died and left him lonely and penniless, removing his only hope of finding the treasure. Never again would they talk through the night beside a campfire or spend the expedition's funds in a filthy cantina at the bottom of some remote mountain. Their chaotic adventures were over.

Bereft and empty, he felt as if he had lost an organ. He reached into his pocket and pulled out the compass Jorge had given him on his deathbed, polishing it with his shirt tail. The battered instrument could be a useful tool but its sentimental value was incalculable.

When Jorge died, Alfredo's first reaction had been to drink all the bars dry, but this hadn't given him the relief he craved. His search for the elusive treasure was the only thing that gave his life meaning.

In one last effort to sharpen his mind, he had given up drinking. Five whole months without a drop. But he had failed to solve the mystery of its hiding place, and the bottle sat on the table, a testament to his weakness.

He had kidded himself that he was buying the bottle for 'guests', not that he ever had any. It took less than a minute to buy, hardly time to change his mind and now he weakened, enslaved again by its siren charms. He imagined the whisky burning a path down his throat and the intake of breath as it hit his stomach. One drink would be enough to calm the demons that tormented him. But that was the problem. It would not be a single glass. It never was.

Why had he bought the damn whisky? Why was he such a failure? He grabbed the bottle from the table, and a glass tumbler from the cupboard, and went to the kitchen to get some ice.

***

Mike dropped an Alka-Seltzer into a glass of water and swirled it around with his finger. He was relieved Sam had come to Calderon. They hadn't exactly gotten off on the right foot but he blamed Edward for that. Edward had put him under pressure in Lindos and treated him as if he was disposable. If things didn't go as planned in Sierramar, he was walking a tightrope.

Chapter IV

When it was light, Sam had a shower in the pristine new bathroom, leaning into the hot water and letting it run down her back, which was stiff from the twelve-hour flight. She dressed in a T-shirt and jeans and put her hair in a bun before venturing out of her room where she bumped into a young mulatto woman who seemed unsurprised to see her and addressed her in Spanish.

'Buenos días. Yo me llamo, Tati,' she said. *'Yo soy la empleada.'*

The young woman spoke with a strong, almost impenetrable accent but Sam understood that her name was Tati and that she was the maid.

'Buenos días. Yo me llamo, Sam,' she said.

There was an awkward silence while Sam searched her memory for another phrase that might suit the occasion but she was too jet-lagged and shrugged. Tati was used to foreigners who didn't speak much Spanish. She was not put off by her mute guest. Beckoning Sam over to the table, she gave her a breakfast of eggs, toast and tea.

At half past nine, Mike's personal assistant, Marta Perez, let herself into the apartment and sat down at one desk. Her legs dangled over the edge of her chair, and, despite her vertiginous heels, did not quite reach the floor. She wore a lot of make-up with clumps of mascara on her long lashes and a huge quiff in her long, wavy, bottle-blonde hair. She had squeezed into a skin-tight skirt and jacket with a frilled shirt spilling out of it covering an ample cleavage. Rings swamped her fingers, and she jangled when she moved due to the number of bracelets she wore.

She stared at the interloper with frank interest before speaking, and Sam felt underdressed compared to someone who appeared to have stepped out of a New Romantics music video.

'Buenos dias. You must be Sam?'

'Um, yes, buenos dias. I'm sorry but I don't know who you are.'

'Marta, Marta Perez. I work for Señor Mike as his assistant.'

'Oh, I see. It's nice to meet you.'

'Did you have a good flight?'

'Yes, thank you. A little jet-lagged. There are no curtains in the bedroom so I couldn't sleep well after it got light.'

'You'll get used to it. I've tried to make Mike buy curtains but he doesn't think they are essential.'

Sam heard the italics and imagined that Marta and Mike had not seen eye to eye on this matter.

'It's lovely and sunny today. Is it always like this?'

'Most days. We are on the equator here so daylight lasts from six in the morning until seven in the evening every day of the year except for the rainy season. Do you speak Spanish?'

'Some. Not well, I'm afraid. You speak beautiful English. Where did you learn?'

'I spent several years in Miami. I can help you with your Spanish if you like.'

'That would be great. My spoken Spanish is rusty but I understand most of it. Does anyone else work for Mike?'

'Hernan Sanchez's daughter, Gloria.'

'And what does she do?'

'*Chica*, Gloria is the daughter of Hernan Sanchez; she does anything she wants to.'

'Is he an important man in Calderon?'

'Yes, he's Mr Big.'

'Mr Big, okay then,' said Sam, feeling out of her depth. 'What time does she get here?' she asked, although she already knew the answer.

'Whenever she feels like it, but I doubt she'll be in today. She had a party last night.'

A dismissive swish of the hair followed this, and question time was over.

***

As predicted, Gloria did not come to work but Mike was not at all fazed by this. He took Sam to eat at a local restaurant so they could meet her there instead. Gloria kept them waiting half an hour before she appeared, cigarette in one hand and expensive handbag in the other. She gave Sam a long, appraising look before offering her face for a kiss on either cheek. Not wanting to appear intimidated, Sam stared right back.

Gloria was petite with a large bosom and skinny legs. She wore a yellow silk blouse with big, red roses, and a pair of skin-tight designer jeans. She had multi-coloured hair that had been a reddish-auburn colour but had succumbed to various experiments in the hair salon. It was long with natural curls and made Sam jealous. Like most of the girls in Calderon, Gloria was made-up to the nines.

The overall effect had originally been sultry but

her mascara had flaked around her eyes, giving her the look of an indignant panda. Sam wondered if she had been wearing it since the night before. Gloria was not the least put out by Sam's inspection, and she pouted with her cigarette held in the air. Then, tossing her head like an impatient pony, she led them into the restaurant.

The place was packed, but when they walked in with Gloria, a table became available as if by magic. There was an air about her that mesmerised mere mortals. She was polite but it was like a veneer over something harder and more threatening. The maître d' almost wet his pants when she sent back her soup to get reheated.

The soup was fine and it had started out hot but her constant smoking stopped her from making any progress. She chain-smoked throughout lunch oblivious to the fact that Sam and Mike were eating, and then, she spoke to Sam, somewhat at random, on the subject of her boyfriend, her husky voice conspiratorial.

'Aye, *chica*. Diego isn't treating me right.'

'Oh?' said Sam, not sure of the correct response to this revelation, voiced with real emotion. There was a vulnerable centre to the onion that was Gloria.

'Not taking me seriously. He's happy to get drunk and do chaka-chaka with me, but last night he disappeared and I heard someone saw him with another woman.'

'How dreadful,' said Sam. Gloria's boyfriend, Diego, sounded like a complete jerk, but it was rather a lot of information for a first meeting.

'Oh yes, he likes to get drunk with me, but I want him to get serious.'

'How annoying. You must be a saint to put up with that behaviour.'

Mollified, Gloria drank her coffee and sucked on another cigarette. Sam felt as if she had passed a test.

'What's the story with Gloria?' she asked Mike on their way home from the restaurant.

'She's the daughter of one of Sierramar's richest and most powerful men. I met him at a cocktail party given by the chamber of commerce. He asked me if I would give her a job to keep her out of mischief. So, I did.'

'Does she work full time?'

'Sort of. Gloria is not the most diligent worker but she's effective. If we go out with Gloria, we always get a table, no matter how busy it is. She helps me on an ad-hoc basis,' said Mike.

From the way Gloria and Mike talked to each other, there might have been some other ad-hoc activity involved from time to time but she didn't comment.

'She certainly seems to get around. That Diego sounds like a bastard,' said Sam.

'Yes, I think he's only using her to make contacts. She's more vulnerable than she looks.'

'Does she have children?'

'No, she's not married, and anyway she told me she can't have children. I'm not sure how she knows. I didn't want to pry.'

***

Gloria turned up the next morning and took Sam to buy maps for Mike at the Geographical Institute perched on a hill at the boundary between old and new Calderon. The only way to get there was by car. Driving in Sierramar was an erratic affair because most of the population bought their licenses on the black market instead of taking a driving test.

Gloria drove as if she were being chased by the four horsemen of the apocalypse, putting on her lipstick and lighting cigarettes at high speed, while nonchalantly throwing the jeep around the corners on two wheels with one hand. Sam gripped her seat with white-knuckles.

'Are we in a hurry?' she said, hoping to alert Gloria to her distress.

'Oh no, *chica*. Mike told me to drive slowly because you were not well and might vomit. I drive a lot faster than this.'

When they got to the gates of the institute, armed guards stopped their jeep and asked them to park in the street and walk up the steep driveway instead of parking in the car park at the institute.

'I have a sore leg, officer,' said Gloria, fluttering her long eyelashes at him. 'I can't climb all the way up that hill in these heels.'

'No one may park up at the institute except the management.'

'Oh, but I would only park for a short time. I have to collect something. Please let me drive up. Or you'll have to carry me.'

The teenage soldiers giggled at the thought but allowed Gloria's blatant flirting to persuade them. They kept the women's identification papers as surety, but for what, Sam couldn't imagine. Gloria drove the car up the hill and parked in a reserved space, a fact she ignored.

They entered the institute through a large door into a cool vestibule lined with kiosks occupied by uniformed staff who dealt with the different stages needed to purchase a map. The maps Mike wanted them to buy were of areas close to the border with Peru, so they had to fill in a form and sign a promise they would not give the maps to any foreigners. Sam found this amusing. Each map had a separate form and they had to fill them in triplicate using ancient carbon paper that did not transfer the writing to the next page, a process Sam found time consuming and irritating.

'You know Mike is dyslexic?' said Gloria.

Sam shook her head.

'He often gives me the wrong reference numbers. There is only one public telephone in the building, so it's difficult to call him and check them. I've had to return to the office and start again more than once.'

When they had filled in the forms with the correct serial numbers, they took them upstairs to Colonel Fernandez, the senior officer on site, for countersigning. He kept them waiting half an hour outside his office before he found the time to sign their form. Sam got impatient.

'This is ridiculous,' she said, 'In England we choose the map we want from a rack, pay and go. Why do we have to go through all this bureaucracy?'

'That is how we do things in Sierramar. You will have to be patient.'

Sam sighed. There was nothing to be done about this stupid system. Gloria pretended not to hear her. When the colonel's secretary beckoned them in, he was in an expansive mood.

'Buenos dias, Señoras, how can I help you today?'

'Please sir, can you sign the form for us so we can get some maps for our work?' asked Gloria, batting her eyelashes with practised skill. The colonel was much more interested in Sam, who fidgeted in her seat, bored by the whole process.

'Do you speak Spanish, señorita?'

'I used to, Colonel. I learned to speak at school, but I'm still trying to remember it.'

'No problem, your friend will translate,' and here he looked at Gloria who gave him a curt nod, her attempts at flirting having been ignored.

'Do you know why I have to sign this form for you?' he asked Sam.

'No, I don't, I'm afraid,' said Sam. *Maybe to annoy them by stringing out the process?*

'During the conflict of 1941, Peru stole a large piece of the Amazon basin from Sierramar. Since then the two countries have disagreed about the border position between them. The government of Sierramar has refused to redraw the border or issue new maps. It's illegal to bring a map into the country with the new border on it.'

Sam remembered the map on the wall of Mike's apartment. It had the new border. *Contraband.* She tried not to smile.

'I thought the war was over forty years ago. Why haven't they fixed the border's position yet?'

'As part of negotiations to end the war, a remote river valley between two mountain ridges was proposed and accepted as the border between the countries. The advent of aerial photography and satellite photographs has led to discovery of a second parallel valley on the Peruvian side which has generated disputes about which river was originally intended as the border.'

Gloria said, 'Sierramar has refused to change its international boundaries to exclude the part annexed by Peru. The hostility between our two countries still simmers and bubbles over.'

'I had no idea,' said Sam.

'The result of all this controversy is that the nearer an area is to this disputed border, the more difficult it is to buy a map. That is why you must come and see me to get permission for copies of any maps in that area. To check that you are not a Peruvian spy.'

Sam felt embarrassed at her attitude, which he had read.

'Thank you, Colonel.'

He nodded and signed the form.

'Have a good day, ladies. See you again.'

He winked at Sam who was unsure how to reciprocate but she winked back anyway. When in Rome...

They went downstairs to queue at the cash desk. This time Sam did not complain. She tried to imagine what it was like to lose a large chunk of your country to an aggressive neighbour. Chastened, she muttered, 'I had no idea about the border.' Gloria did not comment.

***

'Hi, Daddy, it's Sam. Can you hear me?'

'Hello, darling. Yes, you sound as if you're next door. Are you?'

'No, I'm still in Calderon.'

'How is it? Have you been to the field yet?'

'It's amazing. Not what I was expecting. It's not as different, well, superficially anyway, as I thought it would be. There are no parrots in the streets, for a start. I suppose I haven't been here long enough to know.'

'But are you enjoying it? Mike treating you okay?'

'Oh yes, he's generous. We go out most days to eat somewhere in town. Mind you, it's cheap here.'

'Have you met anyone nice?'

'Yes, there's Marta, Mike's assistant and Gloria, she's brilliant. You'd like her, Daddy. She drives like Fangio.'

'Hmmm. I hope you're wearing your seat belt.'

'Of course. And I'm forcing Gloria to wear hers, too.'

'Excellent. I can't have a daughter of mine driving around without a seat belt.'

'I know, Daddy. How's Mummy?'

'She's here, hanging on every word.'

'And Hannah?'

'Oh, you know her, boyfriend trouble again.'

'No surprise there. I won't chat long. It's expensive and I don't want to abuse Mike's hospitality.'

'That's all right, sweetheart. We're happy that you're safe and having a good time. Call soon with news.'

'I will. Bye.'

'Bye, Sam.'

'Should we have told her that Simon is looking for her?' said Matilda Harris, when he had hung up the receiver.

'No,' said her husband. 'Best not to. Water under the bridge and all that.'

Chapter V

Sam's Spanish soon improved enough to communicate with Tati and Marta, to take a taxi and order food in a restaurant. The local accent was easy to understand, and she was soon incorporating local idioms into her phrases. Fascinated by the huge wealth gap in Calderon society, she was desperate to understand more of what people discussed.

Her friendship with Gloria meant people always invited her to social events, but she often felt left out by her inability to speak Spanish as well as she understood it. She worked hard on picking up jargon and local usage. Gloria corrected her worst mistakes and encouraged her as she struggled to string a lucid sentence together. When Sam got frustrated and refused to try any more, Gloria put her back on the horse.

'*Chica*, there are gringos who've been here ten years who can't do more than ask for a beer in Spanish. It'll be worth it. You'll see when you go into the jungle and need a taxi.'

Sam glanced up and saw she was having her leg pulled and smiled. She liked Gloria and her down-to-earth manner. People from Sierramar had their own way of doing things but Gloria was proving to be kind and funny. And Sam needed a friend. She was far from home and she hadn't appreciated how isolated she would feel in Mike's empty apartment. There wasn't anything to do, and they had no television.

'What's the point? All the programmes are in Spanish,' said Mike when Sam asked.

'It would be a good way for me to improve my Spanish and keep up with the news. I could tell you what's happening in other countries,' said Sam.

'The way things are going, I'm happy to live in blissful ignorance,' said Mike.

'Most of them are in English with Spanish subtitles,' said Gloria, but Mike was unmoved.

'Let's wait until we have a sofa.'

But no sofa appeared. Sam sat alone in her bedroom at night listening to her Sony Walkman and trying to read the local newspaper to improve her vocabulary. *Had she had made the right decision coming to Sierramar?*

There was not enough work to do. She did her best to be pro-active and stumbled through a document listing the mineral prospects of Sierramar, with the help of a dictionary and the similarity between English and Spanish geological terminology.

'Couldn't we search for some prospective areas ourselves?' she asked Mike. 'There's lots of interesting geology in Sierramar.'

'As an investor in a bear market, I don't have to go looking for projects. I sit back and wait for them to come to me. Anyway, we don't have the funds to go on wild goose chases. Be patient and one will walk in here all by itself.'

While Sam was waiting for a decent project to amble into the office, she sorted out all the project files already received. She reviewed their contents and made sure she didn't miss anything, but it was a vain hope. Marta took delivery of several new project files which she gave to Sam to review but they were not good enough either.

Their owners were speculators who claimed an exploration concession from the ministry and then held onto it by paying the ground rent without doing exploration work. These people had got wind of the fact that a gringo with lots of money wanted to invest in mining, and the rumour caused them to crawl out of the woodwork. They claimed their explorations concessions contained rich deposits of metals, but on revision they turned out to be moose pasture with no samples analysed.

One owner asserted that he had at least a million ounces of gold in his deposit, a statement based on the analysis of three rock samples found on the surface. This is like claiming a cake contains six ounces of sugar because a few grains of sugar are sprinkled on the top. Sam was not impressed. She used the maps they had bought at the institute to plot the positions of the concession areas and coloured them all in green for grass.

'Are you sure there's nothing worth looking at?' said Mike, examining them with dismay.

'One hundred per cent,' said Sam. 'If nothing better comes in, we could discover one, but it would be expensive to start from scratch on a hard rock mining project.'

'What are we looking for?'

'I recommend we wait for some properties containing alluvial deposits on surface and easy to mine. We can't afford hard rock on our budget.'

'I lost money on an alluvial project. Edward was furious about it.'

'That was before you had a geologist. Trust me, I'll choose us a better one.'

Sam didn't mention the fact that only one exploration project in one thousand becomes a mine. There wasn't much point in discouraging Mike if she wanted to keep her job.

'Have you ever heard about the Lost Treasure of the Incas?' she said.

'Sure, who hasn't? I read about it when I was researching Sierramar.'

'Do you think it's still out there?'

'I thought you were a scientist. It's a myth. Or if it isn't, it's long gone. Let's try to stay focused here. Edward will have my guts for garters if we don't find something worthwhile.'

'Of course. Trust me. I'll find you something good.'

***

Outside the office, her only entertainment was driving around town with Gloria who seemed to act as chauffeur and agony aunt to half the population of Calderon. Her driving scared the pants off Sam. One day they drove straight through a red light in front of a police car. Sam grabbed Gloria's arm.

'There was a police car at the crossing,' she said.

'Oh oh, that's not good.'

'You're lucky they didn't follow us.'

'They did. I can see them in the mirror. Hold on,' said Gloria.

To her horror, Sam realised that Gloria intended to outrun the police car. This could only end badly.

'Shouldn't we stop?' she said.

'Oh no, I've done this before. Watch and learn, *gringa*.'

They turned into a side road at full speed, the jeep seeming to teeter on two wheels. Sam reached for the hand grip above the door and hung on. Gloria laughed like a mad woman.

'*Vamos*,' she shouted as they barrelled down the road at top speed. 'Hold on tight, Sam.'

She slowed down and executed a perfect handbrake turn into an empty driveway.

'Get your head down,' she said to Sam. 'Do you want them to see you?'

They both bent over their knees and listened. The siren came nearer and nearer. Sam imagined calling her parents and explaining why she would stay in Calderon for longer than expected. About five years. She screwed up her face in anticipation but the police car flew past and kept driving.

'Wow, they didn't see us,' said Sam.

'Ha! The *chapas* are not masterminds, you know,' said Gloria. 'They've never caught me.'

Her face glowed with excitement and pride. Sam laughed out loud. 'Evel Knievel has nothing on you. You are bonkers.'

'What is that word, bonkers? Is bonkers good?'

'Oh yes, it's brilliant.'

***

'Get your glad rags on. We're taking you out to experience the local idea of a good time,' said Mike.

'Where are we going?' said Sam.

'The *Discoteca*. You'll love it. The décor screams seventies and it has a dance floor that has flashing squares like something out of *Saturday Night Fever*.'

The Discoteca was packed with Gloria's friends and everyone knew everyone else. Once people discovered that Sam was English, enthusiastic questioners surrounded her, many of whom spoke English with American accents. The revellers operated with a reduced personal space. They came so close to her when they spoke that she felt uncomfortable. This was especially true of the women, who reached out and touched her clothes and hair. She flinched when a man she didn't know put their arm around her waist.

'Was it because I touched you? I've heard that the English are cold people.'

'Oh? I wouldn't say that. Reserved is a better word.'

'How do you cope with all that fog?'

'I don't think I've ever seen fog in London. Perhaps I don't get up early enough.'

'Do you get football hooligans on the streets? Is it dangerous?'

'Margaret Thatcher has controlled that problem. It doesn't exist anymore. Well, not much anyway.'

'We need Margaret Thatcher over here. She would control the corruption.'

'Um, she's not Prime Minister any more. It's John Major now, so maybe you could ask her to come over since she's free?'

'Yes, but she stole the Malvinas. What right have English people to the Malvinas?'

Sam shifted on her feet, uncomfortable with all the attention. Her shoes stuck to the residue of spilt drinks on the floor and her eyes watered from the thick cigarette smoke. Sam looked around for an escape and Gloria noticed that she was being corralled. She stepped in, placing herself between a relieved Sam, and her interrogators.

'Why are you asking her about the Malvinas? She's a woman. She doesn't know anything,' said Gloria, pushing them away.

Grateful for her intervention, Sam left to dance with the owner of the disco. Soon out of breath in the thin air, she retreated to an empty table carrying a glass of water. She saw Mike sitting in the far corner chatting up a pretty woman with long hair, and Gloria propping up the bar and drinking shots with her friends. She was panting due to the high altitude. Gulping down the water, she leaned back against the wall.

A man in a tweed jacket weaved through the crowd and flopped down beside her. He had shoulder-length coarse grey hair worn in a ponytail, and big black eyebrows over sad brown eyes in a rugged face. He looked at her with drunken interest.

'You're not from here, are you?' he said in perfect public-school English. 'Don't worry. You'll get used to the altitude.'

Sam turned to look at him.

'Green eyes,' he said. 'Beautiful green eyes.' He took her hand and crooned a song in Spanish called 'Ojos Verdes,' which was about a man in love with a woman with green eyes. Sam got the gist of it and removed her hand from his grasp.

'Ah, typical cold *gringa* bitch, are you?' he asked.

Sam was taken aback.

'Who the hell are you anyway?' she said, her eyes flashing with anger.

'Ah, the *gringa* has spirit. Permit me to introduce myself,' he said, again grasping her unwilling hand. 'I'm Alfredo Vargas, the treasure hunter, at your service.'

Sam could tell he wasn't joking, as he was in no fit state to make anything up, and her mouth opened in surprise.

'You're a treasure hunter? Which one are you hunting?' She felt a frisson of excitement. *Could it still be hidden?*

'The lost hoard of the Incas, *linda*.'

'I thought they had already found it. What makes you think it still exists?'

Alfredo looked disappointed as if this was not the reaction he expected. 'Please excuse me,' he said. 'The toilet is calling,' and he stumbled off into the darkness.

Sam waited for him to come back but to her disappointment, he didn't reappear. Why couldn't she keep her mouth shut? She had found someone who might share her interest in the treasure and her natural cynicism had curtailed an interesting chat. She could be abrasive and now she was bored instead.

As the night wore on, Gloria got more and more drunk. Sam wanted to go home, so she found Mike, who was also ready to leave. Predictably, Gloria did not agree. She draped her arms around Mike and slurred in his face.

'Let's go to another party, Mike. I want to find Diego.'

'Not the best idea you've had. Why don't we take you home?'

'You can go home. I want to find Diego.'

'We can all go together in the car and find him,' said Sam winking at him over the top of Gloria's head.

'Okay, that's what we'll do. Come on, Gloria. Let's look for Diego.'

Gloria looked sceptical at this change of plans but she wasn't capable of going anywhere by herself. She hung on to Mike's arm and after much procrastination, Mike and Sam manoeuvred her into the car. They set off down the narrow streets of Calderon, driving through red lights and up the hill to Gloria's house. It didn't take her long to realise that they were heading for her house, instead of looking for Diego, and she got cross.

'Hey, we're going the wrong way,' she said and wound down the window and shouted, 'Help, they've kidnapped me.' No one took any notice, and she didn't have the energy to protest much, sinking back into her seat and lighting up a fat joint which she sucked on with a blissful expression.

When they got to her building, Gloria flung open the door of the car and slid out of the back seat onto the pavement where she sat for several minutes, still griping.

'I don't know why we can't get Diego. He's missing me.'

'Gloria, it's four o'clock in the morning and he's tucked up in bed by now. You should be too. Come on, let's go.'

After lighting and smoking a cigarette, she hauled herself up and tried to open the front door, but she was so drunk that she kept dropping her keys. Mike sighed. He left Sam in the car and walked to the front door. Taking the keys from Gloria, he opened it. He then disappeared into the building with her in a practised manner that suggested this was not the first time he had helped her get home.

When he got back to the car, he had an obvious smear of lipstick all over his lips and chin. Sam raised an eyebrow at him.

'Gloria's a hell of a girl but she's not having a great time,' said Mike. 'That boyfriend of hers is a dead loss.'

'How come?'

'Diego Mena belongs to one of Calderon's richest and most powerful families and that makes him the most eligible bachelor in town. All the girls fight over him but he prefers to hang out with Gloria.'

'Do you think they'll get married?'

'No. I think he loves her, in his own way, but his mother is a Class-A bitch. She'll never let him marry Gloria.'

'Why not?'

'Gloria comes from new money. Her father is not from one of the old families in Calderon. They are nouveau riche. Barely tolerated.'

'And Diego? He sounds horrible.'

'On the contrary. He's charming, educated and popular, but he's unreliable and unfaithful. I doubt he has any real intention of marrying Gloria. He's having fun.'

'Does she know?'

'I'm sure she does, but she won't admit it to herself. It's tough being an outsider in your own class. Despite all evidence to the contrary, money does not buy you love.'

Sam knew only too well how it felt to be betrayed by someone who didn't care enough about her. Horrible memories of the humiliation following the revelations about Simon's adventures assailed her, and she felt a kinship with Gloria. No wonder she drank so much.

The next day, Sam, Marta and Gloria went to lunch at the Banana Verde.

'Have either of you ever heard of Alfredo Vargas?' Sam asked. 'I met him last night at the disco. He told me he's a treasure hunter. Mind you, he was drunk.'

'It's true,' said Gloria. 'He's spent many years looking for the lost treasure of the Incas. He may be a drunk, but he has periods of sobriety when he researches it. I heard that he hadn't touched a drink for months.'

'I don't think he's still sober,' said Sam. 'Where

did he learn to speak English?'

'He went to school in England, although he claims he can't remember anything due to the drinking. He's not in my circle of friends so I don't know him that well, but he is handsome.'

Sam had not noticed. Since Gloria was in an expansive mood, she asked more questions.

'Last night the barmen were Indians but none of the clients were. It's the same in this restaurant. Why is that?'

'It's the class system here,' said Gloria. 'The white people are richer than the mestizos who are richer than the Indians and everyone is richer than the black people. A white person wouldn't dream of working in a bar, or as a waiter, and you don't get too many mestizos in a disco, unless they're serving the drinks.'

'Money talks though,' said Marta. 'Possessing a large amount of money can neutralise the disadvantage of belonging to the wrong set. One of my friends is a mestizo whose mother runs the Toyota franchise in Sierramar. That qualifies her as white.'

'The men at the disco assumed that if they wanted a woman, they could have her. Don't women get to choose their man here?' said Sam.

'Not really, *chica*,' replied Gloria. 'We are decorations and not expected to have an opinion.'

'When will women's lib arrive in Calderon?' said Marta.

'It's taking a long time,' said Gloria. 'Men here are the worst.'

They both sighed.

Sam couldn't help herself. 'Do you think it's coming on a plane? Liberate yourselves.'

'Who asked you?' retorted Marta.

'Sam means nothing by it. She has no manners,'

interjected Gloria.

This comment did not impress Sam, who was convinced she had exquisite manners, but she decided not to defend herself. She sighed and rolled her eyes. This turned out to be the correct response as Marta took it as an apology. Gloria left to visit the toilet.

'How come Gloria works at all if her father is Mr Big?' said Sam, when Gloria was out of earshot.

'Her father is unusual amongst the rich here. They inherited their money and haven't worked for it. Senor Sanchez is a self-made man who doesn't mind subsidising her as long as she works too. He believes that you should work no matter how much money you have. Anyway, you know Gloria, she would not tolerate being a lady who lunches.'

'None of her friends work then?' said Sam.

'Ha! They're too stuck up to work. They spend their time partying and getting drunk and drugged.'

Marta looked as if she would spit from disdain. Sam changed the subject.

Chapter VI

When Sam woke up the next morning, she felt like death. Altitude sickness combined with the aptly named Montezuma's revenge meant she couldn't eat or breathe. Her nose was as dry as a desert as were her eyes and throat. She drank lots of mineral water which she threw up, and she spent exaggerated amounts of time in the bathroom deciding whether it was more urgent to evacuate her bowels from the top or the bottom. Mike was unsympathetic.

'For God's sake, Sam. Everyone knows they should take it easy for the first week or two in Calderon. It's over a mile above sea-level.'

'I would have known if you had told me,' muttered Sam to herself.

'You need to be on form this morning. I've arranged a meeting here with Wilson Ortega, a Sierramarian geologist who's been talking about some prospective exploration claims. I want you to tell me if you think they have any merit.'

'Don't worry about me, Mike. I'll be fine,' said Sam with grim determination. She would not fall at the first hurdle. Marta made her a drink to rehydrate her, a disgusting mixture of salt and sugar, and she sat on her bed, waiting for it to kick in. She wondered where

Mike had found Wilson. Probably at a disco.

When Wilson arrived at the flat, even Sam focused long enough to peruse him from head to foot. He was a tall, handsome man with a big, black moustache, which he stroked and adjusted often. Although only thirty-three, he looked older, his skin grey and lined because of chain-smoking Full Speed unfiltered. He had large, dark brown eyes under a mop of thick black hair. He wore a black shirt, black polyester trousers, and short black boots. When he arrived for the meeting, a large black fedora sat on his head. This outfit was his equivalent of a uniform.

They roped in Marta to translate for the meeting as Wilson spoke only pidgin English. She had her head bowed most of the time, but she looked at him from underneath her false eyelashes with something approaching adoration. When he glanced at her for reassurance on some point, she blushed pink and squirmed in her chair. He liked being the centre of attention. He sat back in his chair and flung his knees apart with a smug expression on his face.

Wilson had brought some folders containing official documents giving permission for exploration work on several tracts of land in the province of Esmeraldas in the west of Sierramar. One of them contained terraces of gravel along the banks of a river which flowed into the Pacific.

'The rivers, staked out by the exploration concessions I am offering you, have terraces which contain gold along their riverbanks. We can buy these concessions for twenty thousand dollars each and have all the gold for ourselves.'

'How much gold is there in the terraces?' said Mike.

'Oh, I would say about a million ounces, but there

could be more.'

'Has there been any geological exploration done on these terraces?' said Sam. They ignored her.

'The natives pan the gold from the alluvial deposits for money to buy beer and cigarettes. It must be high grade for them to take out enough to live on with their primitive methods. They don't bother for less than a gram a cubic meter or about six dollars.'

'So, there's no measured resource of gold then?' said Sam.

'Not as such, but it's a rich deposit,' said Wilson. 'We could exploit it straight away if we had the machinery.'

'Where would we get the machinery? How much would it cost to buy?' said Mike.

'Oh, that's the easy part. There is a man who can lease us all the equipment we need. We don't have to buy anything.'

'That sounds like an excellent plan. I could persuade Edward to part with the money if we put a budget together,' said Mike, now several steps ahead of Sam.

Wilson opened his mouth to speak but Sam interrupted.

'Whoa there. Hold up a minute,' said Sam. 'It's certainly an interesting concept, but I recommend that we visit the river to do some sampling before we decide about investing in the project. We need to establish the presence of gold in the terraces and get an idea of the amount per cubic metre as well as the total volume of gravel.'

'Why is that?' said Mike.

'It may cost more to mine than we get out. Wilson might be right about the presence of rich terraces there, but we need a mining plan to determine if we can make a profit before we invest,' said Sam, straining to sound rational but not condescending.

Wilson flashed an annoyed glance at her but changed his expression when she stared right back.

'Of course,' he said. 'Mike can come with me to the area next week and see for himself.'

Mike laughed.

'I'm sorry, Wilson, but you must make do with Sam. I've a dicky heart, and the jungle is too far from a hospital for me if something goes wrong.'

Marta translated. Wilson looked at Mike in surprise. Sam raised an eyebrow but didn't comment. *He's probably too lazy to go.*

'I'm a geologist too. Didn't Mike tell you?' said Sam, knowing full well that Mike had introduced her as his geologist when Wilson arrived at the meeting.

'Women can't deal with the conditions in the jungle. They're too weak. I can't manage Sam's safety,' Wilson said to Mike, ignoring Sam.

His condescending tone floated into the air and stayed there as Marta tried to translate the bald statement into a politer version. His arrogance shocked Sam. She couldn't believe anyone still talked this way about a woman when she was present. She swallowed the bile that had risen to her throat.

'Oh, don't worry about me. I'm as tough as a mule. I'll look after myself.'

'Sam will be fine, Wilson. You won't have to babysit.'

Wilson was not happy, but Mike had not picked up on Sam's fury or Wilson's reluctance, as he was imagining how much gold they would mine from the terraces.

'When can you go, Wilson?'

'I can organise a trip in a week's time, if that suits

you?'

'Yes, perfect. That's settled then. Sam, why don't you go to town with Wilson and buy supplies for the trip? That way you can get to know each other better.'

It was the last thing either of them wanted to do, but if they worked together, they had to communicate.

'Can I have some money?' said Sam.

'Yes, Marta, give Sam some petty cash.'

Marta wiggled over to her desk and returned with a wad of the local currency.

'Please don't forget the receipts,' she said, batting her eyelashes at Wilson.

'Thank you. Let's go,' said Sam.

Wilson was looking at Marta like a wolf admiring a plump sheep.

'See you later,' he said.

***

Not being able to invest straight away frustrated Mike, but he admired Sam for standing up to them both. It surprised him to find that he had chosen a woman who had appeared easy to manipulate, but who had a hidden core of inner steel. He had hired her hoping to prevent any more unfortunate investments, without having much to go on except her availability and cheapness, but he was now convinced that he had made the right decision. Wilson would have his hands full with Sam.

He rang Edward to update him.

'Hi, it's me.'

'Hello, how's it going out there? Any news?'

'Someone has offered me an area of river gravels with gold in them. They sound promising.'

'So did the last lot. How do we prove they're any good?'

'Sam will go there to do some due diligence on the

project before I decide.'

'Sounds like she has taken charge over there,' snorted Edward. 'I'm glad to hear that we're being cautious this time. It sounds promising. Are you going?'

'I don't see the point. Sam knows what she's doing, and she's going with the geologist who found the deposit.'

'If you think that's best.'

'Definitely. I've already proved how little I understand about geology,' said Mike.

'Ha! That's true.'

'I'll call you when they get back and fill you in on our progress.'

'Excellent. Can't wait. Good luck.'

Mike hung up the phone with a smile. With Edward back on board, he was no longer worried about funding, and this time they were on to a winner.

***

Sam and Wilson left to buy supplies in the market at the centre of the old town. They went by taxi as neither could drive and Gloria had not graced the office with her presence.

'Why don't you drive, Wilson?'

'Engineers don't drive a car in the field. They use a driver.'

'I'm hoping to learn to drive here.'

'Women are terrible drivers.'

'Not all women. Anyway, some men are pretty bad too.' She pointed at the taxi driver's back and smiled, but Wilson looked at her and didn't acknowledge the joke. It would be hard work getting through, she thought.

'What degree do you have?' he said.

'A Bachelor of Science in Geology.'

'Ha! A Bachelor's degree. How long did you study?'

'Four years,' said Sam.

'Your degree is worthless here. You would only be qualified as a teacher. My degree was in Engineering Geology, and I studied at the university for seven years. It's far superior to your degree.'

She didn't bother to disabuse him of this theory. Instead she said, 'Probably. I've also got a master's degree in Geology, though.'

It was his turn to be cross as it made her far superior to him by his own terms of reference.

They stopped at a street market that spilt out of a long, low, breeze-block shed with a zinc roof. There were rows of ramshackle stalls with uncategorizable mixtures of products on shaky tables. Sacks of flour jostled for space with footballs and sweets. Boxes of bottled water sat under a table with underwear and socks for sale on it.

Wilson knew exactly where to go for individual items so Sam tagged along and paid up. She had no idea if they were paying above or below the odds but she got receipts for all of it despite him tut-tutting at the waste of time as semi-illiterate shopkeepers struggled to fill them in.

They bought most of the basic supplies they would need for their trip and packed them into another ancient taxi for transport back to the flat in the Avenida Miranda. Sam found the time spent with Wilson somewhat wearing and was a little worried about the prospect of being in his company twenty-four hours a day in the field. There was something about him that made her feel queasy. She would bring lots of batteries for her Walkman.

When she got back to the flat, Marta was waiting to ambush her.

'How did it go with Wilson? He's so handsome. Do you think he noticed me?'

'Of course. It would be impossible not to,' said Sam. 'Wilson is an English surname. How come they use it over here as a first name?'

'Oh, they named him after Woodrow Wilson. The surnames of American presidents are popular as first names here.'

'Adopting the names of famous people is common in Sierramar especially dictators' names, like Mussolini, Stalin, Lenin and Hitler,' said Gloria, who had arrived at the office while they were out buying supplies.

A dictator's name would have suited Wilson much better, but Sam didn't say so. Marta was suffering from a crush.

'What's his surname?' asked Gloria.

'Ortega, I think, why?'

'Oh, no reason.' Sam found this unconvincing. Gloria looked concerned, but she was trying not to let it show. She was well aware who Wilson Ortega was.

When Sam left to make a cup of tea in the kitchen, Gloria took her chance.

'You like Wilson, don't you?' she said to Marta. 'He's not the right man for you.'

'What do you mean?' said Marta.

'He's not suitable for you,' said Gloria struggling to avoid explaining herself.

Marta, who was sensitive to her position in society, took immediate offence.

'And who told you to stick your nose into my business?'

'Ay Martita, I'm sorry, I didn't mean to upset you,'

said Gloria.

'Is he too good for me because he's a geologist like Sam? Just because you are rich doesn't give you the right to control my life.'

'That's not the problem. I've heard that he's not a good person, and I'd hate to see you get hurt.'

'I can protect myself, thank you,' said Marta.

'He has a reputation for violence. I only wanted to warn you.'

'You can't stop me from going out with him.'

Gloria saw that she had made a mistake and instead of putting Marta off, she had probably pushed her right into Wilson's path.

'I'm sorry, Martita, that's not what I meant. Please forgive me.'

Marta harrumphed and returned to her desk with a stubborn expression on her face. Sam came out of the kitchen with the tea and the moment passed.

***

After Wilson left Sam at Avenida Miranda, he was in a great mood. In one pocket, he felt his fat wallet, loaded with an advance in dollars from Mike Morton. It amazed Wilson how trusting Mike was. In other circumstances, Wilson would have pocketed the cash and walked away for good. However, Mike was a lottery win in human form. There was much more money involved, and Wilson intended to milk his golden ticket for all it was worth.

He was clever and well educated but they had fired him from all his previous jobs when money was missing or he went AWOL. An inveterate womaniser and frequenter of bordellos, he was prone to drunken binges that lasted for days. This meant that he was in debt up to his eyeballs.

Meeting Mike in one of the town's classier bordellos had been a stroke of luck. Wilson was being chased by some nasty people who took exception to his inability to pay what he owed. He was only one step ahead of them, and his time was running out. When Mike had mentioned that he could do with some help with his projects in the jungle, Wilson jumped at the chance. They were both happy with the outcome.

Mike needed Wilson as much as Wilson needed the money. He couldn't send Sam in alone yet as her Spanish was too basic. It would be a pain having that woman along on the trip. She would complain about everything and he wouldn't be able to go drinking and whoring like he usually did in the field. One visit to the jungle would be enough for the spoilt bitch. It wasn't all bad though, she was attractive under those boring clothes. Maybe he could persuade her to let him taste her wares. He'd never had a *gringa* before.

In his other pocket, Wilson rubbed a slip of paper between his fingers on which he had written Marta's phone number. Now, there was a project. All coy and girly in her fuck-me heels and her lacquered quiff; Wilson wasn't fooled. Marta would be an easy lay. In his experience, women were all the same. He used them and disposed of them, running a mile from any display of emotion or clingy behaviour. Never wanting to get married, his wife's three brothers had not given him a choice. They had forced him to do the correct thing when they had discovered she was pregnant and had threatened to kill him if he refused.

His wife now regretted every minute of their marriage, but she was Roman Catholic, and divorce was not acceptable. So, they stayed married, although neither could stand the other. Wilson was happy to be separated, so he could carry on whoring and drinking, which was the only thing he enjoyed, instead of being nagged by his wife. He lit a cigarette and headed down the street to the bus stop. The money was burning a hole in his pocket, and he knew where to spend it.

***

'Where can I buy some chocolate for the trip?' said Sam.

'There is a convenience store at the top of Avenida Miranda where the new buildings stop and the old ones start. It sells lots of candy,' said Marta. 'Can you buy me some M&Ms while you are there please?'

Sam walked up the Avenida Miranda passing the tall new buildings and found the shop in a small house with a roof made of brick red tiles. She selected several large bars of Lindt chocolate which she took up to the counter with the M&Ms. To her surprise, Alfredo, the self-proclaimed treasure hunter, was standing there, swaying, and chatting to the shopkeeper. She placed her purchases on the countertop.

'That's a lot of chocolate, *gringa*.'

'I'm going to the jungle,' she said. 'I need emergency supplies. Didn't we meet in the Discoteca?'

'Ah yes. The girl with beautiful green eyes. You should buy dark chocolate. The more cocoa, the less likely it is to melt in the heat.'

'Oh, I didn't know.' She took them back to the shelf and changed them. 'Thank you. Alfredo isn't it?'

'Yes, Alfredo Vargas at your service.'

'If you're at my service, I've some questions, about the treasure, if you've time to talk.'

'Let's sit outside on the bench in the shade. Do you want a beer?'

'No thanks, I'll have a Seven-Up though.'

They sat in the shade with the bright sunlight all

around them sucking the colour out of the street.

'What do you want to know?' said Alfredo.

'Well, I've got this book, and it says that the Incas buried Atahualpa's ransom in Sierramar. Do you know anything about it?'

'More than anyone alive. I've searched for it most of my life.'

'So, you believe it still exists?'

'Yes, I'm convinced. I've done years of research.'

'Where is it hidden?'

'There's a hand-drawn map that shows a hiding place in the mountains near Guayumba.'

'Have you searched up there?'

'Often. I believe it's only a matter of time before I rediscover the treasure.'

'How exciting. Can we talk about it when I get back from my trip?'

'Anytime, *gringa. Mi casa es su casa.*'

***

The brothel was in the southern part of old Calderon on a sordid-looking side street. The trade carried on inside its sturdy door was not advertised on the exterior. The only clue was a large peephole with a shutter that was drawn back when someone knocked. Wilson did not have to wait for long after he banged on the door. A shadow appeared in the peephole and disappeared in one fluid movement.

The door opened so fast that Wilson fell into the gloomy interior. The décor inside the brothel was a cliché, with its red velvet sofas in booths of dark mahogany, the fabric now stained with use, and the cheap chandeliers with dim bulbs. Several world-weary women of uncertain vintage and massive make-up draped themselves around the bar. A tired young woman gyrated without enthusiasm to cantina music on a filthy stage.

'So,' said a voice, 'you have paid us a visit. How nice.' The heavy sarcasm was evident in the gravelly tone. Esteban Nunez stepped out of the gloom and stood under the dim bulb in the hallway, his greasy face shining.

'I told you not to show your face again until you paid me every penny you owe. You're taking a big chance coming here.'

Wilson smiled.

'Brother, why are you treating me like this when I'm here to pay you and spend my money in your establishment?'

'Pay me? Ha!' Esteban opened the door and looked out at the sky. He shut the door and glared at Wilson.

'There are no flying pigs going by,' he said.

'Esteban, would I lie to you?' asked Wilson.

'Yes, and you do all the time.'

'I'm hurt, but I forgive you. Set me up in a booth with Conchita and a bottle of whisky, and I'll forget it ever happened.'

'Are you nuts? Where's my money?' said Esteban, turning purple with fury.

Wilson reached into his pocket and took out his wallet.

'How much do I owe you?' he asked, although he already knew. 'Seven-hundred and fifty, wasn't it? I'll give you a thousand so I've some credit to spend in here.' He handed over the dollars with a flourish.

'Seven-hundred and fifty-six dollars and thirty cents. And that doesn't include interest. Where did you get the money? I heard you got fired again,' said Esteban.

'None of your business. Why are you complaining about your best customer? I always recommend your establishment. Now, where's Conchita? I've got a tremendous thirst.'

Mollified, Esteban waved to a woman at the bar and signalled to her that she had a client with cash. The woman shimmied over to the booth and tried to appear pleased as Wilson joined her.

'Hello, darling,' he said, 'long time no see.'

After making sure Wilson was distracted, Esteban slipped into his office and searched in a desk drawer for a scrap of paper he had stored there. He unfurled it and dialled the number that Pancho Rojas, known as El Duro, had given him.

'Señor Rojas, it's me Esteban Núñez. You asked me to contact you when Wilson Ortega turned up. He's here, and he's loaded.'

'He's got money? How typical of that scumbag that he spends the money he owes to me in a brothel.'

'Have I done the wrong thing?'

'No. I'll deal with this my own way. Thank you for calling me.'

Chapter VII

A week after their meeting, Mike drove Sam and Wilson to San Martin, a town two-hours north of Calderon, from where they would travel into the jungle. The dry landscape through which they travelled supported only a few scrubby bushes and some small dusty towns along winding roads cut through several banded rock formations, whose relief stood out in the moonlight. There was a large multi-layered fold in one of the rock faces. Sam wanted to ask Mike to stop the car so she could take a photograph but he was driving with grim determination and she didn't fancy his reaction.

When they arrived at San Martin, they checked into the Hotel California. Mike took one look at the dilapidated hotel and drove back to Calderon rather than stay the night. With a misplaced sense of economy, he had insisted that Sam and Wilson share a room.

'There's no point wasting money,' he said. 'You'll be sharing in the field, anyway.'

Sam was taken aback at the thrifty attitude, considering the luxury in which Mike kept himself in Calderon.

'I suppose so,' she said without enthusiasm.

'Okay, so I'll see you at the beach, Sam. Have a good trip.'

'I will. Drive carefully.'

After Mike left, they went straight into the dining room, which had a huge poster of the Golden Gate Bridge plastered over one wall. Sam felt abandoned and nervous. Wilson was behaving like he owned the place, clicking his fingers and ordering food for them both. They sat at a table with sticky patches on its dark surface. The plastic chairs were too low for the table so Sam stacked a second one on hers for comfort.

Bare wiring hung from the ceiling and the flimsy, stained curtains did not hide the filthy windows. Several young men sat at a table in the corner drinking beer and smoking unfiltered cigarettes. They flirted with Sam across the room and made her laugh and blush. She enjoyed the Latin lack of reserve more than she had imagined.

'Boys,' sniffed Wilson, and he turned around to glare at them.

After a supper of chicken and rice washed down with Seven-Up, they went upstairs. The room allocated to Sam and Wilson turned out to be L-shaped with a bed at each end and all the supplies stacked up in the middle. This gave a certain amount of privacy, so Sam was less exposed. Wilson left the hotel to get something that she didn't understand, and she took an early night, hoping to avoid talking to him again that evening. She lay in bed shivering under the thin blanket, the nylon sheets sparking under her. Quivering with anticipation about the trip, she couldn't get to sleep.

After an hour or so of tossing about in the crackly sheets she heard singing in the street. She lay in bed resisting the temptation to look out of the window. The singing was insistent, and her curiosity got the better of her. She knelt on the bed and pulled aside the filthy curtains.

There was a dim street light opposite her room, and underneath it stood the boys from the restaurant. They had a guitar, and they were singing up at her window. She wasn't sure what to do, but she liked the singing, so she opened the window and leaned out. The singing became more passionate, and to her surprise, they sang Angie, a song by the Rolling Stones. She smiled at the garbled words they must have learned phonetically from the radio, but there was no mistaking their intensity.

Wilson came back into the room. Noticing her leaning out of the window, he pulled her inside. He smelt of drink and sex, which made her stomach turn. He cursed at the boys, who ran off laughing. Sam was disappointed and furious.

'How dare you? Never touch me again. Go away!'

'You should not show yourself to those boys.'

'I said go away.'

Wilson stepped backwards and then, shaking his head, he turned on his heel and disappeared around the corner to his part of the bedroom. Sam got back under the covers, shivering with indignation. She was not happy at being manhandled by Wilson. It would be an uphill struggle to work on equal terms in the jungle while he considered her to be inferior to him.

She knew herself at a disadvantage as he was the one holding the cards. Her safety was in his hands and her knowledge of alluvial mining was only from books. It would be hard to gain his respect under those circumstances but she would have to grin and bear it. No one said that it would be easy to break into this male world. It was amazing she had a job at all. She turned to face the wall.

***

At dawn the next morning, they paid for the hotel.

'Why were those men singing to me last night?' Sam asked the manager who spoke English because of his time working in *'gringolandia'*.

'The *serenata* or serenade, is a way of winning a girl's heart in Sierramar. When you appeared at the window, you signified an interest in the petition.'

'Wilson told them to go away.'

'You disappointed them. They had good taste,' he said winking at her.

The hotel manager was squat and sweaty but he knew how to deliver a line. Sam blushed and fiddled with her rucksack.

They walked through the empty streets to the ramshackle train station to buy their tickets to the coast. It was freezing and Sam shivered in her thin cotton shirt and trousers. Her new Wellington boots flapped against her cold legs. Their clammy hold on her calves made her wish she could afford a nice pair of leather walking boots. She added them to the list of things she would buy when Mike paid her. The list was growing all the time, and she wondered if it was a fantasy. If he was saving money by making her share a room with Wilson, it was pretty unlikely that she would get paid soon, in shares or otherwise.

They weren't the only people planning on catching the train. They would compete for tickets with hordes of other people, carrying baggage of every kind and shape imaginable. Wilson led them into the crowd. The ferocious pushing and shoving were something Sam had never experienced before. She struggled to stay on her feet. No-one queued for tickets. A diaspora of humanity surged to the window where they were being sold.

Wilson surged ahead and disappeared into a crowd of bodies swathed in woollen shawls against the cold. Sam could see his fedora moving to the small window where the tickets were being dispensed. She was weary, having not slept much on the thin foam mattress over the wooden slats of her bed. Having Wilson in the same room didn't help much either. He snored like a lorry with dirt in its fuel.

'What time does the train leave?' she asked him when he came back with the tickets.

'That depends.'

'On what?'

'It's meant to leave at seven o'clock, but it doesn't leave on time often.'

'So how will we know?'

'When the driver gets into the cabin.'

'So, we can't have some breakfast?'

'No. They will leave without us.'

'Can we get the next train?'

Wilson looked at Sam to see if she was joking.

'There is one train a day so if you don't want to wait until tomorrow...'

While they waited for the train, the platform they were standing on became a market. Local traders arrived from every direction, carrying their entire stalls on their backs and setting up shop. There were several scruffy, black, hairy pigs snuffling around on the tracks. One of their more unfortunate brethren was being cooked over a slow fire by two large ladies. The odour of the burning hairs and roast crackling crept up Sam's nose, both revolting and enticing her. She drooled with hunger as she imagined the taste of the hot pork fat.

It was noticeable that the population now comprised as many black people as indigenous ones. They were the descendants of African slaves brought to Sierramar by the Spanish during their conquest of the Incas. Sam found it strange to hear them speak Spanish. They spoke with abbreviated words, missing entire chunks of sentences, like Tati did.

It had never occurred to her that there would be different accents in Spanish. She hadn't expected this. *What was the point in learning Spanish in one accent when everyone she met spoke it in another one?* The Esmeraldas accent in Spanish was the equivalent of a Glaswegian accent in English and whether she liked it or not, she would be reliant on Wilson's translations to get along on the trip.

When the train reversed into the platform from a siding, it astonished her to see that it was a bus adapted to run on rails. There was a mad scramble as the whole crowd tried to get onto the train at the same time despite the seats being pre-booked. Wilson told her to get on board while he checked that they loaded the provisions on the roof.

Sam looked at the sea of hysterical people pushing and shoving, took a deep breath, and waded in. Unwashed bodies marinated in wood smoke were pungent and, sometimes, nasty. Somehow, she got a foothold on the metal step up into the solitary door to the train. She heaved herself up by holding on to the bars on either side of the door. The bars were coated in the grease from filthy hands.

Sam let go as soon as she could and staggered aboard, trying to avoid crushing the chickens that were lying about trussed up with palm leaves and fibres. She checked her tickets and looked down the bus. Two large men were sitting on her seats. She didn't need the struggle of asking them to move and stayed standing until Wilson arrived. There was nothing malicious about the bedlam that surrounded her, and she relaxed while being pushed aside by the other passengers in their rush to secure their seats.

When Wilson got on, the interlopers gave them the seats without a murmur of dissent, giving the impression that they were merely warming them up. The seats were tiny, designed for the indigenous part of the population. Since the people on board comprised large men and women, as broad as they were tall, it increased the claustrophobic overcrowding. Wilson had to sit sideways with his bony knees sticking out into the thigh of a large mulatto woman perched on a barrel of lard in the passageway.

'How far is it to San Lorenzo?' said Sam, already dreading the journey.

'It's two hundred kilometres.'

'So how long does it take to get there?' she asked, cheered by the short distance.

'The programmed journey time is eight hours but it can take much longer if the train derails.'

'Eight hours? Is there no quicker way?' said Sam, aghast.

'It's possible to go by plane to the coast and come into Riccuarte by car from the other direction but the train's much cheaper and Mike didn't want to pay for flights.'

This did not surprise her.

A small plump man with a Hitler moustache and an ancient cap appeared from behind the ticket office and walked towards the train. Just as suddenly he turned around and went back to the groans of the passengers. Five minutes later he reappeared with what looked like a lunch box and a plastic bag full of clinking bottles. He opened the driver's door and heaved himself up into the cabin. Shortly afterwards, the train set off with a prolonged shudder and shake through the groves of banana trees behind the station and towards the nearby mountains.

Sam sat back in her seat and admired the view from the railway line. The first part of the journey took them through breath-taking scenery made up of verdant knife-edged hills along whose sides the train teetered. They passed through several long tunnels in the pitch black. Every time they entered a tunnel, someone wolf-whistled in the dark, a practice that became more irritating as the trip wore on.

The train made numerous stops along the way, but they didn't last more than a minute or two. There was the inevitable mad rush as people clambered over the luggage and out of the train and pushed past the people trying to get on. The train moved off as the last people were still getting on. It was only a matter of luck that no one slipped under the wheels.

After a short time, they burrowed into the vegetation that heralded the fringes of the coastal jungle. The tiny villages where the train stopped were barely keeping the jungle at bay. In some places, the vegetation had reclaimed the older shacks, and they were being enveloped by branches of the trees in a sinister manner.

'Do these villages have electricity?' she asked Wilson.

'No, they use candles for light at night.'

'Water?'

'They get water from the river for cooking. They wash in the river.'

About four hours into the trip, it occurred to her that if there was no water in the villages, there was unlikely to be a toilet either. She was holding on, but she knew she wouldn't last all the way. Wilson had not mentioned this problem to her before setting out. He was used to this state of affairs and it had not occurred to him. He jumped out now and then when the train stopped, and urinated against a tree, unaware of Sam's growing discomfort.

The scenery continued to change. The land was now flat. Here and there, the vegetation looked ravaged. Banana and papaya trees replaced the matted tangle of vines and other tropical plants. All the people in the villages were black or mulatto. The populations were young and well-nourished. Packs of children swarmed all over the train each time it stopped, and she was usually the centre of attention as the only white person on board. When the train stopped, they crowded around to stare at her, smiled big toothy grins and then looked abashed if she smiled back.

Also present at every stop were women and children selling the local takeaway foods, such as empanadas and fried bananas with cheese.

'I'd love one of those empanadas, Wilson,' said Sam.

'They're full of germs and will make you ill,' he replied. 'I'll buy you something safe.'

It was pretty obvious that the conditions in the kitchens were unsanitary, but this didn't stop Sam from sulking. Wilson bought some boiled white rice, and some unidentifiable cremated meat. She had never been fond of rice and liked to eat meat still in its death throes, so this culinary delicacy did not impress her.

'What meat is this?' she asked.

'I don't know. Peccary? Monkey? No idea.'

'Monkey? They eat monkey?'

'Maybe not. It's probably a pig.'

'It's horrible.'

'You're not in England now. I thought you were tough. Eat the food. You won't get anything better until you're back in Calderon.'

She chewed her way through most of it and ate the rice, which was salty and made her thirsty. She didn't dare drink any water. The lack of sanitary facilities had become a serious problem. She had been hoping that they would pull into a bigger town with a public toilet, but the towns were getting smaller and more primitive, and they never stopped long enough for a pee break.

Just when she thought she would have to apologise to Wilson for flooding the seat, the train shunted into a siding and stopped. Sam turned to him in expectation.

'Have we arrived?' she asked.

'No, not yet. We still have two hours to go. There's only one track for the trains to travel on. Our train has to make way for one coming in the other direction. We may be here for a while, depending on whether they left San Lorenzo on time.'

Sam grabbed her chance and climbed over the other inhabitants of the train in a frantic rush. She dashed out between the shacks on stilts and down to a small pond. People were washing themselves and their clothes in it at the same time. She tried to find somewhere discrete to urinate, but the combined effect of the sprint and the sound of water defeated her abused bladder. She squatted behind a spindly tree and tried to look inconspicuous as the only white person in a black village taking a volcanic leak in plain sight.

Avoiding eye contact with the crowd of children watching her from close quarters, she walked back to the train. She took some photographs of the children and the train in the siding and accepted a banana from one villager. There was a loud tooting noise. The other train chugged past, and the guard pulled the lever to switch the track back so that the train could move out of the siding.

Sam was not concentrating, assuming that the glacial pace of travel would not speed up, and suddenly the train was pulling out again, without her. She stumbled up the bank, only getting a foothold as it moved off. She clambered over the bodies and chickens and bananas with a look of relief that made Wilson laugh. It was his fault for letting her drink two bottles of lemonade at the station before they set out. She had a nagging feeling he had done it on purpose and decided not to drink anything on the way back.

Finally, when the pain in her bottom caused by sitting on the wooden seats for ten hours had reached the unbearable stage, the train arrived at San Lorenzo, a bustling town of wooden huts and mud streets with a similar station to San Martin. Leaving the train was bedlam. A group of local youths offered their services as baggage carriers, fighting over each bag dropped from the roof. Wilson had his work cut out for him, ensuring that one did not go missing in the pandemonium.

When they had claimed all their possessions, Wilson hired a pickup truck for the last leg of their journey. Sam steeled herself for another endless journey squashed between him and the smelly driver who leered at her in a disconcerting fashion. Whatever the driver had in mind remained a mystery as the dirt road was in an appalling state with massive ruts and muddy channels requiring all his skill and two hands on the wheel. It didn't help that the shock absorbers were non-existent throwing Sam and Wilson from side to side in the cabin of the truck. Sam cracked her head on the roof going over a big bump in the road.

By the time they arrived at Riccuarte, a small shantytown in the middle of the rain forest, Sam felt as if she was sitting on a tenderised steak. She slid off the truck seat and jumped to the ground snagging her trousers on the end of a spring sticking out of the upholstery. Swearing, she twisted around and confirmed that the tear wasn't too revealing. The driver sniggered but an icy stare from Sam stopped him in his tracks. A man stepped out of the shadows where he had been watching them and approached.

'You are welcome to Riccuarte. My name is Moises. I'm a member of the village council. There's no hotel but we use some empty houses for people passing through.'

Wilson grunted, looking at Moises with obvious disdain. Sam smiled.

'I'm Sam, and this is Wilson,' she said, sticking out her hand and inspecting their host.

Moises was a mestizo, the dominant group in Sierramar comprising people of mixed European and Amerindian races but he was out of place in this village. He had straight black hair streaked with grey that hung around his wrinkled face in a pudding bowl cut. His wiry body seemed to float above the ground; such was the Zen-like calmness that enveloped him. With his air of solemnity, and a patriarchal bearing that was at odds with his surroundings, he seemed to Sam like a man to be reckoned with.

Ignoring Wilson's rudeness, he directed them to follow him up the main street to a ramshackle house that stood on stilts.

'This is the guest house. I'm sorry that it isn't in a better state but we don't get many visitors around here.'

'It'll do for one night,' said Wilson. 'Can you find

a canoe and some men for us? We want to travel upriver.'

'How long will you need them for?'

'Four or five days.'

'I'll arrange it now. My wife will bring you some rice for your dinner, and some coffee and biscuits at dawn. I'll meet you on the riverbank at dawn with a team of men.'

'Choose good workers. These black people are born lazy. Look at this house.'

Sam winced. Don Moises did not comment and headed into the darkness. They stood on the street gazing through the gloom at the shack where they would spend the night. There was no front door. A lopsided doorframe with interesting fungi springing from the holes in the wood was all that remained. It had only one habitable room, the floors in the other room having caved in. Two log stools made up the lavish furnishings of this palace.

There would be no escape from living with Wilson in close proximity. Sam wondered if this was the best accommodation available in the village. Wilson had not treated Don Moises with much respect and she suspected the two things were linked. Worse still, something was missing.

'Where's the toilet?'

'There is no toilet. Go to the forest or the river. You can wash in the river which runs parallel to the main street over there.'

'But won't the villagers see me?' said Sam, remembering the crowd for her last performance.

'The best time is the early morning before they get up. You can have a quick wash in the river at sunup before breakfast or in the evening as it gets dark.'

'Okay.'

'Be careful when you wash in the river.'

'Why? Are there crocodiles?'

'No, this isn't Africa. There's a small fish in the river. It's dangerous.'

'Like a piranha?'

'No, it's called a Candiru. It likes urine. It follows your pee and goes into your urethra. You have to go to hospital to cut it out.'

'That sounds awful,' said Sam. 'How do we stop them?'

'Always wear tight underwear in the river.'

'Okay, thanks.'

Sam couldn't imagine the point of these fish. What were they doing swimming up the urethra, anyway? She took exaggerated care with her ablutions that evening. This involved many body contortions that ended with her falling head first into the river. She had an audience, despite the hour who gave her a spontaneous cheer. They wouldn't go away no matter how much she tried, and it forced her to wash with her back to the town, wearing her clothes from the day's travels. She made Wilson go outside while she put on dry clothes and she hung the wet ones around the house.

After a supper of rice and a tin of tuna, which was like the nectar of the gods to Sam, they lay on sleeping bags on the floor of the hut covered with mosquito nets hanging from the roof beams. Sam did her best to make a mattress out of some clothes but it was uncomfortable on the hard, uneven floor. Under normal circumstances, she prided herself on being able to sleep anywhere but this was a new experience. She lay down and shut her eyes, trying to breathe deeply and slow her heart, which was racing.

To her intense annoyance, the cicadas competed

with the tree frogs for the title of the noisiest animals on the planet. At least she knew what all the screeching and peeping was. There were a lot of noises coming from inside and outside the hut that she didn't recognise. It was hard to ignore the presence of Wilson, so close that she could feel the heat emanate from his body. All her romantic ideas about living in the jungle evaporated.

Sometime after midnight, something tugging at her head woke her. She opened her eyes with a certain amount of dread and switched on her torch. She found herself face-to-face with a large rat that had been busying himself gnawing off pieces of her hair for his nest. Startled to be caught in the act, and before she had time to react, he disappeared at speed into a hole in the floor. She rubbed her head ruefully finding a small patch of short hair sticking up from the scalp.

No matter what she told herself about nature and all its wonderful creatures, she found it impossible to sleep after that. She wedged herself into a corner and flashed the torch at every creak and groan emitted by the hut. She spent a long night wondering why she hadn't joined a bank instead of being so stubborn. Wilson slept like a log, emitting blissful snores, ensuring that she would hate him even more in the morning.

Chapter VIII

The next morning, they got up before dawn. For breakfast, they drank scalding cups of coffee, thick with sugar, and ate stale pink wafer biscuits. Sam was too tired to explain that she didn't like sweet coffee. Anyway, it came like that in Riccuarte. Drained after her night in the corner, the sugar gave her an immediate boost.

In the near dark, she had a quick pee behind the house, praying that all the snakes were still asleep. Her belongings stuffed back into her rucksack, she followed Wilson down to the riverbank in the cold light. A row of wooden canoes rested on the shingle. On the other side of the river an impenetrable jungle loomed over them, dark and dank. The cicadas made a racket that belied their size.

Moises had selected three more men to travel with them whom he introduced as Carlos, Rijer and Gustino. He was the obvious leader of the group even though he was not black and was half the size of the others. Doña Elodea, an attractive middle-aged woman, also joined the expedition to cook and pan for gold. She tried to talk to Sam but soon gave up when she saw Sam didn't understand her.

Her inability to grasp what people were saying

disheartened Sam. It had been getting much easier in Calderon, and she had been making strong progress there. The local accent in Riccuarte was proving impossible to decipher. She would have to rely on Wilson to translate into Calderon Spanish or pidgin English, and the results did not convince her. Whether he did it on purpose, she couldn't tell. It gave him power over her she wasn't comfortable with.

Don Moises had selected a canoe with high sides, hollowed from a single long tree trunk, big enough to take all seven people with their provisions and bags stowed at the front with ease. It had tool marks on it that showed it was handmade. Comfort was not a priority. There were loose blocks of wood on the floor that served as seats. Her bottom still tender following the train journey, Sam wondered how she would tolerate sitting all day.

She sat down on one block, which rolled over and deposited her in the water at the bottom of the canoe. Hoping no-one had noticed, she grabbed the sides of the canoe and hauled herself back onto the wobbly seat, the damp now creeping along her trousers. It was cold, and the chill moved up her thighs to the back of her knees. She leaned forward, grabbing her knees to take pressure off her back, and steeled herself for a long day.

Wilson sat in front of her with Don Moises at the prow. A flock of parrots passed far overhead chatting to each other like women in a bus queue. Carlos, who was at the back of the canoe, steered it away from the bank with a long paddle at the back of the boat. He then picked up a long pole. At the front, Rijer and Gustino, both with one foot on the edge of the canoe for balance, and the other in the bottom, used long poles to punt the boat up the stream by sticking them in the riverbed and pushing the canoe forward. Carlos did the same at the other end, using the paddle to steer when necessary.

It was a more efficient method of travel than it looked and they made good progress against the current, scything through the clear water in smooth steps. When the canoe arrived at a rapid, they all disembarked and hauled it upstream past the rocks and boiling water and into the main channel.

The canoe was a dead weight, and even with the buoyancy afforded by the water, it took a massive effort from the team to drag it through the rapids against the current and around the rocks. Sam could not help much, but she still tried and was soaked each time by the strong waters of the river. She found it exhilarating to be using her physical strength in this way It reminded her of the old Tarzan movies she had watched as a child. However, there were no friendly elephants to pull the canoe upriver in this version of the movie.

They took six hours to get to the farthest boundary of the mining claim they were investigating. They had arrived at the highest navigable part of the river in the interior of the rain-forest which grew between the Andes and the coast of Sierramar. The region was untouched by human development due to the absence of roads. The only populated places were the banks of the innumerable rivers.

Most of the villages had black inhabitants. They had replaced the local indigenous population, except for isolated villages. The vegetation had built up into huge verdant walls, rising many metres above the riverbanks. Here and there among the trees sat small huts on stilts surrounded by banana trees. The lack of wildlife disappointed Sam.

'Why haven't we seen any animals yet?' she asked

Wilson.

He laughed. 'These people,' he said, gesturing at them, 'they eat anything. Only the parrots have survived. They're not stupid, you know. They fly too high to get shot.'

The jungle was not lifeless. There was an abundance of huge, colourful dragonflies and a few Red Admiral butterflies that looked out of place. Sam took photographs of any wildlife she got close to. From their continuous peeping, frogs were also common, but she didn't see any jungle-dwelling mammals. Frustrated by her inability to decipher the local accent, Wilson translated most things for her. He veered between irritation at her floundering, and a strange leering attention that made her uneasy.

'Wilson, I need something to do; why can't I help Doña Elodea?'

'Here in Sierramar it is not appropriate for a boss to do any manual work. You must not carry your own bags or serve the food. The workers will lose their respect for you.'

His attitude towards her was the main thing causing them to lose respect for her. She coped with the novel surroundings but not the inactivity. Watching other people work all day lost its charm after a few hours, and there were only so many photographs she could take. They were digging pits in the gravel and then panning the samples to test for gold.

Gustino and Rijer did most of the digging, sweating in the humid heat of the river shade. Their spectacular physiques glistened in the sun as they dug out the pits. Don Moises did not seem to do anything at all except supervise. Wilson wrote copious notes about the gravel, the size of the stones, the type of matrix they were in and the composition of the pebbles.

Sam had never worked on alluvial gravels before and paid close attention to this process, asking lots of questions. She looked at the stones that made up the gravel, but apart from being smooth and rounded, they did not look geologically interesting.

'How does examining the gravel help locate deposits of gold? These pebbles don't look as if they come from mineralised deposits,' said Sam.

Wilson sneered, but he explained with deliberation.

'The gold comes from a deposit high in the mountains and it washes down the river with all the eroded stones from the bedrock. Gold is heavy compared to rock, and it falls out of the water into the bottom of the river. The river terraces along the banks are ancient riverbeds that have been moved many times by ancient rivers. The gold tends to concentrate in depressions as the stones are washed down river.'

'So, the gravel with rounder stones has undergone lots of movement and has a good chance of containing areas with concentrations of gold?'

'Yes, round stones, and not a lot of sand and silt, which gets washed away during concentration.'

'So, it would be a good idea to record the different layers in the gravel so we can sample them separately?'

'That's what I am doing,' said Wilson, although Sam had seen no evidence.

'Shall I draw them to scale?'

'Okay, but show me what you have done so I can correct your mistakes.'

Sam ignored this comment. She drew detailed profiles of the pits they excavated in the gravel, measuring the layers of sand and gravel and noting the approximate percentages of pebbles and gravel in each layer. Wilson examined the drawings and didn't comment, but he directed the workers to sample each layer she had identified. Sam noted the number of each sample in a list so they would be able to identify them later.

Doña Elodea and Carlos, tasked with checking the gravel for gold, were experts, and Sam watched them as they loaded their large wooden pans with gravel and bent double to lower them into the water. They swirled the pans on the surface, allowing the water to wash through the top of the gravel to clean out the lighter materials and free any heavy materials to sink deeper into the pans. They floated the pans on the surface of the river and brushed the clean gravel from the top of the materials in the pan out into the river.

The quantity of material in the pan reduced until there was only a patch of black sand left in the indentation at the bottom of the pan. The panner then trickled water across the black sand, washing it down the pan and into the sample bag. Sam saw several flecks of gold in the tail of the black sand. They looked like pieces of glitter, but there was no mistaking their yellow glow. She was dying to try this for herself but Wilson glared at her as if reading her thoughts.

The crew often dove into the river from the canoe as it glided along but Sam preferred to enter the water from the bank. The river was mud coloured but refreshing. She was careful not to swallow any water, contaminated with bowel parasites and amoebas. She also ensured there were no routes open to the Candiru before she got into the river.

It was a pain swimming in her long-sleeved shirt and trousers but she noticed that Doña Elodea kept her clothes on in the river so she erred on the side of caution. Her wet shirt wrapped itself around her torso and neck in the water, making her feel as if she was being strangled.

At the end of a long, hot first day, they arrived at Arenas, a village of indigenous Indian people, the only one on the river. As they approached the village on a bend in the river, the women gathered on the bank and sang for them. The sun slid down a golden sky, and the leaves of the jungle canopy gleamed in the warm light. Sam lay back in the canoe and watched the flocks of far-above parrots winging homeward and the rippling muscles of the boatmen as they sliced up the river through the turgid waters. The jungle amazed her, and she soaked up those minutes into her memory bank.

The sound of Wilson arguing with the women over how much their welcoming chorus was worth in terms of a tip disturbed her reverie. Money changed hands and was stuffed into sweaty crevices. They helped unload the canoes onto the pebble beach and then lifted the bags and boxes onto their backs carry them up the steps on the riverbank back up to the plateau where the village perched. Once they had carried all the goods up to the flat land, they set off through the village with the women still singing, until they reached an open square with playing fields in the middle.

The village had allocated their group a sturdy-looking, two-story wooden civil building on one side of the square, in which to set up their headquarters. It had recently been constructed, and the boards had not yet dried and shrunk enough to expose the insides of the house to public scrutiny.

There was a church at the other side of the square that looked like it had seen better days. The women of the village prepared a dinner of rice and tuna for the visitors while the men all went to swim and wash in the river. Sam waited until the rest had finished and gone back to the square before cautiously removing her clothes. She kept her underwear on in case, knowing it was unlikely anyone would spy on her, but feeling as if she was being watched.

Back at the square, the men and older boys played volleyball. Money changed hands with each point won, which they played to the last man standing. The men and boys had pudding bowl haircuts, and some of them wore loincloths instead of trousers. They played in bare feet. A crowd of younger boys and girls played a rough game of football in front of the church. The women sat out on the open-sided, roofed platforms on stilts watching the games and breastfeeding their babies. Some women with infants were still children themselves. They did not try to hide their breasts from the visitors.

Despite his interest in women, Wilson didn't even glance at the bare flesh on display. He didn't consider Indian women to be worthy of his attention, and it made Sam dislike him even more. He sat beside her on the steps of the house as if defying her to stand up and leave.

'The women here get married at thirteen,' said Wilson. 'Where's your husband? Are you divorced?'

'I don't want to get married. It's not compulsory.'

'But you've a boyfriend?'

'No, not right now.'

'You should go out with a man from Sierramar. We're the best.'

He stuck out his chest and moved closer to her, his hand brushing her breast as he reached for his cigarettes.

'Maybe,' said Sam, feeling uncomfortable and shifting along the step focussing her attention on Don Moises. It was fascinating how the other villagers reacted to him. They appeared to treat him with something approaching reverence. As she watched, women brought their babies to him for a blessing.

Sam was unable ask him why they did this without using Wilson to translate. He was being too friendly and being unable to communicate meant that she could not fathom why he had changed his mind about her. She resolved to work even harder to learn fluent Spanish. Meanwhile, Don Moises caught her staring at him. She nodded at him in respect and got a smile of approval in acknowledgement.

The sun set from one minute to the next, falling out of the sky like an egg yolk sliding off a skillet. Since there was no electricity, this would usually have been the signal for the villagers to retire to their houses and go to sleep, as they all rose at dawn. However, after dinner, someone started the generator with fuel they had brought from Riccuarte, and soon, the bare bulbs hanging from the ceiling gave out a bright light.

A party began on the ground floor of their building. This was mostly an excuse to make the visitors pay for a few bottles of cheap rum to get drunk on, but there was also some music for dancing from a big cassette player.

Children of all ages pulled themselves up onto the porch to spy through the windows on the adults dancing. There was a lot of pushing and shoving and some tears as they fought for the best view. Some bigger children joined in with the dancing. Sam attended the party out of politeness although she was desperate for sleep. The party was in their building, so there was no chance of an early night. A man cornered Sam, grabbing Wilson by the arm and indicating that he should translate.

'Are you married?'

'Um, no, not married yet.'

'Good. Are you barren?'

Wilson looked amused as he somehow conveyed this to Sam.

'I don't know.'

'You're too old to be single. Are you strong?'

'Yes, I'm strong,' she answered and wished she could show him by punching him hard.

'I need a wife.'

Sam was about to inform him about the chances of snowflakes in hell, but Wilson intervened and took the man off to get another drink. The approach was a compliment, but it always depressed her to be reminded of the limited possibilities for women in most cultures. As a guest of the village, she needed to be polite, and she danced with anyone who asked, being careful to dance with the older, more important men first.

The squashed corpses of the jungle moths, which had congregated around the lights and were dying in droves, soon littered the floor. The more enthusiastic dancers skidded across the carnage causing painful collisions. Luckily, Don Moises sent the last of the dancers tottering off to bed before it got too late. Despite their enjoyment being cut short, there was no dissent, and the authority Moises wielded struck Sam as unusual.

The members of the expedition climbed the stairs to go to sleep on the top floor of the building, which contained one large bedroom and two smaller padlocked rooms. Sam realised that they would all be sleeping in one room. She would have preferred to sleep in one of the small rooms with Doña Elodea but at least the bedroom was clean and appeared to be free of wildlife.

The men from Riccuarte all slept in a row, with Doña Elodea at the end beside the wall. Sam had hoped to sleep beside her, but Wilson had placed her at the far end of the room against the opposite wall. He put his gear down between Sam and the workers. She assumed he meant to protect her from any drunken assaults. She set up her mosquito net, attaching it to the wall, and lay under it on top of her blanket, exhausted by her day in the jungle.

As she drifted off to sleep, a hand lifted her net, and someone lunged at her out of the dark. Terror forced the air out of her lungs. She couldn't see who it was but then she smelt the cigarettes. It was Wilson, and now he was on top of her. She struggled under his weight, his foul breath in her face. She tried to push him off but to no avail as he pawed at her breasts and ground against her. He tried to stick his tongue in her mouth, his moustache wet and his breath repulsing her.

A screaming rage filled her chest. She opened her mouth to call for help, but then stopped. *Would she get the right response from the sleeping workers*? She didn't know how the men would react. She couldn't explain what had happened to her in Spanish. *What if they helped him? Or joined in and raped her, too?*

Revulsion made her powerful. She freed her hands, and when he lifted himself up for a second, she pushed him off with her left hand and, swivelling to give herself the room, she gave him a right hook into the solar plexus with all her might. Sam had done self-defence training for fun with a former boyfriend who wanted her to protect herself while he was at sea. She knew to leave one knuckle sticking out when she punched him.

She gasped at the pain in her hand. Wilson rolled off her, bringing down the mosquito net, and lay wheezing on the floor of the hut. When he got his breath back, he stumbled out of the room and down the stairs, bumping off the walls. He left the building and did not come back all night.

Furious and scared, Sam sat on the floor trembling, trying to think of what to do next, if someone else thought she was fair game. *What would she say in her pidgin Spanish to make them go away?* For all she knew, the villagers might think it was Wilson's 'droit du seigneury' to have the *gringa* and maybe theirs, too. Shaking with fury and the after-effects of fear, she wanted to cry, but fear stopped her. She felt dirty and ashamed.

She put her mosquito net up again but she could not relax. She had the sensation that not everyone was still asleep and someone was watching her. She lay down under her net, tense and afraid. The entire night, she lay awake, running through the attack again and again in her head. *Why had Wilson attacked her? Was she safe now?* By the time dawn arrived, she pretended to herself it had been a nightmare, but it hadn't.

Chapter IX

It was difficult to avoid Wilson the next morning. Sam ate breakfast at the far end of the house steeling herself for the day ahead. There was no way of going home or contacting anyone to come and get her. She would have to stick it out. Wilson approached Sam before work started. He did not look as if he intended apologising.

'You shouldn't have provoked me if you weren't going to...'

He saw the fury on Sam's face and stopped speaking.

'Provoke you? By writing things in my notebook?' she spat.

'I don't understand, Sam. Speak slowly.'

'Fuck. Off. And. Die. Is that slow enough for you?' She stalked off towards the canoe.

'It was your fault. I'm a man, I have desires.'

Sam spun around.

'Which you should control. I doubt Mike will be impressed by your behaviour.'

Wilson's cocksure expression changed to one of total panic. *Hadn't he imagined that she would complain to Mike?* She could not understand what was going on in his head. Feelings of indignation and humiliation percolated through her as if she had been injected with shame. She was alone in the jungle, unable to speak for herself, reliant on his good graces to get along, and vulnerable to his whims. He tried to take advantage of her while her defences were down and in front of the team. *What sort of pervert was he? Had she really caused this?*

She was apoplectic but unable to let off steam in any satisfactory language. And now he followed her around like a lost dog, chain smoking and apologising. So much for her fond imaginings of working in the jungle with fellow geologists and being a team and having fun together. It was a nightmare. She tried not to cry.

After a breakfast of sweet coffee and bananas, they packed the canoes and pushed off from the riverbank. Sam remained speechless with misery. She sat apart, steeling herself for the day ahead. When they landed to do the sampling, she stayed as far away from Wilson as possible and did not address a word to him except for saying yes or no. He wore his trademark all black outfit with his polyester slacks tucked into black Wellington's, his face in shadow under his fedora emphasising his smoker's wrinkles.

The morning dragged. Sam pretended not to understand anything Wilson said in either language, shrugging and turning her back on him when he tried to talk to her. Determined to carry on somehow, she focused on making notes, even though she was desperate to get back in the canoe and head home. Although she went through the motions and drew sections of the pits dug in the gravel, a profound feeling of humiliation weighed her down, and she felt lost.

When they rested, she sat apart from the group, listening to her Spanish tapes and mouthed the words.

She had never imagined something like this would happen to her. Memories of his body grinding against her made her feel sick. She was close to tears when she heard a strange, high peeping sound in the jungle.

The men heard it, too, and gesticulated at Sam. They noticed that she removed herself from the group and did not smile or try to talk after Wilson jumped on her, but they did not understand what happened or why. They were worried about their pay if the trip got cancelled.

Until this point in the trip, Sam had displayed an interest in photographing everything that moved or didn't. They knew what the peeping noise was. Rijer approached Sam and gestured into the jungle. He did a pantomime of taking a photograph and pulled her arm. She didn't want to take a picture, but she needed a distraction. She grabbed her camera and said '*Vamos*!'

The men took off into the jungle, dragging her with them. This headlong dash into the darkness frightened her, but she understood the pantomime about the camera, so she ran with them. Wilson and Don Moises showed no interest in the frog noise and did not go. The hunters ran into the vegetation at right angles to the river until they stopped at a wet rock-face. They pointed at a bush. Sam peered into the gloom but couldn't see a thing. The peeping sound was louder now, desperate. She nodded, unconvinced, afraid to move nearer.

They kept pointing with insistent fingers. Then, through the shadows, she saw a bright green snake slithering off into the darkness with a frog's head and legs sticking out of its mouth. The frog peeped in a forlorn hope of rescue, trapped in the jaws of the snake. She cursed her cowardice and snapped a photo of what later turned out to be the back view of a well-camouflaged snake with what looked like twigs in its mouth.

She was remonstrating with herself for being feeble when she looked up through the bushes at the face of the rock. To her surprise, the early morning sun highlighted what looked like worn steps cut into the rock. Concave with use, there were pools of water on the steps with sediment at the bottom.

Rijer grinned at Sam. He took a plastic sample bag out of his pocket and ate the leftover piece of meat he had secreted in it. Then, he turned the bag inside out and filled it with sediment from two of the steps. The other men slapped him on the shoulder and seemed most amused by their trip and pleased Sam got her photograph.

They all walked back out to the river where Rijer emptied the sample bag into a pan and sat in the river. He swirled the contents around the pan, reducing the coarser material until there were only black sands at the bottom. He beckoned Sam closer. As she leaned in, he trickled water across the sand, washing it down the pan. A strip of golden flakes appeared at the bottom of the pan.

'Gold,' he said.

Wilson had been observing and stepped closer.

'From where?' he queried.

'From steps in the rock.'

'Maybe Inca make steps,' he said to Sam, 'to catch gold? You want show me?'

Sam was not aware that the Incas had colonised this part of Sierramar. She thought they were mountain people. Intrigued by the steps, she would have liked to stay and do some exploring, but they had work to do and she had no intention of going anywhere with Wilson.

'We need to get on,' said Moises. 'We don't have time for this.'

His veneer of calm had slipped, and he appeared agitated. *Perhaps he was trying to get home before it rained?*

'Next time,' said Sam.

Wilson shrugged, and they returned to the canoes.

The day passed in the established pattern with Sam now happier after her short adventure but still traumatised.

'I have no luck with women,' said Wilson.

Sam did not reply. Phrases like *why am I not surprised* flashed through her head.

'They forced me to marry my wife.'

'Who forced you?'

'Her brothers.'

'A shotgun wedding.'

Well, that figures. He probably raped her too. She wouldn't marry him even if someone pointed a shotgun at her head. Bastard.

She pretended to be asleep for the rest of the trip home. When they got to the village of Riccuarte, a fiesta raged. All the street lights were on, their variety of size and colour creating quite a show. The boys suggested they go dancing. Sam leapt at the chance to avoid Wilson for the evening. They ate tuna and rice again for supper. No wonder she had constipation. It distended her stomach, and she felt as if she would explode.

They held the dance in the schoolhouse. It was a long, low barn with three or four blackboards on the walls. It was dimly lit with the desks pulled back against the walls, used as tables for the drinks. Most of the desks were occupied, but they found one in the corner where they could sit. Rain lashed down in waves soaking the dancers with a mix of water and sweat. Most carried a large handkerchief or a towel and rubbed themselves down from time to time.

Don Moises bought three beers and a bottle of potent local brew that Sam declined to try. Carlos sashayed up to her. Would she like to dance with him if they put a go-go record on? *She would, even though she did not understand what go-go was.* Go-go turned out to be the local version of pop music. All the records so far had been rhythmic African tunes. They danced stiffly with lots of intricate footwork. Most people stared down at their own feet, checking out their moves. Sam tried a couple of dances but found it hard to tone down her movements.

Wilson danced well and was having a ball. Carlos shimmied back over for another dance. At the same moment, the huge son of Doña Elodea requested one. They stared at each other. Sam looked from one to the other anticipating a fight. Wilson was off strutting his stuff on the dance floor, so mediation was not a possibility. She grabbed Carlos and whisked him off to dance under the glare of the jilted boy.

It was great fun. Sam forgot to dance in the local manner and caused much amusement among those watching. A plump girl in a canary yellow dress collared Wilson and danced right up next to him jiggling her giant body. All the other women perched on the school desks, dying to dance. The women never danced without a male partner and waited for an invitation that only the men could offer. Each invitation was only for one dance, and then the woman returned to her perch on the desk. It was an egalitarian system and most people got a turn on the floor. One mother breastfed her baby while waiting for her next suitor.

If Sam sat down, someone asked her for the next dance, despite her foreign way of moving. By the end of the evening, the dancing had exhausted her. Wilson wanted to go home. Don Moises stayed with Doña Elodea because she couldn't stay alone at the dance, being a married woman. At least Sam thought that's what Wilson said, and she now took his translations with a grain of salt.

***

Sam woke up with a bald patch. Bloody rat! Wilson shook with mirth when she showed him the damage. As they washed at the river, they met Don Moises and Carlos, who were still drinking. Despite their inebriated state, they were raring to go to work, and the day was a success. They set off downriver to pan the terraces in the lower reaches of the concession where the river widened and the terraces contained lots of sediment. They stopped several times on their way back upriver to Riccuarte, but the results were not interesting.

'These terraces don't have gold now,' said Wilson. 'Because they're near the road. Men with diggers can come and take out the gold. None left now, I think.'

'Can I try panning?' said Sam, knowing full well that Wilson would have let her do anything to suck up to her.

'Okay. Carlos, show the engineer how to use the pan.'

Sam noticed that Wilson called her engineer, a tacit recognition of her degree. That must have hurt. *Serves him right.* She used all her strength to guide the pan and swirl it in the river like she saw the others doing. It was harder than it looked but the satisfaction of seeing a couple of tiny flakes of gold in the bottom

108

of the pan made it worth the effort. She made copious notes and drawings, more to annoy Wilson than for any technical reason. As he predicted, pickings were slim, and they found a spade handle at the bottom of one pit showing their previous exploitation. This part of the river would not figure in any mining plan.

After work they swam in the river. Carlos and Don Moises showed no signs of wilting, despite having had no sleep. They got back to the village after dark. As Sam and Wilson sat on the stairs outside their shack waiting for their supper, a big bunch of children congregated at the house across the road. They played a game of concerts.

Each child shuffled up the front steps of the house and did a turn for the critical audience who giggled and wiggled as they sat on the wall in front of the house. They greeted each act with raucous applause, and the children often joined in with the performer in their high-pitched, angelic voices.

The horror of what happened to her evaporated with their voices, and soothed by the jungle harmonies, Sam felt safer again. Wilson did not sleep in the house with her that night which was a massive relief. She did not ask him where he had been.

The next day they left Riccuarte. They loaded their bags into the canoe double-wrapped in bin bags to keep out the water. The crew looked worn out. They worked down the river towards the sea to do their last piece of prospecting. Wilson suffered from serious over-attention to her every whim, trying to get back in her good books before she saw Mike. Sam avoided talking to him and spent the day practising her Spanish with the workers.

When they reached the last village on the concession, Wilson paid the men away from Sam.

Carlos came up to her and tried to articulate a complaint to her.

'Eight dollars.' Carlos held up eight fingers and pointed at Wilson. 'The engineer gave us eight dollars. We earned ten dollars.'

'I don't understand, Carlos.'

'Ten dollars. We need ten dollars. Can you help, please?'

Sam understood the sign language better than the word, but it was clear Wilson underpaid them. She did her best.

'Wilson, how much are you paying the workers?'

'This is none of your business. I know what I'm doing.'

'They have worked for five days including today. I make that ten dollars each. Carlos says you only paid them eight dollars.'

'Sam, they're trying to trick you. This is something they try in this region. They think you're stupid because you're a woman. Leave these things to me.'

She didn't believe him and she couldn't prove it, but he had short-changed them and not the other way around. She couldn't speak Spanish yet, but she could count. Embarrassed she couldn't do anything to help them, she shrugged at Carlos and mouthed 'I'm sorry.'

Wilson was a law unto himself. She couldn't believe he'd cheat people who were so poor of a meaningless number of dollars. That was him in a nutshell. If they ever came back, she would bring the difference and make sure they got it.

The workers set off back to Riccuarte in their canoe, grumbling about their pay, leaving Sam and Wilson to go back to San Lorenzo in a pickup truck that had seen better days. They squeezed into the front seat and were thrown from side to side by the terrible condition of the road. Sam regretted that she hadn't chosen to sit with Don Moises, who hitched a lift into town with them and sat in the open part at the back, looking serene despite being thrown into the air by the potholes.

The ash from the cigarettes Wilson chain-smoked blew into her eyes and made them sore. His polyester trousers pressed against her leg making hers sweaty and damp. Their close contact repulsed her but she couldn't move away as she interfered with the gear stick when she slid closer towards the driver. No doubt he, too, would think she fancied him if their legs kept touching.

Once they arrived in San Lorenzo, they checked in to the only habitable hotel in town, a seedy establishment where Sam could hear the bedbugs rustling in the sheets. Wilson left to eat with Moises, but Sam said she wasn't hungry to avoid seeing him any more than necessary. She took the mattress off the bed and rigged up her mosquito net and her sleeping bag on the plywood base, hoping to avoid the worst of the fauna.

She was about to go to bed when Wilson knocked on the door of her room. He brought her some pieces of cooked chicken and a few stale biscuits. It reminded her of a documentary on kingfishers she had seen on the BBC and she remained cagey, pushing him out of her room without speaking to him. He already smelled of the strong local hooch and would, without doubt, drink himself to sleep.

She didn't know what to do about Wilson. Having never been assaulted before, she wondered if she deserved the attack. Perhaps she gave him some signal without realising it? Customs in Sierramar were still a mystery to her. She had been professional on the trip and tried to help when she could without getting in the way. She had done her job in the jungle as a professional geologist, and her colleague had only seen a vagina on legs.

How did this happen? Maybe she would ask Gloria when she got back to Calderon in case it was something she did. She realised that there was a different culture in Sierramar that was not obvious at first but became more obvious as she came into closer contact with the local people. It would be tricky but Sam was determined to learn how to fit in and get on. Her distrust of Wilson still raw, she pushed a chair under the door handle.

Chapter X

Wilson set off at dawn on the train for San Martin, taking with him all the samples and equipment from the trip. Sam took a taxi in the other direction to the beach where Mike, who had taken a break from work, waited for an update.

As the distance between herself and Wilson grew, her anxiety dissipated and her humour returned to normal. Her whole body ached with fatigue, and she looked forward to speaking English again. Her week in the jungle had been an ordeal and not at all what she had expected.

At least she wouldn't have to work with Wilson again after what happened. What excuse could Wilson have for his behaviour? Mike would take her side. She sat back in the ancient taxi and watched the palm trees whizz by.

Someone had tied the doors of the taxi in place with string, and the springs of the back seat stuck into her legs. Now and then the gears got stuck, and the driver had to grind them into submission. A new clutch might have solved the problem, but it sounded as if a new car would have been a better solution.

'You need a new car,' she said.

'Oh, you speak Spanish?' said the driver. What a

relief to hear an accent she could understand.

'Yes, but I understand better than I speak. Are you from San Lorenzo?'

'No, I'm from San Martin. My car is on its last legs. I'd love a new car but we don't make them here. We have to import them. The import tax is two hundred per cent of the price of the car.'

'Two hundred per cent? That's a lot,' said Sam.

'Too much. I need to win the lottery if I want a new car.'

'So how did you pay for this one?'

'Twenty years ago, cars did not have import taxes, then the government saw a way to make lots of money.'

'You bought this one twenty years ago?'

'No, I was a doctor but the state never paid me on time so I bought a second-hand car from my cousin and became a taxi driver instead.'

'Um, does your taxi meter work?'

'No, we don't use them. We charge fares based on the distance and the customer,' said the driver.

'Will I be paying extra?'

'We always charge foreigners extra.' He turned around and grinned. 'But since you speak Spanish, I'll reduce the price.'

'What about my clothes? Do I look rich?' Sam gesticulated at her dirty trousers and torn shirt.

'We can take that into account, too.'

After paying her gringo-based taxi fare, discounted based on her language ability and her shabby appearance, Sam stepped out of the taxi into the sand in the parking lot. Like all the other hotels on the dunes, they built Las Terraces on stilts because of the risk of high tides during stormy weather. The hotel comprised one main building which had a terraced bar and restaurant on the top floor overlooking the beach and the sea. The bottom floor contained storage and the hotel manager's residence.

Stretching right and left along the beach between the palm trees were some wooden cabins for guests, also on stilts, with tin roofs. They had once been painted in bright colours which had now faded to pastel and peeled off in places. There were small porches on each of the cabins with welcoming but shabby hammocks with tatty fringes. Randomly placed seashells and strange-shaped rocks had been left behind by former holidaymakers who had balked at carrying them in their luggage.

There was a cool afternoon breeze blowing. A coconut fell at Sam's feet, making her jump. She left her bag at the foot of the stairs of the main building and climbed up to the restaurant. She approached the bar, and a small wiry man with a greying beard appeared from what looked like the kitchen.

'Hello,' he said in English, 'you must be Sam. I'm Socrates. Your friends are out on the balcony. Would you like lunch?'

Sam was ravenous. She looked through the well-fingered menu and selected a dish called 'fish at the beach,' which pleased Socrates, who bustled into the kitchen to encourage the cook. She wandered out on the balcony. There was no one there, but evidence of a long lunch was spread over a table facing the sea. A bowl of banana crisps and popcorn sat amid the debris of dirty plates and glasses with soggy lemon slices. Sam pushed the plates to the other side of the table and slid along the bamboo bench to sit overlooking the beach.

The sea sparkled in the afternoon sunshine, gulls swooping and crying above a small fishing boat that was heading for shore. Socrates appeared on the beach below the balcony and made for the place where the boat landed. Three fishermen pulled the sturdy craft up onto the sand with the help of several people who had appeared on the beach, alerted by the seagulls. Socrates helped them land the vessel and then entered negotiations over the contents of two orange buckets in the boat's prow. Sam breathed in the sea air and luxuriated in the feel of the sun on her back as she watched him bargain for her supper.

Mike Morton appeared from behind a bamboo screen beside the bar. He wove his way across the floor in the uncertain manner of someone who had enjoyed a long alcoholic lunch.

'Hola, *chica*,' he said, 'want a *cervesa*?'

He giggled at her tired face. His gentle drunkenness disarmed Sam.

'I'd prefer a fruit juice, please. One of those passion fruit juices would be perfect,' said Sam.

Mike turned to go back to the bar to order the juice. Halfway there, he turned back to Sam.

'I'm here with Alfredo Vargas, a friend from Calderon. He's around somewhere. I expect he'll turn up any moment. I think he went to help Socrates with the fishing boat. You'll love him.'

Sam played dumb. Mike didn't have to know she had already met him.

'Alfredo Vargas? I think I met him in the disco. Isn't he eccentric?'

'No more than the rest of us.' He winked.

She was crabby with hunger and in desperate need of a siesta. She smiled back at Mike and tried to ignore the rumbling in her stomach.

After a few minutes, a drunk Alfredo Vargas appeared in the restaurant with a monkey on his shoulder. From where on earth had he conjured up a monkey when the jungles she had left behind were empty of wildlife? He wore the lopsided grin of someone who had also spent the afternoon drinking.

'Cocos locos,' he said, sitting down with a thump beside Sam on the hard bench. The monkey jumped onto the table and scavenged amongst the scraps of food left over from lunch. Alfredo hiccupped and turned to look at Sam with big, brown, unfocused eyes.

He was so drunk he was struggling to recognise her. She could not move away, as she was already touching the railings around the balcony, so she opted for staring back at him.

'Don't I know you? I recognise those green eyes,' said Alfredo

'I'm Sam. We met in the Discoteca, and in the shop on the Avenida Miranda. I was buying chocolate.'

'Ah, now I remember.'

'How's the treasure hunt going?' said Sam.

'I have new clues. I think I'm close,' said Alfredo, slurring.

Mike's eyes widened. 'You said you were a researcher,' he said.

'You didn't ask. I research lost treasures.'

'Tell us all about it,' said Mike.

'Order me a large whisky then.'

Mike called Socrates over and ordered a round of drinks. Socrates brought them over with one for himself. He had heard the tale before but it didn't get boring. Alfredo's back straightened in anticipation and his voice dropped making them all lean in to hear him speak.

'When I was a young man, I befriended Jorge Vasquez. He was one of Sierramar's richest men, who had made a fortune from bananas and cocoa. I had come across some material referring to the lost treasure of the Incas and I resolved to find it. I told Jorge about it and asked him for money to fund the search. Jorge had no family on which to spend his fortune, and he, too, was fascinated by the tale.

He poured money into the project. I convinced Jorge that a crude map I had found in my research would lead us to it, so he dedicated the next twenty years of his life to trying to find the treasure, which, rumour had it, was hidden in the mountains of Sierramar.'

'Twenty years? Wow,' said Mike. 'That sounds like my relationship with Edward Beckett. Did you ever get close to finding it?'

'We made many, many attempts to get it, and I believe we were not far away. The mountains of the Llanganates are unforgiving terrain and it's easy to get lost. Once Jorge broke his leg when a helicopter crashed in a stream. It stranded him for a week while I went to get help. It took a military expedition to find and rescue him.'

'Are you still looking?' said Mike.

'When Jorge got too old to go to the mountains, he delegated me to go there by myself and I always came back with tales of Derring-Do and narrow escapes to entertain him. We were both infamous drinking men, and many nights turned to day in the telling and retelling of these yarns.'

Alfredo paused for breath and took a large swig of his whisky, his eyes filling with tears.

'But when Jorge died of a heart attack last year, it left me bereft and without funding, and to tell the truth, my hunt's been on hold for a few years now. I've tried to go straight, but running a bar in Calderon was probably not the best way to stay sober. So, there you have it. I'm on sabbatical but not retired.'

He grinned and raised his glass. Sam looked across the table through the maze of empty glasses glistening in the late afternoon sunlight. Transfixed by Alfredo's stories, Mike muttered, 'If only I had the money.' Alfredo accepted the adoration as his due.

'Do you want to hear about our trip to Riccuarte?' said Sam when there was a lull in the conversation.

'Did you find a huge deposit of gold?' said Mike.

'Um, not exactly, but it has great potential.'

'Let's talk about it when we get back to Calderon. Wilson should be there too, don't you think?'

She didn't agree, and she would have liked to tell him about Wilson's behaviour, but it was pointless to argue with a man possessing the attention span of a goldfish who had found a new rock in his bowl.

'It can wait.'

While the men talked about the treasure, Sam slipped off for a siesta in the hammock outside her cabin. She was woken in the early evening by mosquitoes dining on her hands. Swearing, she hopped out of the hammock into the cabin and shut the door. She had a shower with water warmed by the sun in the pipes that lay across the sand. When this warm water ran out, the colder supply of water from the well at the beach forced her out.

She sprayed herself from head to foot in repellent and then dressed in a baggy T-shirt and a pair of linen trousers that were almost clean. She slipped on a pair of flip flops and walked to the restaurant. Mike and Alfredo were back at, or had never left, the table which was clear but for a couple of fresh drinks, and they were involved in an intense debate.

Sam slipped onto the bench on Mike's side of the table, but the two men did not acknowledge her, being so intent on their conversation. Socrates came over to the table.

'So, *linda*, what can I get you?' he said.

'I'd like a gin and tonic and a shrimp ceviche please,' said Sam.

'A double?'

'Yes please. Of both.'

She sat watching the bats, staring at the stars and trying to spot the planets. Her input was unnecessary in the conversation the men were having, and she was too tired to talk, anyway. Her drink arrived, and she moved to a quiet corner table where she ate her food and sipped her drink in peace.

She reviewed the events of the past few weeks in her head, avoiding the horror of the near-rape as something she couldn't process without help from Gloria. She couldn't tell Mike while he was in this state. It would have to wait. She raised a glass to herself and drank deep, the alcohol keeping thoughts of Wilson at bay in the inner recesses of her mind.

A warm thrill ran through her as she considered the luck that had brought her to Sierramar. She could see her future now, tangible. Life with Mike would obviously be rather unprofitable but she was learning to be a real geologist and she would soon be unstoppable. Now she had experience of alluvial geology she didn't need Wilson to show her. Soon they would find a project to run and then she would be in charge.

All the doom and gloom she had felt about her career, after being rejected for her gender, had floated away replaced by a certainty that gave her strength. It rippled through her body making her hairs stand on end. She was on her way and no one would stop her. When she got up to leave, Mike and Alfredo were still talking but it looked as if they wouldn't last much longer, either. She waved her thanks to Socrates and went back to her cabin.

***

Sam looked out of her cabin the next day to see the sun shining on the sand. She was so excited that she ran down to the sea in her T-shirt and knickers and jumped in. The water was cold, and she squeaked when it hit her thighs. She pushed into deeper water feeling the sand with her toes. She was covered in goose pimples as her body fought the cold.

There was a strong current, so she only made a couple of feeble attempts at swimming parallel to shore in shallow water. The waves broke over her head, making her cough and snort. The saltwater ran down her throat burning it. *I hate the sea. Why do I always jump in? Sounds like my life.*

Judging that she had done enough to justify being wet, Sam came out of the water and marched up the beach to her cabin. Alfredo lay in his hammock, watching her from under the brim of his hat, all of his hairy limbs dangling over the edges. He resembled road kill. She waved, and he raised a limp hand to acknowledge that he had seen her.

Sam felt great, and she was hungry, the sea air having done wonders for her appetite. She got dressed and wandered up to the restaurant to see if someone could muster up breakfast. A fat, jolly woman in the kitchen understood Sam's famished look with no need for conversation.

'*¿Buenos días, mi señorita, quieres desayunar?*' she asked.

'Breakfast? Yes, please,' answered Sam. 'Two fried eggs, fried ripe plantains, toast, juice and tea.'

She wanted to ask for yoghurt as well but couldn't remember the word in Spanish. When her breakfast arrived, it had yoghurt anyway with a big spoonful of granola. Perfect. Sam ate everything except the plates. The eggs were delicious. They didn't have that supermarket fishmeal taste that the ones in London had. She had been desperate for something tasty after all those boring meals of tinned tuna and rice.

She forced any thoughts of Wilson back down her throat with an ocean of food. She drank two cups of tea and a glass of passion fruit juice, and then, feeling bloated, staggered back to her cabin and fell asleep in her hammock. The sound of the sea sent her into a deep slumber.

She was still asleep when Mike tapped her on the shoulder. 'Sam, wake up. We're going to the airport now.'

She didn't remember Mike telling her they would leave for Calderon so soon. Surprised and saddened by this news and groggy with sleep, she got to her feet and went inside to pack her bag. She hadn't told him about Wilson yet but the opportunity had not arisen with all the talk of treasure. It would have to wait until she got Mike on his own.

It didn't take her long to get packed, but by the time she walked to the restaurant, Mike and Alfredo were already sitting in a taxi with the engine running.

'Hurry, the flight leaves in an hour,' said Mike, leaning out of the window.

'Sorry, you didn't tell me that. I packed as fast as I could,' said Sam.

Mike looked her up and down. 'Well, you obviously weren't deciding what to wear.'

Wow, that was nasty. Where did that come from? It's not like he hired me for my looks. Despite the urge to say something clever or funny, Sam didn't defend herself and swallowed the insult to avoid conflict like she always did.

'I think the *gringa* looks cute,' said Alfredo, who had noticed Sam's hurt at this remark.

Sam smiled, and it raised her opinion of him a notch. Mike did not notice the effect that his remark had on her and hummed tunelessly, drumming his fingers on the window frame. Sam got into the front seat of the taxi and pretended to go to sleep.

The ancient taxi did not look as if it had the legs to make it to the airport in time, but they got there with half an hour to spare. They were not the last passengers on the plane. A big fat man in a dress uniform stomped up the stairs and evicted someone from the front row about five minutes after take-off time.

Mike and Alfredo sat together talking treasure in hushed tones, and Sam sat beside a woman, who spent the whole flight doing and redoing her makeup in a quiet panic. *We are never pretty enough, or thin enough. There is always a reason to criticise us.*

Gloria was there to collect them, waiting in the no-parking area at the arrival's door. She looked her best, having been to lunch with her friends from school.

'Gloria, this is Alfredo,' Mike said. 'He's a treasure hunter.'

'A pleasure,' said Alfredo, kissing her hand in his most gallant manner. Gloria blushed, and in her confusion, drove off without Sam, who was trying to put her bag into the boot of the car. Sam raised an eyebrow at her when she slammed on the brakes and leaned out of the window with an apologetic shrug.

Gloria dropped Mike and Sam off at the flat in Avenida Miranda and drove off chatting to Alfredo, who had a big smile on his face. Sam crossed her fingers and hoped that Gloria could be distracted from her hopeless quest of the successful Diego by a successful quest for the hopeless Alfredo.

'Home, sweet, home,' she remarked to Mike, who grunted. 'I wonder what's in the fridge.'

She lugged her bag into the utility room at the back of the kitchen. Tati was not there, so she left her dirty clothes in a pile by the large sink.

'How come we don't have a washing machine? Are they expensive?' said Sam.

'No, Gloria told me they put maids out of work. The maids resent washing machines as usurpers and are liable to sabotage them,' said Mike

'Would Tati mind if you bought one?'

'Tati has minimal cleaning to do, and she's had to hand wash clothes since she was a small girl.'

The tone didn't invite discussion. Sam went into her room and shut the door. Soon, she luxuriated in a hot shower and thought about supper.

Chapter XI

The day after getting back from the beach, Sam went with Gloria to the one-hour photo shop to drop off Sam's photographs of the trip to Riccuarte for developing. There was a long queue and Sam got impatient at the glacial pace of the shop assistants.

'I can't see why they are taking so long,' she said, standing on tip-toe and straining to see what was happening at the counter.

'What's wrong with you, *gringa*?' said Gloria. 'It's called the one-hour-photo because you queue for an hour to hand in your film.'

Sam laughed in delight. Despite the difference in their cultures, they had a sense of the absurd in common, and were becoming firm friends.

The next stop on their list was the geography institute where they had to buy more maps. There were no jolly teenage soldiers guarding the entrance this time. The jaundiced men at the gate were immune to Gloria's charm and made them park outside on the street and walk up the steep hill to the entrance.

The purchase of the maps took forever, and the colonel kept them waiting even longer than usual for his signature. This did nothing for Sam's mood, and even Gloria seemed irritated that he had not responded to her best smile.

They returned to collect the photographs, but the shop was closed for lunch. Worse still they got back to the flat to find Mike had given them the wrong map numbers. A final trip to collect the photographs confirmed Gloria's fears.

'The photographs are not ready yet, madam,' said the assistant.

'Can you tell me when I can come and collect them?' said Gloria.

'You could try tomorrow after eleven.'

'Thank you, we'll do that.'

Sam's face darkened, and she glared at the girl behind the counter who tossed her head and went into a back room to gossip.

'Sam, you gotta stay calm. If they notice you're impatient, they'll get nervous because you're a *gringa*. They think you'll shout things they don't understand,' said Gloria.

'But they're slow on purpose,' said Sam.

'It's not that. They're not used to someone in a hurry.'

The pace of life in Calderon frustrated Sam. It was such a contrast to London. The inefficiency was getting to her. Gloria took it on the chest and accepted the 'mañana' culture with good humour and a cigarette.

Her inability to tell Mike about what had happened in the jungle worsened Sam's mood. She couldn't find the right time to broach the subject and the longer it took the harder it became. Meanwhile, she had taken such an intense dislike to Wilson that she couldn't bear to be in the same room as him. He also kept his distance, so much so that even Mike noticed the frost between them.

'What's up with you and Wilson?' he said.

She snapped at him unable to control her stifled emotions.

'Nothing's up, Mike. Unless you count the fact that he tried to assault me during the trip.'

Mike looked bewildered by her accusing tone.

'What? When did this happen?' he said.

'Um, in the jungle, in a house at night,' said Sam, staring at her feet.

'Why didn't you tell me about this before? Do you think I'm psychic?'

'I'm sorry. I couldn't find the right time at the beach but I've told you now.'

'It can't have been that bad if you haven't told me yet. He didn't harm you, did he? He only tried?'

'No, he didn't manage do anything but only because I punched him in the solar plexus,' she said. 'But he attacked me in the night for no reason. I don't trust him. I don't want to work with him anymore. Can't we use someone else?'

Mike looked annoyed.

'Someone else? This is Sierramar, you know. He's the best geologist we've got. I can't magic up another one. You have to realize that the differences in our cultures can cause strange interpretations. Maybe he misunderstood something you did.'

'But I didn't do anything. I worked and minded my own business. Can't you at least talk to him?'

'No, I can't. You must have done something. Figure it out and be more careful next time.'

Next time? How did it turn out to be her problem? Somehow it had become her fault instead of Wilson's. It upset her that Mike dismissed her, but she did not want to make an enemy of him. Why she hadn't told him at the beach? Perhaps she was ashamed.

Anyway, she had told him she could look after herself and now she was demonstrating that she couldn't. She had a job, and that was a lot more than most geologists. She was getting paid, and although it was a minuscule amount, was paying off her university debts bit by bit.

When she realised Mike would do nothing about Wilson, Sam dealt with it her way. She never spoke to Wilson unless she had to and then only in words of one syllable. Oblivious to the damage he had caused and Mike's total indifference to the incident, Wilson was on a mission, sending her cards with pink teddy bears on them, apologising for his behaviour.

There was nothing Sam hated more in the world than disgusting fuchsia monstrosities on cards or cuddly toys. She was allergic to them, and with Sam, there were no half measures. She was not a nuanced thinker at this stage of her life. There were only two colours: black or white.

She considered women who collected cuddly toys to be infantile. She thought men who gave them were paedophiles or morons. Wilson could not have picked a better way to make her feel nauseous and alienate her further. It felt like he was trying to make her feel worse by grouping her with that kind of woman.

Needing advice about Wilson, Sam rang Gloria and asked her to pick her up at the office so they could collect the photographs.

'Oh no, *chica*. I can't pick you up this morning. There is a strike.'

'A strike? Who's on strike? I don't understand.'

'It's a protest about the economy. Most people stay indoors on strike days. The strikers throw stones at private cars that dare to go outside. You can only go downtown by taxi but, even then, they often block the streets with barricades and burning tires. If the strike is bad, the shops can get looted.'

'It's more like a riot, then? What's it about?'

'The government devalued the national currency so the students throw Molotov cocktails at the police who respond with tear gas and baton charges.'

'Are the students interested in politics?'

'The students don't care about the currency. They only love to riot and stone the police so they don't have to go to classes.'

The strike was over by lunchtime, so Sam and Gloria ventured out to the Banana Verde for lunch. Burning tires still littered the centre of town, but the streets were deserted. They tried to collect the photographs on the way to lunch, but the shop was closed because of the strike.

Sam asked Gloria to stay and have a coffee with her in the restaurant before going back to the office. Gloria was easy to persuade and appeared glad that her *gringa* friend was adapting better to 'Calderon time' if not to its glamour. Sam wore an old, blue shirt with the sleeves rolled up and a pair of ancient denim jeans. Her face was free of makeup and her fingernails naked of polish.

'So, *chica*, what's up?' Gloria asked.

Sam hesitated, unsure how to approach this subject, but she wanted to know the truth. Had she done something to provoke him or not?

'It's Wilson,' she said. 'He tried to rape me.'

Gloria's horrified expression alarmed her, so she added, 'Well, not rape me, exactly, assault me, I think. I don't know...'

She trailed off, ashamed, and stared hard at the salt cellar in the shape of a chef with a big white hat. Her face blazed with shame.

Gloria looked shocked but only for a moment. She nodded sagely.

'When was this?'

'In the jungle. He jumped on top of me without warning during the night.'

'I can't believe it. How did you stop him?'

'I punched him in the solar plexus.'

'Good for you. That son of a bitch thinks he can have any woman.'

'But, Gloria, we're equals. We're both geologists. I don't understand what I did to encourage him.'

'Sam, are you so naïve? Do you really believe Wilson thinks of you as an equal?'

It had never occurred to Sam that she was less than human to some men because she wasn't a man, too. She shook her head.

'Has he left you alone since?'

'He sent me a horrible pink cuddly toy and a card with hearts and flowers on it, begging me for forgiveness. I hate cuddly toys.'

'He probably thinks all women like them.'

'He's not stupid. He knows I hate him and his cuddly toys. What did I do to deserve this? I'm so ignorant of the culture here. I'm worried that I'm responsible for it happening,' said Sam, in tears now. 'Please, tell me the truth.'

Distressed now, Gloria's eyes filled with tears, too. She stood up and moved next to Sam on the banquette and gave her a tender hug.

'You poor girl. That Wilson is a monster. He's afraid that Mike will hear about this and fire him. Have you told Mike yet?'

'Yes, but he thinks I provoked Wilson and he won't do anything about it. I couldn't persuade him.'

'Typical man. He's wrong about Wilson. I've

heard things about him you wouldn't believe. You didn't provoke him, not on purpose anyway. That man would jump a giraffe.'

Sam couldn't help smiling at the possibility.

'So, Wilson's a complete bastard?' said Sam.

Gloria smiled. 'Absolutely, *chica*. And that's not all. I heard he frequents brothels and beats up the girls. He has a reputation as a violent drunk. There are rumours he owes a lot of money around town.'

'Does Mike know?' asked Sam.

'I don't think so,' said Gloria, 'but I promise to tell him as soon as I get the chance. I think Wilson has designs on Marta, and that poor girl has no chance against his persistence and brand of full-on charm.'

'Really?' she asked. 'I didn't do anything provocative?'

'Ha!' said Gloria. 'Dressed like that? There isn't a man in Sierramar who would think you were trying to attract him.'

Sam took the verdict on her dress sense on the chin. Glamour was not her forte. Gloria had the ability to make her laugh at anything. Sam trusted her, and she knew she could count on her. Vindicated by Gloria's reaction, she was determined to make Mike see sense. She would also make certain she never slept near Wilson again.

***

Sam and Gloria collected the photographs of the trip. She gave the shop assistants her brightest smile as she left, having learned something from Gloria about how to make friends and influence people in Calderon. Sam ripped the envelope open in the car and devoured the contents, squeaking with delight at the best ones and shoving them in front of Gloria who drove even more erratically than usual.

They went to meet Alfredo and Mike for lunch. The two men had formed a close friendship after their trip to the beach. They were both obsessed with the treasure and rarely spoke of anything else. She found herself in charge of the geology projects that came into the office and, as her Spanish continued to improve, she took owner meetings with Marta.

If Mike got bored with Alfredo, and his hunt for the elusive treasure, Sam was determined to be ready with some good prospects. There was no point in going home. She didn't want to be a secretary and the job market had not improved. Besides, she found that reviewing projects was educational and increased her understanding of what was out there. A spell in Sierramar would look good on her resumé whatever she did there and fluent Spanish would be even better.

Sam could not get Alfredo alone again since the beach, but she got to know him a little better due to his constant presence in the office. The archetypal Byronic hero, he rebelled against convention, was self-destructive, passionate, arrogant and charismatic. Although he claimed to loathe the English, it was a love/hate relationship for him as he dressed his compact frame in the clothes of a Devon country farmer.

A charming man with a history of bad luck that was always self-inflicted, he loved to tell tall tales. He ripped his shirt open in the office one afternoon, making the buttons fly in all directions. He had a large, livid scar on his left shoulder. The flesh was shrivelled, purple and pulled around a central hole, like a large pair of pursed lips or as Mike remarked, an arsehole.

'Do you see this scar?' he asked. 'Want to know how I got it?'

'Whoa! That's some scar,' said Sam, who had a few herself from playing hockey. 'How did you get it? Did someone stab you with a poker?'

Alfredo laughed. 'Ha! Nothing that exciting. I fell into a drunken sleep under a poisonous tree in the Galapagos. The sap of the tree dripped onto my shoulder and ate away at it. My friends found me with a large hole in my flesh, still sound asleep under the deadly tree. They rushed me to the hospital, and an emergency operation saved my arm by cutting out the poisoned flesh.'

'Is the moral of the story never to sleep under a poison tree?' said Sam.

'Or not to get so drunk you don't wake up when your flesh is melting?' said Mike.

In case Sam was in any doubt about the truth of this story, Alfredo made her touch it. She shivered with horror as her finger slipped into the puckered hole.

When they were all seated at the table in the restaurant, Mike and Alfredo reverted to the subject of the treasure. Sam had heard it all before and opened the envelope of photographs which she examined at length. Several of them were classics. She shared them with Gloria, who having ignored them in the car, examined them with little enthusiasm. She was more interested in flirting with Alfredo from under her fat eyelashes.

Sam examined the photograph of the snake with the frog in its mouth. It wasn't great, but anyone could see what it was if they peered at it.

'Mike,' she said, 'you must look at this photograph. Can you tell what it is?'

The interruption was unwelcome. Mike grabbed the photograph and gave it a cursory glance before passing it to Alfredo. Alfredo glimpsed at the photograph and was about to give it back to Sam when he went pale. He brought it up to his face and screwed up his eyes.

'Mike,' he said. 'Lend me your glasses.'

Mike gave him his reading glasses which Alfredo put on. He peered at the photograph muttering 'oh my God'. Mike scrutinized his friend. 'Do you feel all right, Alfredo? You have gone a funny colour.'

Alfredo stared at the photograph in shock.

'Oh, my God,' he muttered. 'Holy crap and all the saints.'

He stood up letting the photograph fall to the floor and ran to the door of the restaurant, pushing his way past the waiters and out into the street. He got straight into a taxi and it drove away at high speed.

There was silence at the table for a moment.

'What the fuck just happened?' said Mike.

'Search me,' said Sam. 'Maybe he forgot something.'

'Maybe he wasn't feeling well,' said Gloria. 'He could be afraid of snakes.'

Sam picked up the photograph from the floor. She blew on it to remove any dirt and looked again at the snake. Great photograph! *What on earth had prompted Alfredo's weird behaviour? Surely it wasn't the snake? Perhaps he had been drinking before he came to lunch?* It wouldn't have been unusual.

'Shall we order?' she asked. 'We'll find out later.'

'Yes, I'm starving,' said Mike. He signalled to the waiter to come over to the table, and they ordered their food. When it arrived, they all ate with gusto and forgot all about the strange incident with Alfredo. Sam and Gloria shared a crème caramel for pudding, and they asked for a pot of filter coffee.

They contemplated their coffees and were basking

in after-lunch contentment when Alfredo appeared at the restaurant's door as suddenly as he had left. He had with him a great sheaf of papers and documents in various stages of repair and a plastic bag full of similar materials and books hanging from his arm. The plastic bag was old and greying and looked likely to split any minute.

Alfredo was sweating, a strange fanatical look on his face. He didn't notice that his appearance was drawing comments from the other diners. He staggered over to the table, and a waiter who had been watching his progress, leaped forward to remove the various plates, glasses and empty cups from the table. Alfredo dropped his documents on the dirty tablecloth, illustrating how they came to be so stained and torn.

'Alfredo, are you okay?' asked Mike. 'What is all this stuff?'

'Treasure,' mumbled Alfredo. 'It's the treasure, Mike.'

'What do you mean, treasure? I don't understand. You said it was hidden in the mountains.'

'It's the photograph. The one of the snake.'

'What has a photograph of a snake got to do with treasure?'

'The cypher. The cypher,' said Alfredo, addressing Sam. 'You found the cypher.'

He was bright-eyed with excitement. Gloria called the waiter over.

'Can you bring us a bowl of pig trotter soup, please? And a large pot of strong coffee?'

The waiter who had been hovering at the table, set off for the kitchen and returned with the soup. Gloria piled the documents together and made room for him to place the bowl. Alfredo was now dumbstruck with what appeared to be shock.

'Alfredo try a little soup. It'll do you good.'

'I'm not hungry. What is it?'

'Wake the Dead soup.'

'Oh, that's my favourite. I might try.'

Soon he was eating as if he had not seen food for days. The soup disappeared, and Gloria poured Alfredo a large cup of coffee.

'Sugar?'

'Yes, lots.'

'Lots it is, then.'

Sam and Mike suffered silent torture while they waited for Alfredo to eat his soup and drink his coffee. After an age, he sighed, patted his stomach and sat back in his chair. He looked around the restaurant. Most people had left to go back to work, and the few remaining occupied tables were out of earshot. He leaned forward and asked Sam to give him the photo again.

She handed it over, glancing at it again but still unable to understand what the excitement was about. Alfredo spoke in a conspiratorial whisper. They leaned in to hear what he had to say.

'The steps—they're the key,' he said, 'the key to the lost treasure of the Incas. Sam, where did you take this photo?'

Sam was flummoxed. 'I've no idea. Upriver from Riccuarte. Wilson would know, or Don Moises,' she said. 'I'm sure we could find them again.'

'What's so special about the steps?' said Mike.

'We can't talk here,' Alfredo whispered. 'Let's go back to the flat in Avenida Miranda. We can spread the material out on the floor, and I'll lead you through the story.'

'Okay,' said Mike. 'I'll pay the bill and let's go.'

He paid and left a large tip for the surprised waiter.

Alfredo stuffed his papers into a newer plastic bag as they left the restaurant and squashed into the car. Gloria took the wheel and set out for Mike's flat. No one spoke. Sam tried to remember if she had noticed anything special about the steps. She had been so focussed on the snake carrying away the frog that she hadn't given them a second thought.

There was a grim determination to Gloria's driving. She swung the car into its space in the underground parking garage, so close to the wall that they had to inch out past the pillars. They trooped into the lift and rose to the apartment surprising Marta when the four of them appeared in the apartment's doorway. She had been planning to slip away for the afternoon and do some shopping, but she recovered.

'What's up, Mike? You look mysterious.'

'We need to use the floor of the sitting room as a large display area. Can you ask Tati to give it a good sweep?'

'Yes, of course. Give me a minute.'

Marta went to the kitchen where Tati was doing a large pile of ironing and put on the kettle.

'Tati, please can you sweep the floor and make a large pot of tea? I think we'll need the big cups.'

The floor swept, and the tea poured, everyone stood back as Alfredo laid his documents out in order on the parquet flooring.

'What's this about, Mike? What are those documents?' asked Marta.

'Tell Tati to go home please, Marta. We won't need her again today. You should go home, too. This is confidential.'

'Oh, Mr Mike, please don't send me home. I love secrets. I promise not to tell.'

'You swear it?'

'Cross my heart and hope to die,' she said.

'It's top secret. You can't tell anyone,' said Mike.

'Okay, boss. I promise.'

Tati did not look at all happy to be sent home. Mike shooed her out and shut the door.

Once they all had a cup of tea and were perched on the low windowsills along the picture window of the sitting room, Alfredo was ready to talk.

'Sorry about lunch. I was so amazed I didn't know how to react. I've spent twenty years looking for this.'

'Looking for what? The snake? I don't understand,' said a bewildered Mike.

'I will fill you in on the background before I tell you. Is that okay?'

'Sure.'

'So, as you may already know, there's always been a lot of talk of El Dorado and ancient treasure troves in Latin America, but one that is historical rather than mythical is the story about Atahualpa's ransom. When the Spanish commander Pizarro captured Atahualpa, the great Inca chief in 1532, he demanded a huge ransom for his release. A great convoy of Atahualpa's people, led by his half-brother Rumiñahui, set off carrying the gold to pay for his freedom.

However, the Spanish reneged on their deal and executed Atahualpa before the convoy could arrive. The news reached the convoy when they were high in the mountains of Sierramar. Rumiñahui hid the riches where the Spanish would never find them. The legend says the hoard was taken up secret pathways and hidden deep in the mountains. Then all the bearers committed suicide.'

'Suicide? That's horrible,' Marta said. 'Why did they do that?'

'To prevent them telling anyone where it was

hidden, of course. Decades later, a Spanish adventurer called Valverde married an Inca princess, a descendant of Rumiñahui. The story goes she led him to the hiding place, and he made a secret map of the route. He may have removed a part of it and returned to Spain a wealthy man.

Upon his death, he left the map, describing the landmarks on the way in great detail. This route had been the blueprint used by all the hunters since then, but no one else has found their way back to it.'

'But how did the princess know where the treasure was, if the bearers committed suicide?' said Sam.

'Nobody knows.'

'Has nobody else come close?' said Marta.

'A British botanist named Richard Spruce (after whom the tree is named), arrived in Sierramar in 1860. His book, *Notes of a Botanist on the Amazon and Andes*, gave further details of the hunts that took place after the death of Valverde. Various adventurers came close or even claimed to have found the treasure over the years, but all perished before returning to claim the booty.'

'Do we know what it contains?' asked Mike.

'The last person who claimed to have found the it died on a ship carrying an expedition force returning to Sierramar to remove it. His name was Barth Blake. He had described the hiding place as being in a cave: "There are thousands of gold and silver pieces of Inca and pre-Inca handicraft... life-sized human figures made of beaten gold and silver, birds, animals, cornstalks, gold and silver flowers. Golden vases full of jewellery".'

'Wow, that sounds amazing,' said Sam. 'What happened to Blake?'

'Blake died before he could give anyone

information on its whereabouts. He'd talked about ascending some steps cut into the rock. He had mentioned no mountains although he had used the Valverde map to get to the treasure. But no one has seen it since. People assumed that it was lost.'

'What has this got to do with the snake in Sam's photo, Alfredo?'

'I spent twenty years researching the mystery of the hoard's whereabouts with Jorge Vasquez but we never got close.' Alfredo paused as if considering this. 'But what if the map is no longer valid? Maybe the treasure was moved after Valverde found it. Had Blake stumbled across it somewhere else?'

'You mean in the jungle where Sam was?' said Mike.

'Blake's description of the steps matched those in the photograph that Sam took. They had a serpent cipher on them not seen on Inca monuments. The cipher represents a king or leader.'

Alfredo stopped talking and fumbled through his papers, producing a line drawing of an Inca design showing the cipher which he held up.

'Where's the cipher?' Mike was breathless with excitement.

'Sam, can you have a look at the photograph of the snake again, please?'

Sam opened her handbag and took out the photograph again. In the background behind the bushes, she saw the same cipher carved into the steps, only visible because the late afternoon sunshine had hit the rock at an angle. Her jaw dropped.

'I-it's identical,' she stuttered. 'Identical.'

They took turns comparing the cipher to the photograph, and agreed that it was the same.

'Does this mean what I think it does?' said Mike.

'I hope so. Sam might have discovered the resting place of the lost treasure of the Incas. Imagine the historical value of something like that,' said Alfredo.

'We'll be rich beyond our wildest dreams. I can't even guess how much something like that would be worth,' said Mike.

'Are we going to search for it?' said Sam, her excitement rising. *A real treasure hunt. Surely, she would go?*

'What do you think?' said Mike. 'Alfredo, we have some discussing to do. The rest of you, go home and please do not talk about this with anyone.'

'Not even our families?' asked Marta.

'Not even with the Pope.'

'What about Wilson?' said Sam, crossing her fingers under the table.

'I don't think you should use Wilson. He's shifty,' said Gloria, unwilling to elaborate with Marta in the room.

'That may be true but we will need his help to get us set up in Riccuarte,' said Alfredo. 'I don't know anyone around there.'

'We don't have to tell him about the hoard,' said Mike. 'I'll tell him we are mounting an archaeological investigation and that we won't need him after he gets us to the river. The fewer bodies involved, the better. People can be odd about money.'

Chapter XII

When the meeting was over, Marta travelled home on the bus. She buzzed with suppressed excitement but she kept her secret all through the evening and into the next morning because there was no one at home old enough to understand the significance of the serpent cipher or the trials of Atahualpa. Her telephone had been cut off because she had forgotten to pay her bill that month.

Marta lived with her three-year-old son, who obsessed over cartoons on the television and always wanted to see *'just one more, Mummy'*. He was a wilful child who took after his mother in character and after his father in looks. Sometimes Marta couldn't bear to look at her son because it brought back all the feelings of shame and humiliation she associated with her ex-boyfriend.

He had left her pregnant at nineteen and run off with another girl who lived one street away and had a green card for the USA. Marta had to face her disappointed family and disapproving neighbours when she discovered that she would have a baby. She got pregnant the first time she slept with him, which was on the night he asked her to marry him. How corny! *How did she fall for that old chestnut and on St*

Valentine's Day, too? Despite all the warnings from her mother about having sex before marriage, she had fallen for the oldest trick in the book, and she had a son to remind her.

He was the spitting image of his father, poor lad. It wasn't his fault she wouldn't look at him. Even worse was the knowledge that Francisco had never intended to marry her. How could she compete with that hussy and her right to live in the States? Life was not fair. Marta had ceased to trust from that day forth, assuming that a lot of her friends and family knew that her boyfriend was playing away but did not warn her.

She got ready for work, taking a lot of time with her makeup as she did daily. She blew her hair dry and fixed it into place with a toxic amount of hairspray. Satisfied that she looked her best, she took the bus into work, bursting to tell someone her secret. She let herself into Mike Morton's apartment and slipped into the kitchen. She was rewarded with the sight of Tati, the maid, bent double over the washing board, punishing Sam's jeans. Tati came from the coast and brought the sunshine with her. Her lithe body danced over the task with all the enjoyment of a job well done. She looked up when she heard the tick-tack of Marta's high heels on the tiled kitchen floor, announcing their owner's hurried arrival.

'Good morning, Señora Marta,' she said. 'How are you today?'

'Well, thank you, Tati,' she said, 'and you?'

'I'm okay. A little concerned about last night. I don't understand why Señor Mike made me go home when the whole team was there. I've come early to clean the clothes with all my might so he can see me working hard.'

'You've done nothing wrong. Mike would have

told me.'

'I took home the remains of a chicken they had for lunch this week. It was mostly bones, but I removed it without asking. I wasn't able to sleep last night worrying about it. I should've asked Mike, but I thought no one would notice.'

'It's definitely not the chicken. You needn't worry. If you make me a cup of coffee, I'll tell you all about it. Okay?'

Tati wrung out the jeans and hung them over a drying rack. She wiped her hands on her apron and padded into the kitchen in her flip-flops. She made them both a cup of strong coffee with lots of sugar. Marta struggled to keep her composure while Tati spooned the sugar into the cups and stirred it extra slowly.

'Thank you,' said Marta, straining at the seams with impatience. 'That's good coffee.'

'So, what's up with Mr Mike and Mr Alfredo?' said Tati.

'This is top secret. You mustn't tell anyone.'

'I won't. I promise.'

'Last night after you left, Alfredo told us about the lost treasure of the Incas. It belonged to Atahualpa, and they intended to use it to pay his ransom, but the Spanish murdered him before the ransom was paid and it disappeared. It turns out that Sam took a picture of a cipher Alfredo thinks might have something to do with the hiding place. I didn't understand that part. I think she said it was in the jungle.'

Tati shifted in her chair.

'Really?'

'Yes, Alfredo's a treasure hunter, and he has lots of books about it, so he must be clever. He seems sure that Sam has found something to do with it, and Mike wants to look for it himself. Well, not himself, but he wants Sam and Alfredo to go, I think. Isn't that amazing?'

She paused, breathless. She sat back and waited for Tati to beg her for more details. She was disappointed. Tati appeared unimpressed by this tall tale.

'Ah, but that story is a myth. I read about it in the newspaper. There's no trove any more. It was all stolen by the Spanish, or someone, I can't remember who. Anyway, I don't believe it still exists. Are you sure you don't know why Mr Mike sent me away?'

'Perhaps because we were speaking English. Aren't you interested?'

'No, it's none of my business. I'm worried about losing my job. I have to finish the laundry.'

'But Tati...'

Tati stood up and marched off to the sink. She was worried about her job, but Marta didn't understand why she didn't seem interested in the treasure and had dismissed it out of hand as a myth. Tati was the first one to gossip about superstitions, rumours and miracles. Today, she had showed no interest at all. This apparent change of heart frustrated Marta, but she had never understood Tati and assumed that she was in a mood or had her period.

Marta remained frustrated, still carrying her secret, which felt as yet unshared because of Tati's reluctance to take part in speculation. She sulked at her desk all morning and sighed loudly when Mike and Sam left to go to lunch with Gloria.

'What's wrong with Marta?' said Sam.

'Probably got her period. Ignore her,' said Mike. 'She'll get over it.'

***

Sam's growing excitement about the treasure was tempered by the fact that Mike had still not told her whether she go with Alfredo to look for it. It seemed obvious she should go, after all, they would never have found the steps without her, but past experience of being left out nagged at her until she got up the courage to corner Mike.

'Have you got a minute?' she said.

'What's up?' said Mike.

'Nothing. I'm just so excited about the treasure.'

'Isn't it great? I've always dreamed of being a wealthy man and having my own yacht. My mother, God rest her soul, was a social climber, and she forced me into social circles where I wasn't able to compete in terms of money or education. Class is something money can't buy, but I wanted to better myself anyway and set about reading any book I could find. I travelled far and wide getting experience in other cultures and countries.'

'How did you get into investing?'

'Rich people like to invest in riskier schemes as a side-line to all those boring bonds and properties. It's like an expensive casino for them. The rewards can be huge—and unlikely—but they like to take a punt sometimes. I'm well placed to put them in touch with my contacts worldwide, many of whom specialize in finding unlikely projects for investment. The lost treasure of Atahualpa is an entrepreneur's dream. It has everything: adventure, history, violence, mystery. I've had no trouble convincing Edward to put up the money to pay all the salaries and office bills in Calderon, funding the trips to the jungle and so forth.'

'That's great,' said Sam. She paused, uncertain.

'What is it?'

'Am I going?' she said.

Mike's eyes opened wide and he laughed, a frustrated bark.

'For God's sake, of course you are. Someone has to help keep Alfredo on the straight and narrow until you get to Riccuarte. He's struggling to cope with the revelation about the hiding place of the Inca hoard being in Esmeraldas instead of the Llanganates. He might become a liability on this trip if he can't stay sober.'

Sam stopped holding her breath. 'I can't say I'm glad Wilson's coming, but I understand.'

'It's only to Riccuarte. Just be careful not to provoke him again.'

Sam swallowed her reply. There was no point trying to convince him she hadn't done anything to attract Wilson's attention. Mike didn't comprehend Wilson's behaviour because he was used to women throwing themselves at him because of his public profile. He had assumed Sam had been starstruck by Wilson's manly appeal.

'I'll do my best,' she said. 'I've taken to Alfredo, despite all the drinking. He's such a charming man, it's impossible to resist him. Wilson isn't the picture of sobriety himself. I hope I can keep an eye on both at once.'

'I wish I was coming,' Mike continued, oblivious, 'but I can't risk it. Doctor's orders. But if it wasn't for that, nothing would keep me away. In fact, it would be the adventure of my life. I can't wait to hear all about it.'

Doctor's orders? Mike was too lazy to come on the trip with them. He only wanted the booty. 'Don't worry. We'll be back before you miss us.'

Despite all her instincts telling her Wilson was dangerous, Sam didn't want Mike to change his mind and leave her at home. She needed the job, and she was desperate to go on the treasure hunt.

***

Sam's reluctance to go on the trip with Wilson made Mike uncertain. She didn't behave like most women he had come across. He had been astounded when she came to him with the revelation about the assault. Before this he had been unconcerned by that aspect of Wilson's character. They had met in a seedy brothel, but that didn't mean much since Mike had also been there.

He'd rationalized it to himself because he needed them both on the trip and he still thought it was the right decision. She'd fought Wilson off the last time, hadn't she? Who knew what sort of teasing went on? No one jumped a woman without provocation; he didn't. The treasure came first. Sam would have to get a grip.

He took advantage of being alone in the office to call Edward.

'Hello?'

'Oh, hi Ophelia. It's Mike Morton. Can I speak to Edward, please?'

'I think he's busy, Mike.'

'He won't be too busy to hear this.'

'He's busy.'

'I don't care how fucking busy he is. Tell him I need to speak to him right now. It's important.'

'There's no need to be rude. I'll see if he can free himself.'

There was a pause. Some muffled, cross-sounding voices were audible in the background. The sound of footsteps approached the telephone. They were not high heels. He breathed a sigh of relief.

'Mike? What's so urgent?' said Edward.

'We've done it, mate. We've hit the fucking jackpot!' said Mike, unable to contain himself.

'What jackpot? How can you be sure? Don't we have to do lots of sampling and measuring? I thought that was the reason you hired Sam. She's pretty expensive for a junior. I hope she's worth it.'

This confused Mike for a moment, then he remembered. He had put a decent salary in the budget for Sam, which Edward had refused to pay at first. What he hadn't told Sam was that Edward had changed his mind. Sam wanted the job, and he needed the money more than she did. She was happy, and he was happy. Why rock the boat?

'Turns out she's a fucking genius. She's only discovered a staircase that leads to the lost treasure of the Incas.'

'What the fuck is the lost treasure of the Incas? Aren't we supposed to be opening a gold mine?' muttered Edward, who couldn't keep up with Mike's changing plans.

'Grab a chair, mate, and pour yourself a large one while I spin you a tale of Incas, murder, suicide and gold.'

***

The revelation about the serpent cipher on the Inca steps had been too much for Alfredo. He disappeared into his study for several days and emerged looking haggard with lack of sleep. Gloria took it upon herself to keep him fed, but her offerings were left to get cold or eaten by Alfredo's dog. He had lost all concept of time and often rang Mike in the early hours of the morning to discuss a new revelation with him.

'Mike, are you awake?'

'Jesus, Alfredo, do you know what time it is?'

'The last Inca used the serpent cipher on one of his seals. It was a royal cipher.'

'That's great. You already told us that. Now can I go back to sleep?'

'But, it's a royal seal!'

'Yes, and it still will be in the morning. Night, Alfredo.'

***

Desperate to improve her relationship with Wilson before they went back to the jungle, Sam decided that the only way to deal with him was to confront him herself, something she found excruciating. Steeling herself, she approached him in the kitchen while he put sugar in his coffee.

'Wilson, I need to talk to you.'

He looked at her with disdain and sighed.

'What is it? Can't you see I'm busy?'

Sam's mouth fell open. She had not been expecting his surly attitude, but it gave her the courage to bite back. 'You had no right to assault me,' she said.

'Assault you? You were all over me like a rash, and then you chickened out. Typical *gringa* bitch.'

'That's a lie,' she said. 'As if I would fancy you. Anyway, Gloria knows all about you. What would Mike think if she told him about your past?'

Wilson looked her straight in the eye.

'She wouldn't dare. Not if she knows what's good for her. Anyway, what about her past? What would Mike say if he knew all about her?'

This was not going the way Sam had planned at all. She lied.

'Gloria told me that she knows why you keep getting fired. She'll tell Mike if you don't watch out.'

150

'If she knows about me, then she knows about my friends. They wouldn't mind a piece of rich bitch for a change.'

He turned away, leaving her standing in the middle of the room, white-faced with shock.

***

Gold fever had infected Edward, and he was beside himself with excitement. He rang Mike daily for updates.

'How much is that treasure worth, Mike? Millions? Billions?'

'I've no idea yet. Enough to retire on I hope.'

'Do we have to share it with the government? What are the taxes? Can we smuggle it out?'

'I think we should cross that bridge when we get there.'

'Okay, but you need to tell me as soon as you get an idea of the value.'

'Naturally mate, you'll be the first to know. I need another transfer. The salaries are due next week and I have to pay the quarterly rent, too.'

'No problem, mate. Ten thousand all right?'

'Ten thousand would be perfect. Speak soon then, mate?'

'Absolutely.'

***

Despite his apparent immunity to Sam's threatened exposure of him by Gloria, Wilson panicked. The job with Mike was nirvana for him; lots of pay and plenty of easy prey. Mike wouldn't mind the womanising, being a man of the world, but he doubted that stealing from his employer would go down well. He had to get rid of Gloria before she spilt the beans and he had a pretty shrewd idea how to do it without suspicion.

'Señor Falconi, it's Wilson Ortega. Long time no hear.'

'Wilson? It has been a long time. Is this a social call?'

'Yes and no. I was hoping you would help me with a problem.'

'Would you like that problem to disappear?'

'Yes, but it must look like an accident.'

'An accident? I think I can arrange that. Does the problem have a name?'

****

There was a lot of work to do in the following days. Sam and Gloria made another visit to buy large-scale maps of the river and some aerial photographs of the area where they stopped to photograph the snake. Without Wilson it was hard to pinpoint the exact bend on the river where they stopped. Sam studied the aerial photographs with a magnifying glass but they were on a tiny scale and she couldn't spot anything of interest through the trees.

'I can't find the exact spot where we saw the steps but Don Moises will remember where they are,' said Sam.

'Take the maps with you. They aren't any use to us here. We can always buy some more,' said Mike.

'Do you want to review the list of supplies with me?'

'You made it with Alfredo, didn't you? I doubt I can add much. Buy them with Gloria.'

'Can I have some money?'

'Ah, you will need to go via the bank. The transfer from Edward has arrived. I'll give you a cheque.'

'Um, talking of money, have you remembered to

deposit the cash in my account?'

'Of course.'

But his face told Sam another story. She faced a dilemma. Now she was part of the gang, she didn't want to make a fuss. She longed to be included more than anything. The money would have to come from somewhere else.

***

The only thing to do in Calderon apart from work was to party, and there was an occasion of some sort most nights for people in the right set. Gloria found out about most of them and she selected a big party in a hacienda outside Calderon as being suitable for Sam to meet people who were likely to speak English. Mike was not pleased that he would miss out, as he had a previous engagement, a dinner with the British Consul, and it was with bad grace he waved them off.

Excited to be getting out of town for the night, they sang along to the music on their way through the dark country roads. When they got to the party, the large garden was decked out with fairy lights and a good selection of drink had been placed around the house. Everyone who was anyone was there and Sam found lots of people who were able chat in English making it much more fun and less effort. They had a fine evening, dancing, drinking and hanging out in the garden.

The party wound down long after midnight. Even the hardened veterans of Calderon nightlife had given in to the combined excesses of drink and coke that formed the backbone of any decent fiesta in the capital. Some people had left. Others crashed where they sat, their necks at grotesque angles on the low-backed sofas. Full ashtrays leaked lipstick-stained cigarette butts onto tables and floors. Cut crystal whisky glasses glinted from under the plants on the veranda.

Outside, the crickets deafened those who had ventured out into the starry, early morning. Sam sat on the stone steps amid the cacophony of competing insects and frogs. She had wanted to go back to the flat for over two hours now but was unable to persuade anyone to take her. Gloria was no help. It was simple to get her to go to a party but persuading her to leave was a different proposition. She had been vomiting in the bathroom most of the evening and kept coming out to refill herself with the same fluids she had expelled.

Sam stood up in the garden in the moonlight and gauged her ability to balance on the wobbly garden steps. She staggered back into the house to look for Gloria. She was surprised to find her in the bathroom snorting coke with Alfredo, who had emerged from his self-imposed exile and was fumbling with Gloria's outer clothing in a way that suggested that he had never undressed a woman without help before.

He was looking at her shirt buttons with disgust and seemed to contemplate ripping the blouse open. Gloria was oblivious. As usual, she was puffy-faced with large, damp circles of mascara around her eyes. There was vomit on her sleeve, and her jeans had a big, red wine stain at the crotch.

'Hello, Gloria,' said Sam. 'Are you ready to go home yet?'

Gloria was leaning against the wall and had lost control of her head, which hung from her neck like that of a strangled chicken. She twisted it enough to see who was talking and smiled malevolently.

'Not yet, Sam. Another half hour.'

This was what she had said every half hour for the last two hours, and Sam understood her well enough now to be convinced that Gloria was staying on to spite her. She developed a malicious streak when she drank. The more Sam wanted to go home, the less Gloria would feel like going.

Sam had returned to wandering around in the garden when Gloria appeared in the doorway and said, 'So, let's go, then.' She spun on her heel and walked into the doorframe before staggering towards the front door. Her friend's drunken state alarmed Sam but she couldn't bear to stay any longer. She would make sure Gloria drove with care.

Slipping out of the party and into the dark yard, she saw that Gloria was already backing out of her parking space. Alfredo had taken possession of the front seat of the car, so she slid onto the back seat where she was enveloped in a cloud of whisky fumes and cigarette smoke.

Gloria took a swig from a half bottle of scotch, which she dangled over her shoulder offering it to Sam. Sam refused with a smile. Gloria passed the bottle to Alfredo in the front seat. Grasping the bottle, he manoeuvred his seat into a supine position so he could leer at Sam. He winked at her and gave her a lovely crinkly smile. He was the very definition of a caution. Sam couldn't help beaming back.

'*Me llamo, Alfredo*,' he said, unaware he knew Sam well.

'*Y yo, Sam*,' she answered, and as an afterthought, 'seatbelts.' Gloria obeyed without demure as she was used to Sam's bizarre obsession with seatbelt wearing. Alfredo fumbled with his in a confused manner.

Gloria set off for Calderon and was soon shouting drunken abuse at no discernible target. The car swerved around the potholes on the rural road. Soon, it was rising through the s-bends that led up over the tops of the peaks that surrounded the main area of the city.

There were a lot of road works near the top of the hills. The steepness of the terrain, the rape of the forests and the torrential rain had all contributed to constant landslides, which were apt to sweep the roads and houses away like a child knocking down a sandcastle at a beach. The present roadwork resulted from the old entry road disappearing down the valley, taking with it a couple of buses full of people during rush hour a few months before.

Faced with the complex one-way system, Gloria's driving became a little more measured. There were no streets lights. A power cut had plunged the valley into gloom, exacerbated by an early morning fog that sat on the road like translucent meringue in the headlights. Alfredo was fast asleep, rocked in his seat by the constant cornering.

The road became wider, and Sam relaxed. There wasn't another car in sight. They were safe enough on this broad back road into town. She gazed up at the vertical walls of rock lining the road and tried to spot orchids, a trick she often used when travelling in Gloria's car at ludicrous speed. Gloria braked for the next corner, but the car didn't slow down.

She shouted, 'Jesus, the fucking brakes have gone!' and swerved to the left throwing the car into a lower gear. She fought the car around the corner, but it skidded. Sam grabbed the seat in front of her. She tried not to panic. *They would crash.* She braced herself for impact.

The crash happened in slow motion. It threw the car in the air which landed on its roof and caved in on one side, almost knocking Sam out. The car spun across the highway and came to a stop on its roof in the darkness. For a moment, only the car stereo broke the silence playing 'You're So Vain' by Carly Simon.

Sam moved. She wasn't dead. She worked this out because her arm hurt and then she heard Gloria singing along to the radio as if nothing had happened. There was a pool of liquid in the car's roof. Gloria giggled.

'Are we dead?' she asked

Sam considered her answer with care before deciding on, 'we'd better try to get out.'

Gloria's window was still open, and her side of the car was not as flat as the passenger side. They got out of their seat belts and lower themselves on to the roof of the car without incident, and Gloria slipped outside through the window. Sam had to fold down the front seat and slide out over it to emerge out onto the road.

They sat on a log at the side of the road dazed by the crash, shock silencing them. Suddenly, Sam realised that they were missing someone.

'Where's Alfredo?' she said.

Gloria swung her head around, eyes wide.

'Jesus, I forgot. Can you look inside the car? I'm too drunk.'

Sam got down on her front and slid back into the car feeling a puddle of warm liquid pooled in the roof of the car sink into her clothes. Fright made her gasp. The liquid under her might be petrol and the car could explode like they did in the movies. She sniffed it and found to her relief that it was the remains of the bottle of whisky.

She reached out and switched off the radio, causing a yell of protest from Gloria, turning on the internal light over the windscreen. In the reduced space between the erstwhile roof of the car and the passenger seat, she spotted Alfredo's leather jacket. He seemed to be still in his seat, hanging upside down. She grabbed his collar and pulled hard, but she couldn't move him. His seatbelt was on as she had demanded. His compliance amazed her since most men in Calderon took the wearing of a seatbelt as a challenge to their masculinity.

She strained to release the catch, and as it gave way, Alfredo fell down onto the roof head first. *I must be pretty drunk to have forgotten about gravity.* The fall revived Alfredo, who had been asleep.

'Shit,' he said. 'Where are we?'

He struggled to right himself enough to see Sam, who sprawled on the upturned roof. She offered him her hand, and then pulling him with one hand, she pushed herself out of the car backwards through the whisky onto the road with the other. Alfredo had a wiry build and slid across the roof with surprising ease.

Gloria was still sitting on the log at the side of the road smoking a cigarette and fiddling with her shirt. She was trying to work out which button went into which hole, a task that appeared to be an insurmountable puzzle in her state. She appeared unconcerned by their situation, and unsurprised to find herself sitting in the middle of the road beside an upturned car at four o'clock in the morning.

She screwed up her heavily made-up face in concentration as she tried to brush off the dust that had stuck to the blood on the material. She was used to being in trouble. As the only daughter of the eldest son of one of the most powerful families in Calderon, Gloria had been protected from the realities of life in Sierramar by a cushion of limitless wealth. She was prone to getting into a pickle and experienced at using her position to extract herself from it.

'What happened?' said Sam.

'The brakes failed,' said Gloria.

'What are we going to do? We should notify the

police.'

'No. You must go now. I'll deal with this. You can't be here.'

'But I can't leave you both here. There must be procedures to be followed.'

'Yes, there are, but you can't be here or, as a foreigner, they'll blame you and try to make you pay a lot of money because you've been drinking. I'm the expert here, Sam. Trust me. You must go now before it's too late. I promise you it'll be all right.'

Alfredo nodded sagely, or maybe drunkenly. Sam was unconvinced.

'But it's the middle of the night. Will you be safe?'

'Sam, my father is a powerful man in Calderon. I'll be fine. You are a foreigner and a target for fines and corruption. You must leave now.'

Gloria, who appeared to have sobered up in an instant, was adamant. She flagged down a passing cab.

'Can you take this woman to 2256 Avenida Miranda, please?'

'But she's been in an accident. I can't take her. What will the police say?'

'The police will not find out. I'm the daughter of Hernan Sanchez. You should do as I tell you.'

'Señora Sanchez! I didn't recognise you. Of course, I will.'

'Good man, take this for your trouble.'

Gloria gave him a twenty-dollar bill, a fortune, and Sam got into the cab. The driver left. Sam was in a state of shock. How had Gloria got her to leave? She had been persuasive but Sam didn't understand why the taxi driver had agreed to take her. It was nice that someone cared about her.

She turned around in the seat and peered out through the back window. Gloria was smoking a cigarette with Alfredo beside the upturned car. She looked perfectly calm and leaned in for a kiss.

Chapter XIII

Sam woke with a start. The sun was forcing itself through the sheets she had wrapped around her head. She sat upright in the bed. It was as if someone was shining lasers in her eyes, dazing her for a moment. Then she remembered the crash. *What a nightmare.* She examined herself but found no bruises. Had it been a bad dream? If so, it had been vivid.

Dragging herself into the shower, she discovered that there was a piece of skin missing from her elbow when the water flowed over the wound and made her yelp. She felt for it with her finger. It was wet and sticky and made her feel sick. She dressed at a snail's pace, frightened to emerge out of her bedroom into the apartment and face the music.

She wandered into the office where she found Marta, who was worrying her quiff with a round brush. Sam kissed her hello and wished her good morning. Mike sat at the dining table eating a slice of toast with a thick butter covering. He looked up. 'You all right, Sam? You look rough, girl. That Gloria will kill you one of these days.'

Sam looked straight into his eyes, which stung like hell against the bright light of the window behind him, but she could see he wasn't joking or angry.

'I feel rough. Have you heard from Gloria this morning?'

'No. I guess she's still snuggling up to Alfredo under her pink eiderdown. She'll arrive in her own sweet time. There's no hurry.'

She had been the only one who didn't know about Gloria and Alfredo. Not for the first time, she wondered why everyone except her had such an easy time pairing off. She also noticed that Mike was conversant with Gloria's bed linen, but she didn't comment. Shuffling to the table, she helped herself to some toast.

She tried to figure out why no-one knew or cared about the crash but decided not to say anything unless she had to. Some dry toast and black tea quelled her urge to vomit and she managed to hide the fact that she was shaking. She noticed Tati hanging around the kitchen door, staring at her as if she was naked. *Maybe Gloria had already told Tati what had happened? Why didn't Mike know yet?*

When no one mentioned the car crash all morning, Sam assumed that it was another example of the odd culture in Calderon. She forced herself to act normally, and got on with planning the trip to Riccuarte.

Mike was both meticulous and miserly with his funds. The trip was being planned to the last cent. Sam, who remembered her shared room with Wilson, and did not want to repeat the experience, organised extra cash to fund the inevitable shortfall. She got Marta's cooperation to raid the petty cash fund.

'What do you mean he's not paying you? Are you married to him or something?' said Marta.

'It's a long story, not one we have time for now. Can you help me?' said Sam

'Give me the receipts later and I'll add them to the

accounts. He won't make a fuss. It's not his money, and it's a genuine business expense.'

Gloria swanned in at lunchtime acting like she always did. There was no sign that the accident had affected her. She did not show any sign of wanting to tell Mike anything about their mishap. Sam caught her eye, and took her into the kitchen without Marta, who hated to be left out of any gossip.

'What happened after I left? Did the police arrive? Are you in trouble for driving drunk?' said Sam.

'Don't be ridiculous. The police wouldn't dare. My father has dealt with them in his own way. They won't make any trouble,' said Gloria.

'Okay, that's great,' said Sam not understanding how he had achieved this and not wanting to ask as she suspected that she already knew the answer and wouldn't approve.

'Doesn't the car belong to your father? Wasn't he cross?'

'My father is glad I'm safe and not at all worried about the car. He has lots of cars and he's given me another car to replace it.'

'Are you going to tell Mike about the accident?' said Sam.

'No, I'm not, and you can't either, in case he fires me for almost killing you both. If Alfredo had died, the treasure hunt would have died, too. Can you imagine Mike's reaction?'

Sam could imagine all too clearly.

'I won't tell him. Will you be okay?'

'I'll be fine. My father's so relieved that I have a job, he's prepared to pay anything for me to keep it.'

'That's great news,' said Sam. 'Your father's a legend.'

'Stop me from drinking so much. I feel awful this

morning.'

'Sure, and get stabbed with a cocktail stick.'

They laughed. Then Gloria looked perplexed.

'It's weird, though.'

'What is?'

'The garage changed the brakes and refilled the brake fluid in my car last month. They shouldn't have failed so soon. I gave the mechanics a severe talking to this morning. They promised to check them today and get back when they find the problem.'

'Hmm. With my limited experience of customer service in Calderon, I'm sorry to say I don't think it's that weird,' said Sam.

This witticism did not induce a smile. Sarcasm was lost in translation in Sierramar. Gloria left the office with Marta to buy the final supplies for the trip. Alfredo arrived soon afterwards. He was still drunk and not making sense. Mike made him lie down in the spare room and shut the door.

***

Wilson came into the office later that afternoon and found all the obvious preparations for a trip. It surprised him to find Alfredo in the kitchen drinking some strong coffee but covered it up by making a coarse joke. He saw the boxes of provisions in the back kitchen and his heart quickened.

'What's happening here?' he asked. 'Are you going on a trip?'

'It's exciting...' started Alfredo but Mike cut him off.

'We are financing a dig for Alfredo. He wants to know if the Incas ever got to Esmeraldas Province.'

'Do you want me to go?' said Wilson. 'I can organise workers and canoes and transport for you.'

'Can you help Alfredo get set up in Riccuarte? He won't need you after that.'

'It would be my pleasure.'

'Okay, then that's settled. Marta, can you budget for another on the trip, please?'

Marta nodded, avoiding Wilson's searching glance. He joined the dots in his head. Bingo! Something was going on, and now it involved him.

***

Wilson and Alfredo were sitting at the kitchen table together when Gloria and Marta came back from shopping. When Wilson saw them come in, he stood up, scraping the chair on the kitchen tiles and stumbling backwards. He grabbed the counter to stop himself from falling. He had gone a funny colour.

'Are you all right?' said Alfredo.

'Yes, yes, I'm fine. I thought I saw a vision.'

Alfredo, who knew all about Wilson's appetite for women like Marta, accepted this as the fine art of exaggeration for the sake of effect and went on drinking his coffee. Wilson appeared unsettled by this incident, and after circuiting the office a few times, he left, muttering excuses.

'What's wrong with Wilson?' said Sam.

'Oh, un coup de foudre,' said Alfredo. 'He likes Marta. Well, he likes all women, I think.'

'Huh,' said Sam, who tried not to show her alarm at this turn of events. On one hand, it relieved her. Their little chat seemed to have convinced him she had no interest in him. It horrified her that he had focussed his attention on his next victim already. Marta giggled and flicked her hair from side to side, glad to be the centre of attention.

***

Wilson left the office in a total panic, hyperventilating and shaking with fright. By the time he reached the street his shirt clung to a veneer of cold sweat on his chest. He leaned against the wall of the building, trying to regain his composure. He removed the packet of cigarettes from his jacket pocket with trembling hands and took one out. Lighting it with the third match, he took a deep drag, which gave him a major coughing fit that almost removed his lungs.

He straightened up, red in the face. He took another drag of his cigarette and had a renewed bout of coughing. A small, bald man with a ferret face who had been watching this from the shadows placed himself right in front of Wilson, uncomfortably close to him, and spoke in a hiss.

'Wilson Ortega?' he asked.

Wilson nodded, trying to hold down the cough, which was forcing itself up from his lungs.

'I have a message for you from El Duro. You have one week to pay him his money, or he'll cut off your dick and stuff it down your neck.'

The small man smirked, pleased with his delivery and the effect it had on his victim. Wilson was still choking but now more with increased panic rather than cigarette smoke. He caught his breath long enough to speak. 'I'll have his money soon. I promise. A week is not long enough. If he'll give me a month, I'll pay fifty per cent on top. I swear.'

'Double it, and I'll see what I can do,' said the man. He was planning on taking a large cut of the extra money.

'Okay, okay, give me a few weeks. I'm on to something big. It's a done deal if you let me get on with it.'

'I doubt that. However, El Duro has a soft spot for

you. He will give you two extra weeks to save your manhood.' He stuck out a child-sized hand and spat in the palm.

'Shake on it,' he said.

Wilson shuddered as he felt the spit transfer to his hand and stopped himself from wiping it clean. The man turned on his heel and strolled down the street with his hands in his pockets. Wilson rubbed his hand on his trouser leg to remove the drying spittle and took another drag of his cigarette.

He couldn't believe what a nightmare the day had been. José Falconi, the man he had paid to rig the brakes on Gloria's car, had called early in the morning to tell him about the car crash on the outskirts of Calderon.

'The job on the brakes was a success, Mr Ortega. The car was a total wreck. No-one could survive a crash like that.'

'I should hope so, too, considering how much I had to pay to get it done. Is Miss Sanchez dead then?'

'I am not privy to that information yet, so I can't confirm any casualties but I can find out for you later.'

'Casualties?'

'Yes, I believe there were two people in the car. A Miss Sanchez and a Dr Vargas.'

'Jesus! Two people? Are you sure?'

'That's what my source says.'

'Okay, thank you. I'll call you later.'

This was terrible news. Wilson couldn't believe his bad luck. Filled with trepidation, he had gone to the office to find out what was happening. He was flummoxed when he met Alfredo there, and he hadn't mentioned the car crash at all. *Maybe the police officer was mistaken? Perhaps only Gloria had been in the car?* It stunned Wilson when she also waltzed into the office as if nothing had happened and chatted to Marta. The woman must be made of steel. She hadn't a scratch on her, and she hadn't even mentioned the crash.

Wilson couldn't understand it. *Had Jose fixed the brakes on the wrong car?* He didn't know people even wore seat belts. Most people in Calderon cut them off where they attached to the frame of the car and threw them out. That meant car crashes were often fatal because people drove too fast and were ejected from the car if they crashed, hitting the road or a tree at one hundred and twenty kilometres per hour, which didn't leave much for the undertakers to work with.

His failure to silence Gloria was a disaster. He worried she would tell Mike about his debts and other shady dealings, but if he didn't hold on to his job and get money fast, El Duro would make him pay. There was still the chance he could sell one of the mining concession areas to Mike if he could get rid of Sam. He would play it by ear for a few days and only act again if he had to.

Mike still treated him like a long-lost brother and had even forwarded him some of his salary. This was not the behaviour of a suspicious man. Now he was going on the 'secret' trip he might make real money, money which could save him from the wrath of El Duro and for which he was prepared to kill.

Chapter XIV

On the other side of Calderon, the mechanics in the garage surveyed the wreckage of Gloria's car, which they had hauled over the engine pit. It was a complete write-off.

'How did she survive this?' asked Felix, the head mechanic.

'I can't imagine. Can you smell the whisky? They must have been drunk as skunks,' said Angel.

'Miss Sanchez says the brakes stopped working. How is that possible? I replaced them and refilled the brake fluid a few weeks ago. Perhaps she was driving too fast. It wouldn't be the first time.'

The other mechanic snorted.

'She's some woman. I wouldn't mind taking that firebrand into my bed.'

'The boss would kill you.'

'Yes, but it'd be worth it.'

They both laughed. The head mechanic slid into the pit under the car and poked around underneath it. His companion leaned against the crumpled vehicle and smoked an illegal cigarette. Suddenly, there was a commotion under the car, as the head mechanic hit his head on the axle and swore. He emerged, rubbing his head. He looked shocked.

'Holy fuck, Angel. Someone tampered with the brakes,' said Felix, shaken.

'Seriously? Are you sure it wasn't the accident that did it?'

'No. Someone's made a small hole in each brake line. They must have used a gimlet or something similar. The fluid would've leaked out bit by bit each time someone used the brakes until it ran out. Oh, my God, someone tried to kill Miss Gloria. We must tell her father straight away in case they are still trying.'

'Tell Don Sanchez? Are you kidding me? What if he blames us? He'll make us disappear,' replied Angel.

'It'll be much worse if he finds out, and we aren't the ones to tell him.'

'You're right. I've heard he's a man who likes to take revenge. Okay, call him now. He should be at home for lunch. I'll take photographs of the damage to the brakes. We need to cover our butts on this one.'

'Yes, that's a good idea. You never know what might happen next.'

Felix crossed over to the grease-covered workbench and moved piles of stained paper and random wiring out of the way. The telephone was under a pile of copies of invoices for money owed by the rich clients who used the garage, but didn't bother to pay their bills. He riffled through them for the telephone number of the Sanchez residence. Then he pushed them aside and grabbed the receiver.

He got through to the Sanchez household and asked to speak to the boss. The indignant grumbling caused by his interruption of Señor Sanchez' lunch was audible, a sacrilege unlikely to be forgiven. He almost hung up the phone but decided that the damage was done. Heavy footsteps made the wooden floor creak as Hernan Sanchez made his ponderous way to the telephone. There was a bout of laboured breathing and then the sound of a chair being pulled up.

'What the devil do you mean by disturbing my lunch, Felix? This had better be important.'

'Señor Sanchez, it's a matter of life or death,' replied Felix. 'Someone tried to kill your daughter last night.'

There was a long silence punctuated by more heavy breathing.

At last, Hernan Sanchez said, 'But she crashed the car. Are you sure about this, Felix? And I mean certain?'

Felix understood what he meant, but there was no going back now, and he had the evidence in his workshop.

'Señor Sanchez, I swear on the virgin. Someone tampered with the brakes.'

***

Hernan Sanchez hung up the telephone without saying another word. He called over to the maid who had returned his lunch to the oven and was hovering in the kitchen waiting to take it out again.

'Agatha, bring me my contact list.'

The tiny maid scurried into the study and returned with an ancient address book, dropping several loose pages on her way and bending down to pick them up. She was illiterate, so she wasn't able put them back in the right place. She looked at her boss in supplication. He waved the problem away and beckoned her forward.

He had soon shuffled the pages into the right order and looked for the correct number. In the book, Hernan Sanchez had contacts from the old days who were au fait with dodgy goings on in Calderon. Someone who might use them to find out who had rigged the brakes on Gloria's car and why. He grunted with satisfaction as he found the number and dialled it.

After several ring tones, someone with his mouth full answered the telephone, having also been disturbed at his table.

'Hello. Who's calling me at this hour?'

'Segundo, it's me. Hernan Sánchez. I'm sorry to disturb you at your meal, but I need your help and it can't wait.'

The tone of voice at the other end of the line became apologetic and obsequious.

'Señor Sanchez, you do me a great honour. How can I help you?'

'Segundo, my daughter crashed her vehicle last night. She was lucky to survive. It wasn't an accident. Someone tampered with the brake lines. I need you to find out who it was. Can you ask around? Use your discretion. Someone will have told someone who told someone else, if you get my drift.'

'Of course, boss. I'll get right on it. The scum who did this will pay.'

'Don't do anything foolish. We need to find out who paid him to do the job and why before he pays for his savagery.'

'Yes, sir. I understand. You can rely on me. Thank you for asking me. I'll not let you down.'

'Thank you, Segundo. Quick and quiet, please.'

Señor Sanchez hung up and signalled to the maid he would now like his lunch. Agatha brought the food to the table and served him a new platter. Unusually for him, his appetite had now quite disappeared, and he toyed with the food for some time before abandoning it. He felt sick with worry for his beloved daughter.

What sort of trouble could she have got into that

had led to such extreme measures being taken against her? Even worse, it might be someone trying to get revenge for one of his deals? He decided not to tell Gloria for the time being. The poor girl had enough problems in her life without this. He took his coffee into the study and was soon snoozing in his big, leather chair.

***

To Sam's surprise, Alfredo appeared to be less enthusiastic about the trip than she had expected. He was distant and distracted. He was unwilling or unable to accept that his search had ended, checking and rechecking his documents and staring obsessively at Sam's photo of the serpent cipher. She wondered if the shock of discovering that for years he had been searching in the wrong place had been too much for her alcoholic friend.

Alfredo had a fragile grip on reality at the best of times. He preferred to talk about literature rather than current affairs and was happiest with a glass of wine in one hand and a book in the other. As the time came to set out from Calderon, he seemed to doubt his own reasoning.

'But what if it's not there? I can't be sure. If only I had more time,' said Alfredo, flapping his hands about.

'Alfredo, you can find the treasure. After all these years searching, you may find what you're looking for.'

'Be careful what you wish for, because you might get it,' he replied.

The treasure hunt was Alfredo's entire existence, and she was unsure what effect finding an answer to the riddle would have on her friend. Gloria tried to help, but even she could not reach Alfredo in his lost world.

The next few days were manic. To make matters worse, Tati announced that she was going away to attend to some family business.

'But Tati, we need you here. Can't you go another time?' asked Mike through Marta.

'I've got to go now, my aunt is dying,' said Tati.

Marta questioned her and shook her head at Mike.

Since Tati had taken no time off before and was desperate to go, Mike decided they would cope without her. Gloria got her own maid to come to Avenida Miranda and cook a constant supply of food for the 'troops' in the office over the weekend. Mike had planned to take the team to San Martin on the evening of a national holiday to catch the train to the jungle the next morning.

They bought the usual boxes of bottled water, tuna, rice, cooking chocolate (which survived in the heat better), Ritz crackers, raisins and peanuts for snacks to take with them. Sam packed tea bags and powdered milk for herself as the locals only drank coffee. She double-wrapped all her clothes in plastic bags so they wouldn't get wet in the canoe. Also contained in her bag were a dozen rolls of film for her camera, a big bottle of insect repellent and some mints for the train journey. Finally, she put in a woollen hat to wear at night to prevent hair loss.

She could hardly contain her mounting excitement about the trip. *What if they found the treasure? Would she be famous? Maybe even rich?* It had dawned on her this was no ordinary search and that they might solve one of the biggest mysteries of South American history. No wonder Mike was so disappointed to stay behind. She wished for a positive outcome even though the cynic in her believed someone had found the treasure and divided it up years before.

But what if it hadn't? If they found it, whose would it be? Mike would take the lion's share for Edward Beckett, who had financed the trips. He would doubtless take a large share for himself, too. Would the team who found the treasure benefit as well? Alfredo would expect something for his discovery. *Would she get a proper salary? And what about the State? There must be laws about historical troves?* And if she was mulling over this, the others were, too.

Perhaps because of the excitement, she had not yet rung her parents except to say she had arrived in one piece. She didn't want to use up goodwill where phone calls were concerned but she wanted to talk to her family before setting out. She asked Mike if she could call home.

'On one condition,' he said.

She expected his next comment.

'Don't mention the treasure, okay? If you can do that, you can have ten minutes.'

'I can do that. Thank you,' said Sam.

She took the phone from Marta's desk and pulled the cord to its full extension so she could shut herself in Mike's bedroom. She took ten minutes to get hold of an international operator and ask for a call to England, giving the number and hanging up. The phone rang minutes later, and she grabbed the receiver.

'I have your international call.,' said the operator. 'Please speak now.'

'Thank you. Hello?'

'Sam? Where are you?' Hannah's voice.

'I'm in Calderon.'

'How is it? Are you having a good time? Did you meet a nice man yet?'

'Um, no. But I'm having a great time. I've been to the jungle and I'm going again in a few days.'

'Did you have to eat strange things there?' said Hannah.

'Mostly rice and tuna and some bananas straight off the trees. How are things at home?' said Sam.

'Routine. Mum and Dad are both in good form but they're not here because they left to have tea with friends. I didn't fancy it and stayed here. By the way...' she hesitated.

'What?'

'Simon rang me,' said Hannah.

'He rang you? Why?'

'He's been looking for you. He wants to apologise, try again...' Hannah's voice trailed off.

'Try again? Is he on drugs?'

'Look, he sounded sorry. I was cross with him but he wouldn't back down. He says he has tried and tried but he can't face life without you.'

'That's weird.' *And annoying. Talk about bad timing! Like she needed distractions right now.*

'Yes, I was pretty stunned when he called,' said Hannah.

'I can't consider that now. I'm off to explore the jungle,' said Sam.

'I'm sorry. I didn't want to upset you in the middle of your adventure.'

'I'm not sure how I feel about it now, but I've got plenty of time to mull over it. There's no telly here.'

'No telly? I'm not going there.'

'It is amazing, though. It's the best thing I've ever done. I've taken loads of photographs.'

'I'm so glad it's all you hoped for. I'm dying to see the photos. I'll tell Mum and Dad you're okay. They'll be sad to have missed your call,' said Hannah.

'I'll try to call again soon. Oh, can you ask Daddy to please deposit one hundred pounds in my account? I'll explain later,' said Sam.

'Why do you need money? I thought Mike Morton was paying you.'

'Just tell him please.'

'That man is a bastard. Stand up for yourself.'

'And lose my job? Don't worry. With this on my CV I won't have to accept this arrangement again.'

'I'll tell him. Bye, sis. Please look after yourself in the jungle.'

'I will. Bye.'

Sam sat on the bed for several minutes digesting the news about Simon. She wasn't too sure how she felt. Vindicated? Perhaps. But she had assumed that part of her life was gone for good and now the corpse was reviving. Would it be different this time? Can a leopard change its spots? She remembered the nights of passion and let out an involuntary moan as Mike opened the door. He looked startled. 'You okay?'

'Um, yes, sorry, I'll be right out.' *How embarrassing!*

Chapter XV

They set out for San Martin in two cars. Sam's excitement was only momentarily extinguished by Gloria running over a stray dog who wandered into their path. She had no choice as the oncoming cars and pedestrian traffic on the side of the road gave her no chance to avoid it. There was a gasp in the car as it bounced over the body of the dead canine.

'I hope that's not an omen,' said Alfredo.

'Don't be ridiculous,' said Gloria, driving on as if nothing had happened. This show of bravado didn't convince Sam as Gloria lit a cigarette with shaky hands.

They reached the town in the late afternoon and parked outside the Hotel California where the goods were unloaded and placed in Sam's room, leaving a small space for her to reach the bed. She was happy she didn't have to share her room with Wilson again. He was sharing with Alfredo.

'Okay, good luck. Call us from San Lorenzo when you are coming out and we'll come and get you,' Mike said, proceeding to shake first Alfredo's hand and then Wilson's. He didn't mention the treasure because of Wilson but his eyes shone like black diamonds in the dark night. He stood in front of Sam uncertain of the protocol. Gloria reached out and gave Sam a big hug.

'Be careful,' she whispered. 'Keep a rock beside your bed to hit him with.'

'I will.'

Mike and Gloria got back into their cars and drove back to Calderon in convoy. Sam stood outside the hotel looking at the lights disappear. She desperately wanted to discuss the treasure with Alfredo but they had to get rid of Wilson at Riccuarte first. She caught his eye and knew he had read her thoughts.

'Let's get something to eat,' Wilson said.

They went straight to bed after dinner. Sam had hoped for a repeat performance from the love-struck troubadours, but they did not materialize.

***

Back in Calderon, Señor Sanchez's fixer, Segundo, had been busy in the streets of the old town following a trail that led him to the home of a certain José Falconi, a well-known thief and violent lowlife. He had heard talk on the street that Falconi managed Gloria's car crash and now he would find out who paid him to do it. He knocked on the door and waited. A battered-looking young woman answered the door. She was thin and bruised with a new black eye. She wrapped her shawl tighter as the cold evening air hit her frail body.

'Yes?' she said. 'What do you want?'

'I'm looking for José Falconi. I'm an old friend. I'm here to repay a debt.'

'He's not here at the moment. He should be back soon. Would you like to wait?'

'No, thank you. I'll wait in the cantina around the corner. Would you be good enough to direct him there when he gets home, please?'

'Señor. I'll do that as soon as he arrives.'

Segundo noticed how the expectation of some money had lifted her spirits. It was pitiful. She would never receive anything again from Jose, not even punches. He could imagine from the state of her, the pittance Falconi was giving her to survive on. He stuffed two generous notes in her hand. Señor Sanchez would approve. To her protestations, he assured her he had come into some money and that God had told him to be generous with it.

'God bless you and keep you, sir,' she said.

'Now, don't go telling him about the money,' said Segundo, but he could see from the way she stuffed it down her bra she had no intention of telling Falconi. As she shut the door, he walked away. She would be much better off without him. That black eye she had was not from walking into a door. He rounded the corner and entered the small cantina that smelled of deep-fried tripe and old cooking oil. He ordered a soup of pig's trotters and settled down to wait.

***

Wilson had hired a boy with a barrow to carry their supplies to the station in the morning. They were soon standing on the platform, shivering in the cold dawn light, waiting for the train to arrive. Alfredo showed unexpected efficiency organizing several porters into making a pile of their supplies next to the tracks ready for loading onto the roof. Wilson had pushed his way through the normal melee at the ticket office, and he had made his way back clutching the tickets. He gave them to Sam and told her to get on the train when it arrived.

Sam stood on the platform in a crowd of people. There were even more of them than the last time. It got worse as the train shuffled into view. She held firm and got ready to mount the steps. There was a lot of pushing and shoving around her, and claustrophobia almost overwhelmed her. The train stopped with the steps right in front of her.

She grasped the handrails with relief and pulled herself up out of the crowd. People pulled at her clothes. Suddenly, her money belt slid mysteriously from around her waist, and in a flash, it was gone. Sam gasped and looked around. All she saw was a sea of eager faces and jostling bodies. It was hopeless. She struggled back down the steps and through the throng to where Wilson was helping Alfredo.

'What are you doing here?' he asked crossly. 'Didn't I tell you to get on the train?'

'Someone stole my money belt.'

He hadn't understood her. He shrugged and tried to turn away.

'My money. My passport. Stolen.' She watched his expression change as he understood what she was saying.

'Stolen? Shit! Wait here.'

He turned back towards Alfredo, who was directing his porters to lift the boxes onto the roof and shouted something. Sam could see him gesticulating at the men, who lowered the boxes back down to the ground. Alfredo looked over at Sam and shrugged apologetically.

'We can't go without your passport,' he said. 'You can't travel anywhere in Sierramar without identification. We won't be going to Riccuarte today.'

A terrible sense of anti-climax hit her. She gazed at the train which was now full and ready to go. The passengers crammed in even more than usual, and some people were hanging out of the glassless windows for air. Then, she saw a face she knew. Tati!

Tati was on the train. But why?

'Tati!' she shouted, but the train was moving away, and there was no reaction from the face on the train. She tried to push through the crowd but it was too late. The train had left the platform. Sam was still standing there with a startled look on her face when Wilson came over with Alfredo.

'What now?' he asked.

'Tati, she was on the train. I'm sure,' she faltered, less certain under the scrutiny of Wilson and Alfredo.

'Why would Tati be on the train? Don't be stupid, Sam. All black people look the same,' said Wilson dismissively in Spanish. 'You're confused because they robbed you. Tati is in Calderon doing the laundry.'

She flushed red with fury and her knuckles whitened as she struggled to contain her emotions.

'But she's on holiday. It was her. I know what Tati looks like. Almost sure anyway...' Sam trailed off, embarrassed, as Wilson had made her look stupid. Wilson had turned away and was attracting the attention of a local policeman who was loitering at the coffee stall. He walked over to the man, taking bills out of his pocket. Alfredo rolled his eyes at her.

'Don't worry, Sam,' he said. 'The local police know the pickpockets who work the station. They'll get your passport back by this evening.'

'Seriously? How can you be certain?'

'I'm from here.'

It was a grumpy group that returned to the hotel to book rooms for another night. Alfredo did not improve their humour by singing the Eagle's hit song, Hotel California out of tune.

'Shut up, Alfredo,' said Wilson.

They all returned to bed for a few hours and re-emerged for a lunch of chicken soup and rice with tripe. The two men munched their way happily through this culinary feast, but the chicken's feet floating to the top of her bowl of soup when she was about to tuck in, put her off her food. When Alfredo translated the second course as tripe, nausea rose in her throat. She had rice and a fried egg instead, having had enough culture for one day.

After lunch Sam called Mike to tell him about the robbery.

'For fuck's sake. You should be more careful. Did you swap the tickets for tomorrow?'

'Yes, we did.'

'No harm done I suppose. It's been there hundreds of years. I guess one more day won't make any difference.'

Sam noted the complete lack of concern for her wellbeing. Mike was only interested in one thing—money. She determined to find the treasure and get his attention for once. She longed for his approval and to be a member of the team, one of the boys.

They were all sitting in the front lobby of the hotel in the late afternoon when someone pushed Sam's money belt through a gap at the bottom of the entrance door. She saw it sliding into the lobby and ran over. There wasn't anyone outside. She looked out into the street. It was full of local people bustling about their business and local buses picking their way through the crowded streets spewing out clouds of exhaust fumes. There was no one who looked remotely suspicious.

She picked up the money belt and ran the strap through her fingers. Someone had sliced it through with surgical precision. She shuddered as she imagined how sharp the knife must have been and how close it was to her skin. She unzipped the purse and gasped in amazement. Not only was her passport inside but also her money.

'I told you, Sam. It's traditional. The police always get it back for you if you pay them,' said Alfredo, who had not moved from his chair.

'But the money's still in it,' protested Sam. 'What sort of pickpocket leaves the money behind?'

'Never mind the pickpockets,' said Alfredo. 'What sort of policeman would return the money belt with the money inside?'

Even Sam knew this was an unlikely scenario. The police in Sierramar were not famed as beacons of honesty. Wilson shook his head in disbelief. He reached for the money belt and marvelled at its contents. He showed Alfredo the cash.

'Okay,' said Alfredo, 'that's weird.'

'Perhaps the pickpocket was looking for something else? A document or credit cards?' Wilson appeared keen to dismiss the incident as a freak occurrence. Maybe he was eager to get out and about and see if he could find entertainment.

'It's a mystery,' said Alfredo.

'I'm going out for a walk around town,' said Wilson. 'Alfredo, are you coming?'

'Yes. Let me get my coat.'

Sam was standing near the door of the hotel, but he didn't include her in the invitation. She couldn't think of anything worse than a night with two drunks, but hurt at being excluded made her sulk. Even Alfredo had not asked her if she wanted to come. She swallowed her disappointment.

'Have a good time,' she said, but they wouldn't. They would get hammered and talk about how badly life had treated them and then come home in time for a rotten hangover on the train. For once, she didn't know if it was because she was a woman, a foreigner, or they didn't like her. Maybe it was all three reasons. This was not reassuring, as there was nothing she could do about any of them, and Sam craved acceptance more than air.

She stomped off to her room and hid under the ancient blanket. Down in the street, people were shutting up shops and going home to their families. It rained. She sat up in bed, with the blanket wrapped around her, itching her skin, and watched the rain wash the rubbish off the streets and into the drains. The old town with its wooden balconies hanging over the streets full of laundry and flowers reminded her of the Wild West.

She wondered where Wilson and Alfredo had got to and wished she wasn't so sensitive. *Could Alfredo keep a secret when he was drunk?* She didn't want Wilson knowing about the treasure but he was suspicious about the motives for the trip. No-one who worked for any period with Mike would swallow the story about him paying for a trip to do archaeology.

Something else nagged at her. With all the excitement over her money belt, she had forgotten but now she was convinced. She had seen Tati on the train. She had not imagined it. *What was Tati doing there? Was she following them? Was it a coincidence?* She would have to keep her wits about her as things were getting more complicated by the minute.

***

Alfredo was sloshed. Wilson had made sure of that. He leaned over and refilled Alfredo's glass with some cheap aguardiente.

'Drink up, there are no bars in the jungle.'

'I've had enough. I promised Mike that I'd try to

stay sober.'

'Mike, Mike, who cares about Mike?'

'I do, he's funding this trip.'

'And how come he's so interested in history all of a sudden? He always struck me as a money man.'

'History is the key to our future. There may be precious artefacts.'

'Are they valuable? Or precious because of their history?'

'Both I hope.'

'And do you think Mike will let them stay in Sierramar? Ha! You, my friend, are living in cloud cuckoo land. He'll take the whole lot and sell it abroad.'

'But he promised me.'

'And you believed him? You need to work with me on this. I'm a patriot. Let me help you save the artefacts for the nation.'

'But I promised him.'

'At least let me come with you. We can decide what to do if we find anything.'

'You won't interfere with my work?'

'No, of course not.'

'Okay, but don't tell Sam that you know what we're doing. The hunt for the treasure is too important.'

A tiny slip of the tongue, a massive mistake where Wilson was concerned. Alfredo did not notice that he had dropped the t-word. Wilson did not react and stood up, pulling Alfredo up with him.

'Let's go. You're right. Mike's paying us to work, not drink. Let's get back to the hotel. We have to get up early.'

***

'It's all gone.'

'Edward? What's up mate? You sound funny.'

'It's all gone Mike. My whole fortune.'

'What's gone? I don't understand.'

'Don't you watch the bloody news?'

'We don't have a television. Anyway, it's in Spanish.'

'Black Monday. The stock exchanges crashed in New York on Friday and now it's happened here.'

'I don't understand. How come your brokers didn't tell you then?'

'The storm. It was the storm on Thursday.'

'What storm? Have you been drinking?'

'Yes, I have. Christ! Don't you know anything? There was an epic storm over Britain on Thursday. They say it may have knocked down one million trees. One of them landed on my car and cut the electricity and phone lines in my street. Ophelia and I lit the candles and hunkered down. Hardly anyone in the City managed to get to work; it was impossible to get in or out. Our electricity came back on Friday night and it was all over the news. Wall Street was down by one hundred and nine points.'

'Jesus! That's terrible. What did you do?'

'I had to wait until today to get hold of my broker. Only the junior was there. He was crying. I couldn't get any sense out of him. Finally, he admitted that he had panicked and sold my whole portfolio at a huge loss. The London markets finished three hundred points down. I'm cleaned out.'

'So, what do you want me to do?'

'Find the treasure, Mike. It's our only hope.'

'I'm sorry, Edward.'

'I know, and that's not the worst thing.'

'It isn't?'

'They've cancelled all the grouse shooting because of the storm.'

Edward laughed, a nasty hollow sound and hung up.

Chapter XVI

Hernan Sanchez received the call as he was getting ready for bed. He had been waiting with growing impatience and trepidation for confirmation about the identity of the man who had tried to kill his daughter. Someone was taking revenge on him for some dodgy deal he had done in the past, like cutting corners on a building contract, or failing to reinforce a road before applying tarmac.

He had withdrawn from that business and was planning to live out a comfortable old age with his vast fortune. Gloria was his future. The sabotage of her car had been a massive wake-up call for him. He had neglected her in the past and her bad behaviour resulted from this. It was time to make up for it before it was too late. He had sprung into action in the only way he knew how. He lumbered back into the hallway to pick up the ringing phone, having a good idea who would risk his wrath by calling at such an hour.

'Segundo?' He grunted. 'What news do you have for me?'

'Boss, forgive me for disturbing you so late. I thought I shouldn't wait until the morning. Your daughter may still be in danger.'

'Nothing is more important than her. Tell me what

you know.'

'I discovered that a certain low-life scum, who would murder his mother for a few dollars, was the man who tampered with the brakes. His name was José Falconi and he was well known in criminal circles.'

'But did you find out who was behind this? Who paid him?'

'Finding out who paid him was more complicated. I'm afraid I had to use persuasion to get him to talk. I hope that's all right with you.'

'Anything you had to do to protect my daughter is legitimate in my eyes, Segundo. I'll shelter you from any consequences. Where's this Falconi now?' said Sanchez who had noticed the use of the past tense.

'I understand that he's at the bottom of Yanacocha Lake.'

'Excellent. No more than he deserved. And who's the scoundrel who ordered him to murder my daughter? Tell me his name,' said Don Sanchez.

'Wilson Ortega,' said Segundo. 'He is not a criminal, but he is well known about town as a frequenter of brothels and low-life bars. I understand that he owes a great deal of money to some dubious people, including Pancho Rojas, El Duro. I don't yet understand why Wilson targeted your daughter. I haven't located him yet as he is travelling to the coast. Do you want me to find out where he is or wait for him to come back to Calderon?'

Hernan Sanchez hung up without answering. He dialled his daughter's number. He felt sick, and there was a cold prickling at the back of his neck. No one answered. *Where was she?* He shuffled to his room and pressed the service bell. After about five minutes, Agatha appeared in disarray with her long pigtail hanging down her back.

'Aggie, wake the driver and tell him to get the car ready out front as soon as possible.'

'Is there anything wrong, sir?'

'No, nothing to concern you. Go back to bed once you have told him.'

Sanchez struggled out of his pyjamas and into his clothes, panting with exertion. Despite his unwieldy body, he felt heroic. He would rescue his daughter and for once in his life, show her she mattered to him. Praying he was not too late, he took the lift downstairs and opened the front door.

The driver sat outside in the car with the engine running. He held open the door and waited while his boss slid into the back seat.

'Good morning, sir.'

'Good morning. I need you to drive to Miss Gloria's apartment.'

'Of course, sir.'

The expensive sedan glided through the silent streets of Calderon, noticed only by the security men standing guard outside the high-rise blocks. Most people were in bed or huddled inside bars with their friends, drinking imported whisky or cheap local rum, depending on their pocket.

They came to a stop outside Gloria's apartment block, and the driver pressed the doorbell. When there was no answer, he tried again but in vain. It didn't surprise Hernan when no one answered the doorbell. The maid slept like a brick and there was only one place that Gloria would be at this time in the morning.

His daughter liked to get drunk with her friends and he didn't begrudge her a little fun. She would be safe enough in a bar. He leaned into the leather seats and breathed in the smell of his new car, judging it easier to let her come to him. He drifted off to sleep.

***

When Gloria got home in the early hours of the morning, it surprised her to find her father's car waiting outside. Mike had once again been her willing chauffeur, but she had no intention of inviting him in now she had found Alfredo. Even Gloria had her limits.

She walked over to her father's car and knocked on the window. Mike followed her over, still hoping to break her resistance. His embarrassment was extreme when the window rolled down to reveal Hernan Sanchez. Mike wiped his hands on his trousers in anticipation, but Sanchez was not in a social mood.

'Gloria, you're in danger,' said her father. 'I must speak to you.'

'Right now, Papi? What makes you imagine that?'

'I have my sources. Have you come across a man named Wilson Ortega?'

Gloria looked surprised. Mike spoke no Spanish, but he understood that.

'Wilson Ortega works for me,' he answered, and Gloria translated, slurring.

'That man's a menace. He tried to kill Gloria.'

'Tried to kill her? When was that?'

'The car crash last week was not an accident.'

'What car crash?'

Mike looked bemused. Then Gloria remembered that she hadn't told him about it.

'Um, I was going to tell you, Mike.'

'What the hell is going on?'

'We had better go to your office right now and I will fill you in. Perhaps you have information that could be useful.'

There was no doubting the seriousness of the matter. Mike was no fool even though he had drunk his habitual skin-full.

'I can't believe you were in a car crash and didn't tell me about it,' he said to Gloria. He sobered up, dread creeping into his bowels. 'Travel with your father. I'll meet you there,' he said, clambering back into his car. He set out for the office followed by the black sedan.

Once his precious daughter had got into the car with him, Sanchez became emotional. He took her face in his hands and kissed it. Big fat tears fell on his cheeks as he gazed at her. Gloria squirmed under this unexpected attention.

'Papi, what's wrong? Are you ill?'

'Ill? No, I'm not ill. I'm so glad you are okay. I've waited for hours for you to come home. I was so worried about you, my darling little girl.' He choked back a sob and searched his pockets for a non-existent handkerchief.

Gloria took a tissue out of her handbag and dabbed his dear, plump face, which wobbled with emotion. Then, she leaned against the seat and rested her head on his shoulder, while he crooned sweet nothings at her like he had when she was a small child.

***

Twenty minutes later, they sat at the table in Mike's apartment drinking strong coffee. Mike and Gloria had sobered up somewhat, and Sanchez had calmed down now that his daughter was safe.

'So, what's this about a car crash?' said Mike. 'Why's Gloria in danger?'

'I should have told you but I thought you might be angry,' said Gloria.

'Angry? Why would I be angry?'

'It happened on the way up from the party in the

valley. Alfredo was in the car, and Sam, too. I was worried you might be cross and blame me for driving when I was drunk.'

'But no-one got hurt, right? It can't have been that bad.'

'Um, we wrote off the car, but we were all wearing our seatbelts because of Sam. She won't let me drive without one.'

'Good old Sam. Miss law-abiding saves the day. I don't understand though. How are you certain this wasn't an accident?'

'The car crashed because the brakes had failed. I had changed them recently, so I assumed the mechanics had made a mistake when they installed them,' said Gloria.

'They called me two days ago and informed me that someone had tampered with the brakes on the car,' said Hernan. 'They had made holes in the brake line and the fluid had leaked out.'

'Two days ago? Papi, why didn't you tell me?'

'I'm sorry. I wanted to find out who did it first in case it was something to do with me. Someone looking for revenge against me, perhaps. But it wasn't.'

Mike looked shocked, and Gloria had gone white. She added another sugar to her coffee.

'But who'd want to harm Gloria?' said Mike.

'My sources tell me it was a man called Falconi who tampered with the brakes. Someone named Wilson Ortega, who you say works for you, paid him to cause an accident. What do you know about him, Mike?'

'Señor Sanchez, Wilson is our geologist. Little more than that, I'm afraid, although...' Mike stopped in mid-sentence. 'Oh, my God,' he said. 'Poor Sam. I should have listened to her, not sent her into the jungle with that man.'

'The fault is mine, Mike. I should have told you about Wilson before. I thought he was only a macho pig. He had money problems but not grave enough to make him that desperate,' said Gloria.

'But why try to kill you?' asked Mike.

'The treasure,' Gloria said, having a moment of extreme clarity. 'He wants it for himself. He must've imagined I was going to tell you the truth about him and stop him from going on the trip.'

'But he wasn't told about the treasure. He's only going as far as Riccuarte. Who told him?'

Gloria had a good idea who the leaky vessel in the office was, but she didn't tell Mike. 'I guess he must have heard someone talking about it. Maybe he got drunk with Alfredo?'

'It doesn't matter right now how he knows. We have to telephone the hotel in San Martin and stop them from going into the jungle with him.'

'There's still time. The train leaves at dawn although it's often late. I don't have the number of the hotel though,' said Gloria. 'Only Marta has it.'

She ferreted around in her bag for her address book containing the number of Marta's neighbour, who had the only working telephone on the street. To save time, she tipped the bag onto the table, and there was temporary chaos as lipsticks, pens and coins shot across the surface onto the floor. Gloria retrieved a small dog-eared booklet from the contents and thumbed through the pages.

'Aha! Here it is. I'll call now.'

Gloria ran over to Marta's desk and dialled the number.

'You're looking for treasure? Aren't you a miner?' said Hernan Sanchez.

'It's a long story, Señor Sanchez. I'm not sure there's any truth to it. We got carried along with the excitement,' said Mike. 'It may be nothing but Wilson believes it's real and he's a desperate man.'

Gloria held the telephone to her ear and frowned with concentration. The telephone rang and rang until a grumpy voice answered.

'What do you want? Has someone died?'

'Hello,' said Gloria. 'Good morning. Sorry to disturb you. I need to speak to Marta Perez right away.'

'Are you crazy? Do you know what time it is?' said the voice.

'Yes, and I'm sorry to wake you, but it's a matter of life or death. I must speak to her right now. Can you please ask her to bring the phone number of the hotel in San Martin?'

'Life or death? The phone number of the hotel in San Martin?' The voice weighed up the options. 'Okay, but this is the last time.'

There was the noise of a door being opened and closed accompanied by exaggerated huffing and puffing. A long silence followed. Finally, Gloria heard the door being opened again. A breathless Marta came on the line.

'Hello, who's this?' she asked.

'It's me, Marta,' said Gloria.

'My neighbour told me you need the telephone number of the hotel in San Martin. What's so urgent that you're calling me at this hour?'

'I can't tell you, but it's a matter of life and death. I need it now.'

'Sacred Virgin! Okay, but promise to tell me later?'

'I promise. What's the number?'

'I don't have it here. It's in my desk in the top

drawer. It's on a Post-It note that says Hotel California.'

'The drawer's locked. Where's the key?'

'Oh dear, it's in my handbag.'

'Get into a taxi and come straight here,' said Gloria, who looked at Mike for confirmation. 'Mike will refund you.'

'I'll be on my way shortly.'

'Don't do your makeup first,' said Gloria, who understood what Marta was like concerning her appearance.

'But I can't come out without makeup.'

'If you don't come straight away, I'll tell Mike about you and Wilson,' she hissed.

'Okay, please don't tell him. I'll be right there.'

Marta hung up.

Gloria made more coffee for the others and then she took the lift downstairs to wait for Marta and smoke a cigarette out on the steps of the building.

By the time that Marta's taxi drew up to the pavement, Gloria had smoked three cigarettes and was contemplating a fourth. The taxi driver wanted to charge extra for the early hour but one look at Gloria's face changed his mind.

The two women got straight into the lift and ascended to the apartment. The difference in Marta's appearance without her normal thick makeup took Gloria aback. She looked ten years younger.

Once in the apartment, Marta crossed straight to the desk and opened the drawer. She handed the number to Gloria without comment. Gloria telephoned the hotel and waited for someone to answer. The phone rang and rang and cut out. Gloria rang again with the same result.

'Are you sure this is the correct number?' she

asked.

'I'm positive,' she said, and mumbling greetings to the room, ran for the toilet with her head down so she could use the mirror.

'Keep trying, Gloria,' said Mike. 'Someone will answer soon.'

Chapter XVII

Sam was still sulking when they left the hotel. The phone in the lobby was ringing when they checked out, causing the men to moan about the effect the noise was having on their hangovers. Sam couldn't understand how the night manager could ignore it. He didn't acknowledge the phone or the complaints, and after they had paid the bill, he returned to his room behind the reception to sleep.

They could hear the telephone as they walked up the street to the station in the silence of dawn. She wondered who would ring the hotel at this hour. Maybe someone he didn't want to speak to. Fantasies about who could be calling and how they were connected to the theft of the money belt occupied Sam's thoughts until they arrived at the station.

After the usual chaos, they loaded their supplies onto the roof of the train which they boarded before it set off for the coast. Sam wrapped her money belt around her hand and gripped it as she mounted the steps even though she wasn't expecting lightning to strike twice.

Wilson and Alfredo were oblivious to anything except their horrible hangovers. They sat together, leaving Sam wedged against the side of the train by a large, smiley local lady who had an assortment of poultry at her feet. They had their claws tied together, so they lay on the floor under the seat in front unable to move, squawking in protest if someone came too near to them with their shoes.

Sam put her small rucksack on the window frame as a pillow with the strap wrapped around her arm to prevent it from falling outside. She lowered her head onto the makeshift pillow and tried to shut out the noise and cigarette smoke.

The train jerked into action and set off at its usual snail's pace into the early morning mist shrouding the banana plantations. Dogs followed the train, barking and running alongside. They ran through the rotting, rat-infested rubbish on the side of the tracks, skipping around the large pigs digging for scraps with their snouts. Finally, even the slow pace of the train exhausted them, and it left the dogs panting with their tails wagging at the joy of the chase.

***

The night manager answered the telephone when he realised whoever was calling would not give up.

'Hotel California. Good morning. Who's speaking, please?'

'Finally,' said Gloria. 'I need to speak to Alfredo Vargas or Sam Harris right away.'

'They checked out about an hour ago, lady. You missed them.'

'This is urgent. Do you want to earn twenty dollars? I need you to stop them from getting on the train.'

'But the train leaves in five minutes.'

'Has it ever left on time? Please, run down to the station and stop them from boarding. It's a matter of life or death.'

'Give me your number, and I'll call you when I get back.'

'Okay,' she said and dictated the number. 'Have you got it?'

'Yes, madam,' replied the manager and then added, 'I'm leaving now,' with the urgency of a corpse. The call cut out.

The manager stuffed his feet into his shoes, shuffled to the door of the hotel and out onto the street. He was not a man accustomed to being in any hurry, and he was a heavy smoker. After trotting down the road for about twenty metres, he slowed to a rolling gait and then to a slow walk, puffing and panting his way to the station.

He arrived within five minutes, in time to see the end of the train disappear into the distance followed by a pack of yapping dogs. Throwing his hands in the air, he shrugged and walked at a snail's pace to the hotel, stopping to buy fresh bread from the baker on his way.

When he arrived, he attempted to call the number Gloria had given him. Still cuddling the warm soft rolls with one arm, he tried to dial the number with his other hand, but the telephone kept slipping across the counter. He dealt with the problem by eating the bread while it was hot with a nice cup of sweet coffee. The telephone rang when he was on his second roll.

'Hotel California. Good morning,' he said.

'What happened? Are they with you? Did you stop them from leaving?'

'No, my lady, they left. The train left on schedule for the first time this year, I believe.'

'They already left. Oh, no. That's terrible.'

'What about my twenty dollars?' he asked, but there was only a dial tone in reply.

***

Gloria replaced the phone on the receiver and shook her head at Mike and her father. A tear rolled down her cheek. Sam and Alfredo were at the mercy of Wilson in the jungle.

'Papi, what can we do? How will we rescue them?'

'I don't know, sweetheart. There's no way to contact them. There are no telephones in the jungle. Mike, do you know where they were going?'

'I believe they were going to a town called Riccuarte, but the journey onwards from there was secret and known only to a certain Don Moises, who comes from an isolated Indian community upriver from there. We would never find them in time. We must hope Wilson is only planning to steal and not to kill.'

'I can send someone to Riccuarte to make inquiries, but they won't get there until the day after tomorrow when it may be too late,' suggested Sanchez.

'Papi, there's always someone who is spying on everyone else in those small communities. I'm sure there's a person in Riccuarte who can help us find them. They may be abandoned or injured. We must save them.'

Mike, who couldn't imagine explaining to Mr and Mrs Harris how he got their daughter killed by a man that had already tried to rape her, nodded in agreement.

'Okay, I'll call someone today and send him to San Martin to take the train,' said Sanchez. 'He'll be in Riccuarte tomorrow, and he will find our friends. Don't worry, darling. This guy's the best. He's never failed me.'

Sanchez enfolded his now weeping daughter in his arms and kissed the top of her head. The tender gesture struck Mike as unusual, as if she were a small child, and he guessed that for Sanchez, Gloria would never grow up. She would always be his little girl. He wondered how it would be to hold your own child like that.

Mike had to turn away before emotion got the better of him. The turn of events had upset him and blamed himself for listening to Sam but not hearing what she was saying. The treasure had lost its allure, and his hangover was combined with exhaustion. Sanchez appeared unaffected by his sleepless night. He shook Mike's hand and kissed Gloria goodbye.

'I've got to organise things now, hija de mi alma. Stay with Mike and Marta, so I know you are safe. Mike, do you mind if Gloria stays with you for the time being? I'd feel a lot better knowing where she is, and I'd prefer she doesn't get further involved with this business. I'll deal with it my way.'

Sanchez could deal with Wilson without his help and Mike was certain he didn't want to know what that entailed. Honoured to look after Gloria, on whom he had a large crush, despite her defection to Alfredo, he decided he would protect her with his life.

'Of course, Señor Sanchez. It'd be my pleasure. We'll be fine here. Please keep us up to date with any progress you make.'

'Excellent. We'll speak later.' Sanchez squeezed into the lift and was gone.

Gloria sniffed and was comforted by Marta, who had sat in a corner observing the whole process. Mike told them to make breakfast as Gloria's maid had not yet arrived. He sorted through all his files on the trip, trying to find clues to the location of the steps.

There was also a pile of Alfredo's files in the office, which had potential as a source of good leads. Mike spread the information onto his bed and examined it piece by piece. He made notes on some scraps of paper he stored in a jar so they wouldn't get lost.

He had made good headway by the time the two women had prepared a breakfast of eggs, bacon and fried bread. They were starving and devoured the lot. Mike hoped that Sanchez was having better luck than him at finding clues to their whereabouts.

After breakfast, Marta appeared at the door of the bedroom. She looked as if she had something to say and it distracted him from his review of the papers.

'Yes?' he said. 'What is it? Can't you see how busy I am?'

Marta looked like he had slapped her in the face, and tears threatened to escape from her un-made-up eyes. Mike hadn't meant to be so brusque. He put his hand on her shoulder.

'Come on now, Marta, this is upsetting for all of us. It's been a long day already.'

'Oh, Mr Mike,' she said, 'I'm such a fool. You've been so good to me, and I have rewarded you by being silly and allowing someone to seduce me into a confidence.'

'Whatever are you on about?' asked Mike, flummoxed by this confession.

'I told him,' she whispered. 'I told Wilson about the secret and behaved like an idiot. Now I've put dear Sam and Alfredo in danger. I'll never forgive myself.'

A wave of anger ran through Mike, replaced by compassion when he saw her expression. He was as guilty as Marta of putting Sam in danger.

'I don't doubt that he knew already. Wilson is a desperate man who will stop at nothing to pay back his debts. Maybe Alfredo let the cat out of the bag when he was drunk. I don't want you blaming yourself and getting upset. Sam is tough and clever, and Alfredo resourceful. They'll get through it together. Don't worry.'

'Really?'

'I'm sure. Now help Gloria clean up the breakfast.'

Marta was as deep as a puddle, and nothing bothered her for long. She sniffled and tried to smile and went to the kitchen to help Gloria wash up. Soon, she was putting her war paint back on, applying thick coats of mascara to her bare lashes and lacquering her quiff.

He should ring Edward and tell him what was happening, but he couldn't face it. After Black Monday, Edward would be desperate for good news and this would not help. Mike didn't consider himself a dishonest man, but he was economical with the truth at the best of times. Good news he spread thick and fast, but he parcelled out bad news in small portions. He had the entrepreneur's faith his plans would turn out right. He believed uttering bad news out loud made it real, and until then it was only one of many possibilities. Edward could wait.

***

Sanchez had gone straight home to find Agatha the maid in a state of distress as he had not been out all night for several years. He had long ceased to seek comfort for the death of his wife from cancer in the arms of certain courtesans in Calderon and she had feared that some horrible fate had befallen him. He calmed her down and asked her to make his favourite lunch. She bustled off, pleased with this return to normality.

Then, Sanchez rang Segundo's number from memory. The man answered straight away.

'Hello, who is calling?' he asked.

'It's me, Hernan Sanchez. I've another favour to ask of you. I will reward you well.'

'Boss. I'm always at your service. What can I do for you this time?'

'There's been a change in plans. I want you to travel to San Martin tonight and take the train to San Lorenzo tomorrow morning. From there, travel to Riccuarte where you'll try to locate our Mr Ortega before he does any more harm. I believe he'll be travelling in the company of a certain Don Moises, an Indian from upriver. Wilson believes the expedition to be a treasure hunt and he is desperate for money. I need you to find him as soon as you can. I'll provide funds from the usual source. Ask for as much as you need. Questions?'

'What should I do when I find him, Señor Sanchez?'

'You'll think of something, Segundo. I leave it to your good judgement. He's a dead man walking in Calderon. El Duro has a contract out on him if he does not pay a certain debt. Perhaps we could gain advantage if we deliver Wilson to him? Allying with El Duro could be favourable for our businesses.'

'I hear you, boss. I'll not be able to send you any news, but when it comes, it'll be good.'

'Thank you, Segundo. I'm grateful to have such a man on my side.'

'You do me a great honour by confiding in me, boss. I won't let you down.'

Sanchez replaced the telephone on the receiver and then picked it up again to call his intermediary about giving money to Segundo. There was never any direct contact between the men. It was a matter of principal for Sanchez that he didn't get his hands dirty in these matters.

He could smell his lunch being cooked in the kitchen. This galvanised him into taking a quick shower and putting on some fresh clothes. He would take an extended afternoon nap, so he told Agatha that he wasn't to be disturbed after lunch. He then sat down to enjoy his potato soup.

***

The train wended its slow way through the countryside, inducing Sam into a torpor. She glanced over at Wilson and Alfredo and discovered that they had both fallen asleep, and Alfredo's head had fallen onto Wilson's shoulder. She got her camera out of her rucksack and took a photograph of the sleeping beauties. It cheered her up, and she enjoyed the trip again. The large palm leaves swished over the roof of the train, depositing bizarre and interesting insects in Sam's lap. Ever the scientist, she photographed them before flicking them back out of the window with her pencil.

At one stop, she bought a big bag of banana crisps, which she shared with her cheerful neighbour. The two women made a dash for the nearest bush when the train pulled into a siding to let the oncoming train pass. They took turns to shoo away nosey villagers.

Her neighbour got off two stops later, and Sam bought sweet fried plantain with bits of over-cooked pork, which she ate with relish. Sam always felt better after having something to eat. By the time they pulled into San Lorenzo, her mood was upbeat, unlike her travelling companions, who were dehydrated and grumpy.

Sam sat with the supplies while Alfredo and Wilson went to buy refreshments and commandeer a pickup truck. When they got back with the truck, a large group of children surrounded Sam, sucking boiled sweets and giggling. Wilson shooed them away and made sure he got to ride up front in the truck by getting in and staying there while Sam and Alfredo loaded the supplies into the back. Alfredo had got hold of an old foam mattress, which he folded up against the cabin and floor of the truck.

'Madam, your throne awaits,' he said, hopping up into the back and offering Sam his hand.

'Thank you, kind sir,' said Sam, climbing over the piled-up boxes and falling onto the improvised sofa. Alfredo sat down next to her and gave her one of his big smiles. He was in his element. She had never seen him look so content.

'We'll do it, Sam. We'll find the lost treasure of the Incas,' he said.

With that, the truck started for Riccuarte, throwing them both in the air and making them giggle like small children. Alfredo's good humour and the two helpings of banana, which were both sweet and savoury, made Sam feel like a new woman. She dismissed the snub of the previous evening as two men looking for an excuse to get drunk together and bond. The merry presence of Alfredo protected her from Wilson's advances. They were on a real adventure, and the fun was just starting.

They pulled into Riccuarte in the late afternoon. Don Moises, who welcomed them, showed them to a different house from their first visit. It was a lot more habitable. Sam had her own room at one end of the house with a primitive bed placed to avoid any leaks from the rather ratty looking palm-leaf roof. Wilson and Alfredo shared the other bedroom, and they stored the supplies in the middle room.

Doña Elodea came to the house with a pot of rice

and some fresh fried fish for their supper. No one spoke as they ate their fill of the delicious crispy fish with forkfuls of fluffy rice. Wilson, muttering something about organising things for the morning, walked off down the street afterwards, leaving Sam and Alfredo to clear up.

'He appears to think he's coming with us,' said Sam after Wilson left.

'Oh, yes, didn't I tell you?' asked Alfredo. 'I decided that we might need him, so he's coming to Arenas with us.'

'But didn't Mike say Wilson should only come as far as Riccuarte?' said Sam, rolling her eyes.

'That was the original plan, yes, but I changed it. I haven't told him about the treasure. He thinks it's a historical trip. Anyway, Mike put me in charge,' said Alfredo in a way that challenged Sam to disagree.

Sam took a deep breath and went with the flow. Wilson would never attack her now that Alfredo was on the trip. She suspected that Don Moises might also have something to say on the subject. She would enjoy the biggest adventure of her life and not let Wilson spoil it.

'Okay,' she said. 'You're the boss. I'm going to bed now. See you at the crack of dawn.'

***

Wilson was not ready for bed. He needed a drink and having already started on his emergency bottle, he had to save the rest for the trip. He walked through the village looking for the inevitable cantina. Footsteps disturbed the gravel behind him and he turned to see Don Moises, who was clutching a bottle of cheap rum and two glasses. The sudden appearance of alcohol did not faze Wilson who was too desperate to wonder at the coincidence. He was as superstitious as most of his countrymen and a great believer in fate.

'Good evening, Wilson,' said Moises, 'can I offer you a drink?'

'That sounds like an excellent idea,' said Wilson. 'Where can we sit?'

'I know the perfect place. Follow me.'

Moises led Wilson to an abandoned house with a raised porch overlooking the river. There were two wooden chairs on the porch and a log table. The two men climbed the rickety stairs and sat down in the chairs. Wilson's chair creaked and threatened to collapse, but it held up. Moises poured them both a generous helping of rum.

'Your great health,' he said, handing Wilson the glass.

Wilson took the glass and drank like a man rescued from the desert. Moises refilled his glass without comment. He sat in his chair and waited for the alcohol to take effect, watching the river glint in the moonlight. It was dark on the porch, and well camouflaged in his black clothes, Wilson almost disappeared. So much so that when he spoke, his teeth appeared in the gloom like disembodied dentures.

'You're a man of the world,' said Wilson. 'Have you ever heard of the lost treasure of the Incas?'

'Of course. Why do you ask?'

'Aren't you surprised that we're here so soon after our last trip?'

Moises grunted.

'Has Alfredo told you why we're here?'

'He said something about an Inca ruin that Sam found last time she was here.'

'Ha! That girl couldn't find her own arse. I don't know why we have to have useless women hanging around when this is men's work. They're trollops. Didn't you see the way she led me on last time she was here? She's nothing more than a prick tease. I bet she slept with her professors at university to get her degree.'

'Oh, yes, I know what you mean. I saw her. They're all the same,' said Moises.

There was a loud creaking sound as Wilson threw himself back in his chair and drained his glass. He leaned forward and thrust the glass out to be refilled, which it was. Moises waited. Wilson gulped down most of the rum. He was sighing and snorting, considering whether to confide in Moises.

Wilson was in a quandary. He needed an ally for his plan, but he wasn't sure if Moises would support him. Perhaps it was too early to find out. He considered himself superior to the man sitting opposite him. Like most humble people, Moises would accept the orders of an educated man with a degree without question. He had thrown in the comment about Sam to gauge his support. The fact that Moises had not defended Sam, but had recognised her for what she was, encouraged him to believe he was ripe for conversion to the Wilson Ortega philosophy of life.

'It's not only her,' he said. 'That Alfredo is a typical example of a spoiled rich brat who belongs to those few families that rape our country and take it all for themselves. Don't you agree?'

'Oh, yes,' said Moises. 'He makes me sick. Those rich kids are all the same. Over-privileged and under-educated. It's disgusting.'

Wilson warmed to his theme.

'It's the rich who get richer, while we labour for them. It's time we stood up for ourselves.'

'Ah, but how do we do that?' asked Moises.

'They've got the power.'

There was a silence as the little mestizo filled the glasses again. Both men sat contemplating the river. Wilson emptied his glass again and sat forward, moving his chair so that his knees touched those of Moises. He looked him straight in the eye.

'This expedition is about a lot more than history,' he said.

Torrential rain thundered down on the tin roof of their house. Sam watched through the window as lightning pierced the treetops, illuminating the dark foliage. It might have been taken as an omen, but she was not superstitious and had fantastic memories of a particular thunderstorm spent with a French exchange student at university before she met Simon.

She lay in bed, letting her mind roam back to those passionate nights. What was his name, anyway? Jules. That was it. Jules, with the sexy French accent and a cheeky smile. Sam hadn't even considered turning him down when he propositioned her out of the blue in the pub one night. He was not deep, but he was sincere in his passion, and she spent a few torrid weeks under the sheets with him. She could still imagine the thrill of his marauding tongue. Smiling to herself as she dropped off to sleep, she moaned as the thunder cracked outside and the rain poured off the roofs.

Moises, who had been watching over her in case Wilson got any new ideas in his drunken state, leaned against the doorframe and wondered who on earth she was thinking about that made her smile and sigh like that. She was an attractive young woman and he could imagine why Wilson wanted her.

He watched her fall into a deep sleep, her breathing so shallow she looked like a corpse. He made sure that everyone else was asleep, too, before he curled up like a dog on a blanket outside her door and fell asleep himself.

Chapter XVIII

It was pitch black inside the house. Moises had already slipped away to the riverbank to supervise the packing of the canoe. Sam had trouble finding her things in the gloom, the dim light generated by the single candle in her room only just penetrating it. She felt around for her penknife, which she had heard fall off her bed during the night. She used her feet in case there were any millipedes or scorpions waiting to give her a nasty nip.

Wilson and Alfredo shuffled around doing similar explorations in 'braille' in their room. She found a small packet of peanuts in her rucksack and ate them to prevent her losing them. The salty taste made her even more hungry and thirsty than she had been before. She tried to rationalise her feelings of excitement but found no reason to quell them. How many of her peers were about to embark on a real-life treasure hunt? Alfredo poked his head around the door.

'Are you ready, Sam?' he asked.

'More than ready.' She winked at him.

Alfredo's answering smile told her all she needed to know about his mood. It filled the room and illuminated the dark corners where the scorpions had gone to hide. He handed her two finger-sized bananas.

'Breakfast,' he said, and disappeared again.

Sam sat on the edge of her hard bed and peeled one banana. She bit into it and enjoyed the harder, sweeter taste of the lady's finger species. There were twenty-four species of banana in Sierramar, and she loved them all. They could pound even the bland cooking bananas into flour that made exquisite, fluffy, fried drop scones with melted cheese in the middle. She was sitting there musing on the wonders of the banana when Wilson shouted at her from the front door.

'Are you coming or not, *gringa*?'

She didn't dignify his question with a response. Instead, she flipped her rucksack onto her shoulder and sauntered outside at her own pace. She grinned at Alfredo, who rolled his eyes. This was going to be fun.

***

Segundo braved the chill air at the train station in San Martin. He had bought his ticket with ease, the crowd parting before his intimidating presence. He was not a tall man, being a mestizo, but he had a powerful build with taut muscles that quivered with anticipation. The scars of former battles decorated his face, including one that dropped the left side of his lips downward, giving him a sinister appearance.

Some women made the sign of the cross as he walked past them. The locals were superstitious, and Segundo radiated evil. He was well aware of the effect he had on these credulous people. He used it to good effect when he wished to get information out of someone. Rarely did he have to resort to torture as he had with José Falconi. Segundo was wary of meeting the man who had frightened Falconi into silence.

He had picked up lots of gossip about Wilson in the brothels. He got the impression Wilson liked to punch women and avoided confrontations with men, but Segundo was going to be cautious anyway to avoid any unpleasantness.

The train pulled into the station, and he climbed aboard and sat in the window seat of his row. A small boy clambered up beside him. He was young enough to be without fear, and he reached out and touched Segundo's damaged face.

'Did you fall down?' asked the boy.

Segundo gazed down at this little warrior, and his eyes twinkled.

'I did,' he said. 'I fell off a horse.'

The boy's mother, who was wrestling with two other small children, grabbed him when she heard him talk to Segundo.

'How could you be so rude?' she said, 'Apologise to the gentleman.'

Segundo, who was not used to being addressed as a gentleman, was startled. The small boy's eyes filled will tears, and his bottom lip quivered.

'Don't worry, madam. He was only being curious.'

He searched in his pocket for a sweet and found willing recipients for several, despite them being covered in fluff. The little boy sat on his lap and look out of the window as they cut through the trees and headed for the coast.

***

Sam made her way into the jungle to a secluded spot where she could relieve herself without an audience. Reciting an incantation against snakes, she squatted in the undergrowth and hoped that no one else would choose that moment to do the same. Privacy, as she understood it, was not something that anyone in Sierramar respected. A piece of grass tickled her bottom, making her jump and some urine splashed on her boot. Not a good start to the morning but no one would notice a wet boot in the hubbub surrounding the launching of the canoe.

Emerging from the foliage, she squinted into the low sunlight. A crowd of people, including a group of what looked like thirteen-year-olds, had assembled on the riverbank beside a large canoe. Sam tried to spot Carlos, Rijer or Doña Elodea but she couldn't recognise them. She was looking forward to hanging out with them again.

As she approached the party, Sam realised that the silhouettes she had imagined were teenage children from far away were short, stout Indians wearing minimal loincloths and blank expressions. They stood close to the canoe similar in length to the one used on the last trip but deeper drafted containing low wooden seats with small backs instead of blocks of wood–an improvement. They had packed the supplies into the front of the canoe under the bow wrapped in plastic.

A heated discussion was going on between Wilson and a tall, thin mulatto with a pencil moustache who shook with indignation.

'What's that about?' Sam asked Alfredo.

'The mayor of Riccuarte is pissed off because we are using imported labour.'

'Imported labour? Where are the workers from?'

'Arenas.'

'Arenas? But that's the next village. They're hardly imported.'

The mayor of Riccuarte didn't agree. He stood between Wilson and the canoe, his arms outstretched as if to block the way.

'Work is non-existent in this region and sharing it out between the villages is good politics. It is not

Riccuarte's turn this time and the mayor won't get his cut. Leave it to me. I'll sort it out.'

Alfredo went up to the mayor and took him aside. They had an animated conversation. She saw him give the mayor some money, and the problem disappeared as quickly as it had arisen.

'What's the plan today, then?' said Sam.

'We'll do an initial visit to the site, to clear and photograph the steps so we can see if they lead anywhere. I need to document the site in detail for the sake of history and completeness,' said Alfredo.

'And where are we staying tonight?'

'In Arenas. Wilson told me it's easier for the crew to stay in their own homes and cheaper for us if they do. I believe you stayed there last time.'

'Yes, we did.'

Sam did not want to be reminded of her last stay in Arenas. She had not told Alfredo about Wilson's attempted assault and she wondered if Gloria had. Alfredo got on fine with Wilson so he was unaware or didn't care about the attack. She didn't want to ruin her adventure by bringing up the incident for no reason and annoying or distressing Alfredo when he had other more important things on his mind. She would deal with Wilson in her own way.

After smoothing the mayor's ruffled feathers, they got into the canoe and set off for the site of the Inca steps. The sun was not yet high in the sky when they left, so the air felt cool below the shade of the trees bordering the river. The water levels had risen because of the previous night's rains, and the canoe skimmed over the minor rapids with no need for the passengers to get out.

Clouds of tiny flies hung over the water like old lace curtains moving in the breeze. Alfredo poked Sam in the shoulder and offered his legs as a backrest. She leaned back against his skinny shins and looked up at the sky, which was azure blue. Her head was full of fantasies about Indiana Jones, who looked like Simon. Her anticipation rose as they got nearer to the site.

A fish jumped and plopped back into the water, stirring her from her reverie. She looked up from the floor of the boat into the jungle, and to her stunned surprise, saw a big cat lapping water at the river's edge. It lifted its head as the boat glided by and flicked its tail in annoyance before disappearing back into the jungle. Sam lunged for her camera but to her eternal regret, it was double-sealed in a plastic bag at the front of the boat.

One man propelling the boat through the water stopped poling, raised an imaginary rifle to his shoulder and shot at the vanishing feline. No wonder the wildlife hid from them. She glanced around to check if Alfredo had seen it, too. He mouthed 'puma' at her. She nodded and beamed.

After a couple of hours, they arrived at the place on the river where they had been working when Sam had run into the jungle with the workers to photograph the snake. She was dozing and woke up with a start as the canoe nudged the riverbank. They clambered out onto the shingle, a little stiff after sitting in cramped conditions for so long.

The Indians who had crewed the canoe dived into the river, laughing and joking together in the water. She was tempted to join them, but she didn't want to get her clothes wet, as the day was not hot yet. She didn't want to take them off, either, because she couldn't bear the thought of Wilson leering at her in her bra and knickers. Wilson leaned against a tree, smoking with his hat over his eyes. He had been silent the entire trip. He let Alfredo give the orders.

There was something strange going on, but Sam couldn't work out what it was. She took her satchel out of the plastic wrapping and revised its contents. Her notebook, a penknife, some pens, a compass, a camera and some cooking chocolate were there. She wouldn't make the mistake of putting her camera in there again.

Eventually, when the crew had dried off and stretched out, they set out into the jungle, Don Moises leading. Sam was surprised until she remembered that he knew about the Inca steps the first time and was not interested in seeing them. Wilson followed close behind him, chain-smoking his packet of Full Speed cigarettes, forcing the others to walk several paces behind the two men to avoid the smoke and flying ash.

'Filthy habit,' said Alfredo to Sam. He was one of the few people she knew in Sierramar who didn't smoke.

'Full speed to the grave.'

It didn't take them long to reach the steps, which were in the shade at this time of day. They looked dull and nondescript, like a blocky rock formation. *Were they on a wild goose chase after all?* Then, she heard Alfredo gasp. He shuffled forward through the group and was up at the rock face, caressing it with his right hand. His cheek pressed against it and his eyes shut in ecstasy. He muttered to himself.

Sam waited with the others while he recovered and pulled away from the surface where she could see he had been running his hand over the carved stone cipher of a snake. Alfredo was pale, and his eyes glistened. He turned to look for Sam, and catching her eye, he nodded. He was overcome and sank to his knees. One worker ran forward with a log for him to sit on. He sat with his head in his hands, talking to himself.

'Hey, are you okay?' said Sam.

'Yes, it's a shock. It's so real,' said Alfredo.

'We're not there yet.'

Sam gave him a piece of her precious chocolate, which helped to revive him. He gave orders for the men to clear the rock face with machetes. They set to work removing the vines and creepers.

It took about an hour to complete this job. When they finished, the bottom of a stone staircase was revealed, cutting through the ancient river terraces stacked up into the jungle. There were serpent ciphers on the vertical part of each step and concave indentations on the tops of the steps filled with sediment, which Alfredo ordered the workers to collect in plastic bags.

He took copious notes at this stage and pointed out key locations for Sam to photograph. He logged and measured every aspect of the stairs. When they had documented the bottom of the staircase, Alfredo directed the workers to clear the upper reaches. Painstakingly and halting at each step for more photographs and measurements, they cut their way up the slope.

Startled lizards shot into the jungle in all directions, their early morning sunbathing cut short by the invasion of their habitat. At one point, the machetes disturbed a viper which slithered away in alarm. The workers wanted to kill it, but Don Moises stopped them, causing a momentary pause in the work for a vigorous debate. Sam missed the chance to get a photograph as she had her back to the steps.

'Why are they trying to kill the snake? It's running away, isn't it?' she asked.

'Did you see the markings on its back?' asked Alfredo. 'They look like an 'X', so they call the snake

Ekis. They're poisonous and can kill small children. The workers wanted to kill the snake in case it goes to their village.'

'What do they do to protect themselves from snakes who get there?'

'They've a secret weapon.'

'And what's that?'

'Did you see the pigs that the villagers keep under their houses? They are immune to snake bites because of the thick layer of fat on their bodies. They kill the snakes and eat them.'

'The pigs eat the snakes?'

'Yes, pigs will eat anything.'

Moises assured the workers that their village was too far away for the snake to reach and that it was not right to disturb the balance of nature in the jungle by killing the predators. He restored the peace, and they went back to their task of clearing the vegetation.

***

Segundo arrived at Riccuarte in the late afternoon and set about finding somewhere to stay. They offered him the same decrepit hut where Sam and Wilson had stayed on their first visit to the village. He left his belongings in a dark corner and ventured out into the dusk. Bats were swooping to catch the insects gathered around the bare lightbulbs lit by small generators in newer dwellings.

He went to look for a cantina. He met Doña Elodea on the main street and asked her if there was a cantina in the village and where he could find it. She had a villager's suspicion of strangers, and there was something about the man that made her shudder.

'I haven't seen you around,' she ventured. 'Have you got business in Riccuarte?'

'My name is Segundo Duarte. I came to Riccuarte to look for someone. His name's Wilson Ortega. I don't suppose you've come across him? I believe he arrived yesterday afternoon.'

Doña Elodea let no recognition cross her face.

'Maybe he's in the cantina,' she suggested. 'Most visitors eat there in the evening.'

'Can you tell me where I can find it please, Señora?' asked Segundo.

'Follow this street and the first turn on the right.'

'Thank you, Señora. Have a good evening.' He was gone.

There was something sinister about Segundo. He made her flesh crawl with that nasty scar on his face. *Why would someone follow Wilson into the jungle?* Segundo could not be trusted. She took the initiative as Don Moises was not in town. She didn't want the stranger to get away upriver before she sent a message to Moises in the morning asking him to find out what was going on. Her friends in Riccuarte knew how to deal with dodgy strangers.

She picked up her skirts and hurried down the street to find Carlos and Rijer, who had worked on the original crew with Sam and Wilson. She found them playing cards on the porch outside Rijer's house.

'Chicos, I need your help. There's a stranger in town looking for Wilson. He's evil looking. I think he might be dangerous.'

'Where's he now?'

'I sent him to the cantina to buy his supper. Can you please come with me and capture him?'

'But where'll we keep him?'

'The old prison room will be perfect until morning. I'll question him then.'

'Okay, let's go.'

The three vigilantes strode down the street to the cantina where Segundo was enjoying a bowl of soup. He didn't finish it. Carlos and Rijer grabbed him from both sides, and they caught him unaware. Despite this, he was a match for the two strong men and wriggled like an eel between them. Another local, who liked a good brawl, came up behind Segundo when it looked as if he might struggle free. He hit him on the head with an empty beer bottle. He went down with a thump.

The boys lifted his arms over their shoulders and dragged him down the road to the village lock-up. They placed him on a wooden bench inside the hut and locked the door from the outside. Doña Elodea asked them to fetch his belongings and throw them in, too.

By the time that Segundo came around, he had an old foam mattress, a cold bowl of soup and his small rucksack in the lock-up with him. He was groggy and couldn't imagine what had happened to him. The last thing he remembered was eating soup in the cantina.

He tried the door, but despite pulling and kicking with all his might, it did not budge. He shouted his lungs out, but no one came to his aid. Deciding that he was unlikely to get an explanation until morning, he lay down on the bed. Despite the discomfort of the thin mattress and the mosquitos buzzing around his head, he was soon asleep.

***

They had finished the staircase, and it was clear that the terrain flattened out into a small plateau at the top of the steps. Large, black clouds rumbled into sight on the horizon, signalling a major storm was going to break. No one wanted to get caught outside, as these storms sometimes contained large, painful hailstones that could bruise anyone foolish enough to stay out in the open. They made a decision to stop work for the day and set out for Arenas.

The team descended the stone staircase onto the floor of the jungle and walked in single file to the riverbank. No one spoke. Most were exhausted by the hard, manual labour, others by speculation. They had not mentioned the treasure hunt to prevent rumours from spreading all over Arenas. Alfredo was posing as an archaeologist with an interest in the ancient steps and they had not given the workers any further information.

No-one could be sure if the treasure existed, but the steps were significant in their own right and logic suggested that they had to lead somewhere. Sam tried to remain as calm as possible, as if she went searching for treasure every day, but inside her was a cauldron of emotions. She had hoped that the job with Mike would be a stepping stone to a geological career. She had never expected to take part in a treasure hunt. If there was no treasure, she would try to get more field experience working for Mike. She wasn't sure that treasure hunting was a legitimate entry for her resume.

The canoe fought with the river all the way to Arenas, which was close to the site, but it was slow going. The crew had stopped laughing and joking and there was a grim concentration on their work as they forced the canoe through the torrent of brown water. They landed at the village as the first large drops of rain fell from the sky, which was already black even though the sun hadn't gone down yet.

They made their way to the main square where they had been housed in the same civic building in which they stayed before. They had given Sam one of the small rooms off the main upstairs accommodation. It had a primitive lock which relaxed her. She sat on the steps watching the rain pouring down. Children ran about, shrieking with laughter, and she was struck by the contrast to London where the mothers would have called the children inside instead of encouraging them to enjoy the rain.

The visitors had an early supper and went to bed soon afterwards. The storm strengthened and the rain came in sheets, which prevented any transit between the houses. Sam could see the raindrops bouncing off the volleyball court and running off into the gutters dug into the red clay.

The rain was torrential throughout the night, thundering on the tin roofs of the houses. She could hear it streaming off the roofs onto the ground as she lay in bed. The houses in the village were all on stilts to keep the snakes out but also in case of flooding. Random thoughts coursed through her head. *What did the pigs do when it rained? Why was Simon looking for her? When was Mike going to pay her?*

Chapter XIX

Segundo did not get much sleep in his impromptu prison in Riccuarte. The rain clattering on the tin roofs and the thunder cracking overhead meant he was awake for most of the night. The roof had rusty holes in it through which the rain trickled and dripped onto the mattress where he slept, making him damp and stiff. His empty stomach growled loudly.

It worried him he wouldn't get the chance to explain his presence in the village to the formidable Doña Elodea. Wilson might hurt someone while he was locked up in this hut. Elodea interested him despite the treatment he had received. Now, there was a woman you wanted on your side. She was attractive, too. He spent a pleasant hour fantasising about the charms of his captor before she knocked on the door, startling him out of his reverie.

'Good morning, Señor Duarte,' said Doña Elodea. 'I trust you slept well.'

'I've slept better,' he replied with a smile in his voice. 'That rain of yours is noisy.'

'You will get used to it.'

'You don't trust me, and I can understand that. With its evil aspect, my face does not engender confidence. I wonder if you might give me the chance to explain what I'm doing here,' he said, trying to appeal to the soft heart he imagined inhabited her curvy body.

He felt her struggle to reach a decision. The suspicion of strangers in these remote parts was endemic. He was used to people assessing him based on his deformed appearance. Throwing a man in prison because he looked evil could be considered an over-reaction, but she was being protective of her village.

Finally, she sighed.

'Are you hungry?' she asked. 'I'll make you some breakfast. You may eat at my house if you promise not to try anything. Remember that I have two strong, young neighbours who can help me if you try to escape.'

Breakfast sounded good to Segundo. He wouldn't get far if he made enemies in Riccuarte. Doña Elodea knew exactly where Wilson was, and he was sure she would help him if she could.

'It's a deal,' he said. 'You have my word I'll not try to escape. I'm starving as I didn't get the chance to finish my dinner last night. I promise to explain exactly why I'm here over breakfast, and I think you'll want to help me once you have heard what I have to say.'

There was a short silence and then some huffing and puffing outside as Doña Elodea dislodged the large pieces of wood that barricaded the door. The door fell open on its hinges, and Segundo squinted out into the bright morning. Doña Elodea stood with her hands on her hips, ready for trouble. Segundo smiled. A formidable woman, the kind that made him lose all concentration. He shook himself free of those thoughts.

'Lead on, Señora,' he said.

***

Mike plucked up the courage to ring Edward.

'Hi mate, how are you?'

'About time you called me! Where have you been? What's happening? Have you found my treasure yet?'

'I didn't want to disturb you with Black Monday and all that going on.'

'Oh, that's been sorted.'

'Sorted? How?'

'There was a dead cat bounce today. One of the senior brokers got in before the market closed and re-bought my shares at the bottom on Monday before the market closed and he sold them into the recovery today. Now we have bought them again at the bottom. I haven't lost more than a quarter and I expect the market will recover now.'

'That's great news.'

'Yes, well never mind that. Water under the bridge. I'll be richer when we find the treasure. How's the search going?'

The words hung in the air. Mike took a deep breath.

'There's been a slight hitch. I don't think it'll affect the outcome but it may delay it.'

Edward was used to Mike's inability to be straightforward.

'Spit it out, mate.'

'We have a problem. One of the team is planning to keep the treasure for himself, and the rest of the team don't know. He tried to eliminate Gloria and Sam by sabotaging their car.'

'Why didn't you stop him going?'

'We didn't realise that it wasn't an accident until it was too late. It's a long story.'

'Jesus, what a cockup! Can't you ring them?'

'They're in the jungle.'

'In that case, what the fuck are you doing in Calderon?'

'We've sent someone down to sort it out.'

'And what if he takes my treasure as well? I can't believe you're sitting on your arse in the office. Why aren't you on your way to the jungle?'

Mike hesitated. He had never told Edward about his heart problem as he was afraid Edward would cut him loose. Ruthless when it came to money, Mike was Edward's plaything but he had no interest in broken toys.

'Well, mate, we've only just found out, and the flight to the coast isn't until tomorrow so I was calling you to let you know.'

'I should bloody think so. Don't let me down, Mike; my wife will have my balls for this.'

'Don't worry, it's under control. I wanted to keep you informed.'

'Okay, well, let me know as soon as you're near a phone.'

'Bye, then.'

'Don't fuck up, Mike. I wouldn't want this to be the end of a beautiful friendship.'

He hung up.

Mike was in a quandary. It was fine for Edward to order him to the jungle, but Mr Sanchez's man should be able to deal with Wilson without help. Anyway, what about his heart? Could he risk going so far from a hospital? Wilson wouldn't need to kill anyone to get the treasure. He couldn't help worrying, though.

Later, he drank a coffee in the office with Gloria. They had their coffee without milk, as no one had remembered to buy any with Tati away on holiday. Marta was not there as she had stayed at home to look after her son, who had picked up a cold at school.

Mike fiddled with a ballpoint pen, clicking the top in and out. Finally, the pen broke and the insides shot all over the table. The spring landed in Gloria's coffee. She gave him a look that would have melted plastic. He shrugged.

'I can't help feeling responsible,' said Gloria.

'Responsible? You? Seriously though—how and for what?' asked Mike. It irritated him to be reminded that he felt the same. He couldn't imagine why it was Gloria's fault that Sam and Alfredo were in the jungle with a desperate man who might do anything for money.

'I heard things about Wilson, but I didn't tell you because I thought his private life was his business,' replied Gloria. 'I didn't know he was so indebted to such dangerous people. We could've stopped him from going on this trip.'

Mike sighed.

'Gloria,' he said. 'Sam told me that Wilson had tried to assault her, and I sent her back into the jungle with him. What I did was far worse.'

They both sat in silence.

'The worst thing is that we won't hear what has happened for days,' said Gloria at last. 'I'm not sure I can stand sitting around here. We may never find out the truth.'

Mike decided. He needed Edward to finance his projects, and to keep him on his side. He had to stop Wilson.

'Do you want to go to Riccuarte? I'm not sure if we can do anything about this situation, but we might stand a chance of getting news.'

'And your heart?' asked Gloria.

'Bugger my heart. It's not that bad,' said Mike. 'I need an adventure. We can fly to the beach first thing in the morning and hire a car to San Lorenzo. That should be less strain than taking the train for hours. We can hire a truck or car to Riccuarte and be there by evening. What do you say?'

'*Vamos*!' said Gloria, her eyes flashing. 'Let's save Sam and Alfredo.'

Mike laughed. 'They can look after themselves. We need to save the treasure from Wilson or Edward will have my guts for garters. Sitting here is no longer an option.'

'I'll call Papi and ask him to get us seats on the plane. He has friends who can arrange a car from the airport to San Lorenzo,' said Gloria.

Gloria went to ring her father, and Mike packed a bag. His heart pounded in his chest with excitement. He couldn't tell if this was good or bad, coming out in a sweat with the thrill of joining in the adventure. The danger didn't worry him. He was far more concerned that the stress of waiting for news would make him more ill than a quick jaunt to Riccuarte. Letting Edward down could have worse consequences and at least he didn't have to field his calls if he was in the jungle.

***

Segundo leaned back against the wall and patted his full stomach.

'Wow! That breakfast was delicious, Doña Elodea. I thank you, and my stomach thanks you.'

'I like to see a man enjoy his food,' she beamed, leaning over the table to take his plate away. 'Do you want a cup of coffee? You can drink it while you explain what you are doing here and why you are looking for Señor Ortega.'

'Yes, please. Make it nice and sugary to sweeten

my day.'

Doña Elodea poured them both a cup of hot coffee from the gas burner. They sipped it. The scalding coffee burned its way down his throat and Segundo wondered where to start. He decided not to beat around the bush.

'What I've got to tell you is important. I need you to believe me when I tell you this. Wilson Ortega is a dangerous man. He tried to kill the daughter of my boss by ordering someone to sabotage the brake lines on her car. She was lucky to survive.'

Doña Elodea gasped and covered her mouth to prevent herself from swearing. She crossed herself, eyes wide with anticipation for the next revelation.

'The problem is that Wilson's boss did not know about this before he sent him on this trip with Don Moises, Sam and Alfredo,' continued Segundo. 'They're in danger, as Wilson thinks they're looking for treasure, and he wants it for himself. He has major debts and several of the big crime families in Sierramar are looking for him.'

'And is there any treasure?' asked Doña Elodea, breathless with expectation.

'Of course not,' replied Segundo, more brusquely than he meant to. 'It's a myth. There are only ancient stones out there. Wilson is desperate for money. He'll do anything to get himself out of trouble. I must stop him before it's too late.'

'This man Wilson sounds like a liability. I want to believe you but it's quite a story. I'm not sure what to do.'

'We have to stop him. Let me go. I can do it.'

'That would not be a good idea. I know what to do. You must trust me. Is that all right with you?' she asked.

'I'm in your hands,' replied Segundo. 'I can see you are a determined and intelligent woman. What can we do now?'

'I can help you in your search, but you must heed my advice and stay in Riccuarte. If you go looking for Wilson upriver, you'll make things worse.'

Segundo protested, but she held up her hand to silence him and continued.

'I'll send a messenger to Don Moises. He is the leader of the Indian tribe at Arenas where they are staying. He'll know how to deal with Wilson without causing trouble as he's a brilliant man. I guarantee you he'll sort this out. It isn't right to disturb the Indians, as they can be vengeful if someone gets hurt. Leave it to Moises. They will deliver Señor Ortega to you, dead or alive.'

Segundo pondered this offer. He was not used to taking orders from anyone except Señor Sanchez, and he had never taken orders from a woman before. However, he was not a stupid man and he was out of his depth in these remote coastal communities where he had no allies or experience.

'When will you send him?' he asked.

'Carlos will leave now if I tell him. He can inform Don Moises that you're looking for Wilson Ortega and that he should send him back to Riccuarte. Don't worry; Wilson will come, either of his own free will or trussed up like a suckling pig.'

She smiled. Behind her, Rijer had appeared in the door. He had an ancient gun by his side.

'Until then, I'd like you to stay in the lockup. Is that fair?'

'Yes, that's fair,' replied Segundo, thoughts of making his own way to Arenas evaporating. 'I'll stay there until you let me out.'

He followed Rijer out of the house and down the road. Doña Elodea watched them go. She trusted him but not enough to let him roam free in the village. Don Moises relied on her because she had good instincts. She shut the door of her house and set off to find Carlos. Afterwards she planned to go to the market. She would make a nice fish soup for her guest to take the edge off his captivity.

Five minutes later, Doña Elodea bustled up to Carlos, who stood in some grey mud on the riverbank beside a small canoe, which could hold two passengers or a small amount of freight. He leaned on his pole with one hand and smoked with the other. He looked up as she approached and raised his eyebrows. Doña Elodea beckoned him to join her on a dryer part of the bank and leaned in to speak to him so that no one else would hear.

'Carlitos, there's an emergency. That man we locked up says Wilson Ortega is a dangerous man who is intending to harm anyone who gets in his way. You must go straight to Arenas and find Don Moises. Tell him about Wilson, and that a man is waiting to capture him here in Riccuarte. Tell him that the message is direct from me. Have you had breakfast?'

'Yes, some fried eggs and corn patties.'

'You'd better take these bananas, as I doubt you'll eat again before evening.'

'Thank you.'

'Don't forget; this is top secret. No one must know why you are going.'

'You have my word.'

With that, Carlos skipped across the mud, grabbing his pole and landing on the slim vessel in one practised movement. He had no trouble balancing the canoe in the strong current and poling away from the shore with no sign of a wobble. He pushed the canoe out into the river and started his journey to Arenas. Doña Elodea watched him until he rounded the first bend and was out of sight. He turned and smiled at her before he disappeared. She was watching him and wringing her hands. He gave her a cheery wave and was gone.

***

Sam and the rest of the team returned to the site to supervise clearing the small plateau. It was a simple job, as there were no large trees growing on it. There were young trees and bushes, but it was mostly lianas and creepers, which dangled down from overhanging trees surrounding the plateau. They stopped for lunch, and Sam wondered what they would eat. Alfredo and Don Moises set up a fire, but Wilson showed no interest in helping.

The workers got back on the canoe and indicated to Sam that she should come with them. She looked to Don Moises for an explanation, but he waved her on. Alfredo laughed. It mystified her. They sat her in the middle of the boat and give her a paddle, which, they indicated to her, was not for immediate use.

The workers moved the boat downstream a few hundred metres to a deep pool at a bend in the river and stopped the canoe in the middle. One man held the canoe steady using his pole. One of the others rummaged around in a bag, and to Sam's surprise, took out a stick of dynamite. He cut a small piece off the end and stowed the rest back in the bag under the bow. Another man cut what could only be a piece of fuse from a reel and stuck it in the dynamite.

Suddenly, she realised what they were doing but it paralysed her with fright. She tried to object, but she

236

couldn't find any useful Spanish words. Rising panic had her rooted to her seat, unable to protest. The worker lit the fuse with a box of matches he had retrieved from his boot. He held the dynamite in the air close to Sam's head. She noticed with horror he had only two good fingers on his right hand.

They counted to three, and he threw the dynamite stub into the water. It exploded as it hit the surface with a loud bang. Sam put her hands over her ears too late and was left with a ringing noise echoing in her head. Stunned fish floated to the surface.

With cries of excitement, the crew all leapt out of the canoe, leaving her sitting there with her mouth open. The last to leave indicated that she should use her paddle to keep the boat in the middle of the pool. She grabbed it, her ears buzzing, and stuck it in the water, using all her strength to keep the canoe steady.

The workers swam back and forth, finding and dropping the stunned fish in the boat. Sam could see from their bright colour and rows of sharp teeth they were piranhas. She remembered the times she had swum in the river with no idea that these were lurking under the surface. And she had been worrying about the Candiru fish?

Within three minutes the men were all back on the boat and they asked Sam to stop paddling, even though she fancied doing more. The man with the damaged hand sat next to her, extending his hand. She took it and examined the finger stumps. Their eyes met, and Sam said, 'Boom?'

'Si. Boom!' shouted the man, and he threw himself backwards into the water. The other men roared with laughter, and seeing that this was his party trick she joined in. She held out her hand to help him back onto the boat.

The canoe glided up the river to where Don Moises had a good fire going with an improvised grill made of twisted wire. The men jumped out of the canoe with their booty, and Sam followed. She must have been ashen because all three men who had stayed ashore roared with laughter.

'Why didn't you warn me?' Sam hissed at Alfredo, who was doubled over with mirth.

'Priceless,' he said.

They gutted the fish and threw them whole onto the grill. They cooked quickly and were flipped over and ready in less than ten minutes. The smell of their crispy skins made Sam salivate. They presented her with the first one wrapped in a palm leaf and she nibbled on the fleshy bit by the fin. It was delicious. There was a myriad of bones, but it was worth it.

Silence reigned until the fish were finished and the last finger was licked. Then, they made themselves comfortable and had a half-hour siesta on the riverbank. This was the experience she had dreamed of in university. She was finally at home in the jungle.

Chapter XX

Carlos made good time in his light craft and arrived in the village of Arenas at midday. He pulled the canoe up onto the shingle and pushed it under the trees at the edge of the riverbank. He arranged the low-hanging branches over the top of the canoe so it was not visible from the river; he hid his pole underneath it.

Satisfied with his work, he walked up the slippery clay steps to the raised, flat piece of land on which they built the village. He headed straight for the civic building, but, as he expected, there was no one there. Most of the women and children had gone to pick plantains for the evening meal. He sat on the steps of the house and waited for them to return. One woman who had stayed in the village gave him a bowl of rice and fish and soon he had a young audience to watch him eat his lunch.

No sooner had he finished his food than a football appeared, and they forced him to play with the children in return for his meal. Carlos didn't mind. He had three children of his own and spent a lot of time playing football with them when he had no work. Doña Elodea may have chosen him as her messenger but he wasn't used to having such important jobs. It was better than sitting around smoking and playing cards with Rijer all day. He tried asking where the others had gone, but was met with blank stares and understood that it was none of his business. After playing football for the requisite couple of hours, he climbed into a hammock on the porch of the civic building and fell asleep.

***

Mike and Gloria arrived at the coastal airport that morning to find a battered four-wheel drive waiting for them outside the terminal building with the engine running. The driver did not say much. He indicated that they should get in and showed interest only when Mike insisted on putting on his seat belt, which the driver had tied up and shoved under the front seat.

It took a good five minutes of pulling and swearing to get it untangled and ready for use. It was filthy and oily, but Mike put it on, anyway. Gloria told the driver that all gringos were like that, and he shrugged. There was not much danger of crashing on the way to San Lorenzo. The road was so bad they didn't go above thirty kilometres per hour. The driver took exaggerated care with his passengers as he had the daughter of Señor Sanchez in his vehicle. He was hoping for a promotion, and he wanted good reports to get back to his boss.

Gloria sat in the back seat, puffing away at her cigarettes and handing Mike cassettes to play in the well-used tape machine in the dashboard. The journey took a few hours along the coast road, including a stop at a small beach restaurant for some delicious shrimp in coconut sauce on a bed of sticky rice. They arrived at San Lorenzo in the afternoon where they parted company with the driver who could not go upriver with them, so he turned the vehicle around to go back.

Mike was not up for another bumpy trip that

evening. The rain was sheeting down on the town, and it was easy to persuade him to wait until morning. They set about finding a hotel for the night and settled on the same decrepit one that Sam and Wilson had stayed in on their last visit.

'Are you sure this is the only hotel in town?' said Mike.

'I'm afraid so. The accommodation won't get any better in Riccuarte,' said Gloria.

'Sorry, it's new to me, this adventure thing.'

Wasn't he an entrepreneur? Weren't adventures his forte? Gloria shrugged.

***

By late afternoon, the plateau was almost cleared of vegetation, and the workers had removed some soil. Alfredo had gone silent and paced around the plateau like a caged tiger. He had stopped taking notes and was having an internal debate. He muttered to himself, and occasionally, his arms flew out from his sides in a shrug. Sam approached him and tapped him on the shoulder. Alfredo spun around in fright at her touch as if roused from a nightmare.

'Alfredo?' said Sam. 'Are you all right?'

'All right? Yes, I think so. I assume so. That is…' His voice trailed off.

'Do you understand what the plateau is yet?' she asked.

'The plateau? Oh, yes. No. Well, I don't. There are no signs of construction. It is a random platform for worship or something. It's not what I expected. I must think. I need to wait until they clear off the earth. Maybe there'll be an indication of the purpose or its relation to the treasure. We'll find out tomorrow, I hope.'

Alfredo lapsed back into his reverie and paced the plateau again. Sam left him to his thoughts, seeing he needed space to figure them out. Perhaps it was a wild goose chase. What if it was only a place for offerings or human sacrifice and had nothing to do with treasure? She felt disappointed for Alfredo but not for herself because most of the fun for Sam had been in the adventure and being in the jungle. She was still exhilarated after her close encounter with dynamite fishing.

When Don Moises declared that another storm was coming, she was looking for unusual insects to photograph. They downed tools and descended the stairs to the jungle floor as it was safer to stop work and return in the morning. The path they were using was becoming wider and flatter and, despite the muddy surface, it took no time to walk to the canoes.

The rain started before they got to Arenas, and they were soaking wet by the time the canoe beached on the riverbank. Sam looked up from under the hood of her jacket and noticed Carlos standing under the trees beside a small canoe. She waved at him but he didn't appear to see her. She remembered that Wilson had underpaid him and she resolved to slip him some money later. He gestured to Don Moises, who ran across to the shelter of the large leaves to join him.

The rest of the group walked up to the house where they were staying and changed into dry clothes. Sam stored her used camera film in her bag and wound a new one onto her ancient Canon. She liked to get ready for the next morning when she was wide awake as she had a habit of forgetting important stuff at dawn.

The ladies from the village arrived soon after dark with their supper of fish soup, patacones (slices of plantain boiled and then squashed flat for frying) and grilled crayfish. There were also some fresh avocados. Sam drooled with delight.

'I wouldn't eat the crayfish if I were you,' drawled Alfredo.

'Why not?' she asked.

'They catch them in the river.'

'So?'

'The crayfish are easy to catch because they all swim over and eat the poo we leave in the river during our morning evacuations. Isn't it wonderful how nature recycles everything?'

'Yuck, I can't believe it. I'm not eating these.'

'You won't mind if I eat yours, then.'

Sam shook her head in horror and transferred her crayfish onto Alfredo's plate. She lost interest in her food and picked at her fried plantains. As Alfredo munched on the crayfish, it was clear she might have fallen for one of his tall tales, but she was not able shake off the vision of those crayfish coming to eat breakfast. She would check his story next time.

Moises reappeared as they were finishing their food and asked Wilson if they might have a chat. Sam was rather uneasy about the subservient way Moises behaved towards Wilson. It didn't fit with Sam's high opinion of him, and she didn't like the smug look that Wilson threw back at them as he left. Something wasn't right, but she couldn't figure out what it was. *If Wilson knew about the treasure, was he going to tell Moises? What if they plotted to take it? What would happen to her and Alfredo?*

'Alfredo, I'm worried about Wilson. He's behaving strangely, and he has Moises wrapped around his finger. Are you sure he hasn't found out about the treasure?'

'Don't be ridiculous. Moises is not the kind of man

to let Wilson tell him what to do. You don't like Wilson; you make it obvious. We have enough problems without you inventing conspiracy theories.'

His barbed comment hurt Sam, but she reasoned that the empty plateau caused his irritation rather than her theories, and she didn't hold it against him. It didn't do much to assuage her doubts but if Alfredo didn't think there was any treasure, there probably wasn't any. Wilson would not be a threat if there was nothing to steal. She was tempted to spy on the pair, but since the villagers were already suspicious of their motives in being in the region again, she decided against it.

***

Wilson couldn't wait to get away from the others. It was hard to believe Mike had sent a drunk, a woman and a half-breed to look for something so important and had intended to leave him out. After their chat in Riccuarte, Moises had made it obvious whose side he was on and now he wanted to discuss arranging the disappearance of Sam and Alfredo. Wilson congratulated himself on reading his man well. Moises was also expendable, but Wilson would deal with him after he had eliminated the competition. The treasure was so close. His troubles were over.

They shook hands and walked to an old house on the outskirts of the village. The roof was only just withstanding the rain, which fell in sheets. Big drops bounced on the rotten wood of the floor, turning it to mush. They stepped onto the veranda and sat on wobbly stools made from fat slices of a tree trunk.

When Moises offered him a bowl of chicha to drink, Wilson accepted it as a sign of trust. He was not keen on chicha. Like many traditions, the truth about its manufacture was unpalatable. The women of the

'Alfredo, where are you going?'

'I'm coming back from a pee.'

'I thought you went to bed.'

'Well, you thought wrong.'

'Are you drunk?'

'What's it to you, *gringa*? Wouldn't you be drunk in my position?'

'I don't understand.'

Sam moved over to sit on the top step and patted the floor beside her. Alfredo lurched over and sat down with a big sigh.

'How would you understand? You're a success. You have a career. I'm a failure, a drunk. Gloria will leave me.'

Sam couldn't help smiling. *Alfredo thinks I'm a success? It was amazing how other people perceive me.*

'Don't be silly. You're not a failure. Why would Gloria leave you?'

'She's the daughter of Hernan Sanchez. She's clever and beautiful and organised.'

Sam stifled a snort of derision.

'Why would she go out with a drunk? And a failure.'

'Why do you keep calling yourself a failure?'

'I don't think there's anything on the plateau. What if I've made a terrible mistake? Mike will kill me. Gloria will think I'm an idiot.'

'What if you haven't? What if you're about to be a massive success? Don't count your chickens yet, Alfredo. Go to bed. Things will look better tomorrow.'

'How do you know?' said Alfredo

'I'm a failure, too. I always feel better with a new day ahead of me.'

Sam put her hand on his shoulder and squeezed it.

***

Bound and gagged, Wilson lay on the floor in the dark hut. Someone had tied his hands together, pushing his face into the dirt. There was grit in his teeth. He was conscious, but his body was not under his control. *How could he have been so stupid?* That bastard half breed had poisoned him. If he ever got out of there, he would kill him. But he was trapped.

As the drug took hold, he hallucinated. Large ants crawled across the floor of the hut toward him and swarmed over his prostrate form biting his body, but he could not brush them off. He tried to scream but the gag almost choked him. El Loco threatened him, holding out a pair of rusty scissors. Mocking women surrounded him taunting him with their breasts.

He lay in a heap on the floor, drowning in his own nightmares, but the horror was only beginning. He prayed for death. Only when dawn broke did the horrors cease and then the door opened.

Chapter XXI

Carlos pulled his canoe out from under the trees and into the shallows. Chilly drops of dew fell from the leaves onto his back causing him to shiver in the cold dawn light. He wanted to get away from Arenas before the others saw him because Wilson Ortega lay in the bottom of the canoe, trussed up like a turkey, and pale as Christmas snow. Carlos had gagged him but he was now awake with his eyes open. They widened in fright as Carlos leaned in to check on his cargo.

'Good morning, engineer,' he whispered. 'We will take a little trip to Riccuarte to see a friend of yours. If you promise not to shout, I'll take off the gag and give you some water. If you shout, I'll drown you like a rat. It's your choice. Nod if you want me to take it off for you.'

Wilson nodded with relief, and Carlos took off the gag, and, supporting him with his hand, he tipped river water down Wilson's throat. He gulped it down, choking in his anxiety to quench his thirst. Carlos laid him back down in the canoe. Wilson's night in the hut had traumatised him and he would have agreed to anything to lie on the floor of the canoe in peace. He had not given up though. There must be a way to escape.

His blood boiled as he remembered how Don Moises had deceived him but he slowed his breathing so that his captor would not notice the change in his awareness. A bunch of primitive Indians would not outwit someone as smart as him.

Then he saw it. His rucksack sat at the other end of the canoe half covered with a hessian sack. He had left his gun in there, wrapped in a piece of canvas to keep out the damp. Maybe Carlos had not found it. He tried to fall asleep, needing to restore his strength so he could try to escape once he got the chance. He wasn't out of the game yet.

A block of wood was pushed roughly under his head raising it above the dirty water on the bottom of the canoe and he grunted his thanks. Carlos pushed the canoe out into the rushing current, keeping an eye out for floating debris. He jumped aboard and glided off into the cool morning. It was a skilled job keeping the canoe on course in the strong current, but he was an expert. They made slow progress through the turbulent waters.

***

Sam and Alfredo had woken up to find Wilson was missing. Sam remembered that he had gone with Don Moises for a chat after their evening meal, but she couldn't remember seeing him come back. She wondered if they had got drunk together and slept where they were drinking. At least Alfredo was in better form, cracking jokes and poking her in the ribs. After a quick breakfast of scrambled eggs and salty crackers, they picked up their rucksacks and fought their way through the mud down to the river's edge.

The usual crew of workers were there, indulging in horseplay that involved dumping each other in the mud and then throwing the victims in the river for a wash. Sam was struck by how carefree they were. She looked around to see if Wilson was having his usual pre-travel cigarette on the shore, but there was no sign of him. Don Moises was checking their supplies and busying himself for setting off. He looked up as they approached.

'What a storm!' he said. 'Did you get any sleep, Sam?'

'What storm?' asked Sam, 'did it rain? You look tired though. Are you okay?'

'Oh yes, I'm fine thank you. A touch of insomnia.'

'Where is Wilson today?' asked Sam. 'I haven't seen him since he left to chat with you.'

'Wilson? I think he went with Carlos to get supplies in Riccuarte. I expect he'll be back tomorrow.'

'Honestly,' tutted Alfredo. 'That man is a law unto himself. If I'd known, I could have asked him to buy a few things I need.'

'I don't think Wilson is too interested in what other people want,' said Sam.

They got into the canoes and set off into the brown waters of the rain-swollen river, back to the stone plateau.

It was difficult to walk up the path through the jungle to the stone steps. The hard, brown path had become a boot-deep quagmire of sticky mud, which sucked them down and slowed progress. At one stage, Sam lost a boot in the mud and had to stand on one leg with her socked foot in the air while they dug it out. Despite her valiant attempts to keep it off the ground, the sock was soon coated in mud, too.

It was a relief to reach the steps and climb up to the plateau. Debris, twigs and leaves that had washed down from it blanketed the steps. The leaves were as slippery as fish and deadly underfoot so they scooped them off the steps with their spades. The stone steps under the debris had been washed clean by the force of the water cascading down them. Serpent ciphers decorated them all.

They emerged out of the trees onto the plateau. Some earth covering the platform had been swept away by the storm waters. The straight edges and flat contours revealed by the rain made it more obvious that the plateau was a man-made structure but there was nothing to break the flat surface. It was a flat featureless area about the size of a basketball court.

Sam walked around it and tried to spot any anomalies but if it had any secrets, they were not showing. She took photographs from various angles in case there was something she had missed. Alfredo was pacing up and down with his compass.

'Can I borrow it?' she said. 'I want to make a note about the orientation in my sketchbook.'

'I don't know why you would bother,' he said.

She took the reading and handed back the compass.

'What do you think?' she said, more in hope than expectation. 'Are there any clues?'

He looked right through her and kept pacing, his head hanging, his shoulders slumped in defeat.

The rest of the team hung back, unwilling to get in his way. Don Moises had an inscrutable look on his face. No-one spoke. Alfredo searched through his notes and made measurements and muttered and squatted. Finally, he said, 'Let's go back to Arenas,' and started down the steps followed by the crew of the canoe, Don Moises and a disappointed Sam.

They made the journey upriver in an unearthly

silence with none of the usual banter. The rain fell again, pounding on them in the canoe. They got back to their house soaked to the skin, their clothes dripping on the hardwood floor of the balcony. Alfredo disappeared inside. Sam followed him.

'What do you want to do next?' she asked.

'What do you mean?' said Alfredo.

'Shouldn't we dig pits or make a trench across the platform?'

'What for? It's as flat as a pancake. You can't dig pits into solid rock.'

The food arrived early but Alfredo showed no inclination to come downstairs and eat. Sam could hear him pacing the floor and muttering. She hoped that he wasn't drinking, too.

The rain stopped and the dark storm clouds hugging the jungle parted to showcase the stars. Alfredo appeared on the stairs.

'We should go home tomorrow,' he said. 'It's over.'

Don Moises, who had been sitting with Sam awaiting instructions, shrugged and set off through the mud to his house in the village. He showed no emotion but Sam sensed a sigh of relief held back or stifled. He must have thought they were crazy in the first place but at least he and his men would get paid.

She had no idea how Mike was going to take this. Or Wilson. There could be a way of making her shoulder the blame for the whole fiasco. After all, she was the one that found the steps. Perhaps her adventure was over. Going home was not an option she wanted to consider. The spectre of Simon loomed over her arrival back in England. *What if he wanted to apologise and get back together for real? Could she resist? Would it be déja vu all over again?*

***

The added bulk of Wilson and his rucksack disturbed the natural balance of Carlos' canoe and the torrential rain lowered visibility to danger levels with all the debris swirling in the chocolate waters of the river. Carlos had only travelled about a kilometre downstream past the excavation site when he decided to beach the canoe for the night.

He pulled the canoe up onto the sand and helped Wilson out, lying him on a dry bank under the shade of some thick mangroves. Carlos removed his boots and stuck his feet into the sand. They sat in silence as the rain petered out. Carlos smoked and Wilson gathered strength for his escape attempt.

Eventually both men slept. They were woken by the mosquitos feasting on them. Wilson assessed the situation. The river flow had reduced but it was still too high for him to navigate in the canoe. The only way back to the site was to skirt the edge of the river, but first he needed to get away from Carlos. He grunted.

'Can you release me please? I need to go to the toilet and these mosquitos are killing me.'

'Do you promise not to escape?' said Carlos.

'And where would I go? I can't use the canoe. I don't know how.'

'Okay, but no funny stuff.'

Carlos released the lianas from Wilson's hands and feet.

'Get on with it,' he said

'May I get a clean shirt from my rucksack?'

Carlos sighed.

'Sure, but hurry up, I want to leave soon. And I need to tie you up for the journey.'

He stood over Wilson with a thick branch ready to strike him as he removed his shirt from the rucksack.

There was a rustle in the bushes and a peccary dashed out onto the sand bank. Momentarily distracted, Carlos did not have time to react as Wilson pulled out a gun and pointed it at him.

'Get on your knees,' he said.

His tone did not invite discussion. Carlos sank to the sand. Wilson walked behind him and pistol whipped him, knocking him out.

'Fool.'

Wilson spat on the sand and stuffed his feet into Carlos' wellington boots, wincing at their cold sweaty interior. He took his flashlight out of his rucksack and zipped up the pocket, shoving the gun into the waistband of his trousers. Then he put the rucksack over his shoulders and grabbed the machete from the bottom of the canoe. He pushed the canoe out into the river and watched it wash downstream, before slipping into the shallow water and wading upstream towards the plateau.

Chapter XXII

Mike and Gloria were both grumpy after a night at the awful hotel in San Lorenzo. Gloria was covered in red welts where the bedbugs and mosquitos had bitten her. They had travelled without mosquito nets, forgetting that these insect-ridden local hotels either had ancient nets full of holes or none at all.

'I didn't get a wink of sleep,' said Mike. 'A pair of courting cats chose the spot beneath my window to sing the entirety of La Traviata cat-style.'

'This hotel doesn't have breakfast. I must eat in the morning to keep my blood sugar up,' said Gloria. 'I'm likely to have a sense of humour failure early on if I don't get my breakfast.'

After traipsing around for twenty minutes, they found a local cantina that rustled up two omelettes with peppers and onions, and some stale bread rolls.

'This coffee's like a cross between engine oil and molasses, but it's doing the trick,' said Mike.

'It's revolting,' said Gloria. 'Stay here. I'll get us a ride to Riccuarte. Don't move.'

'Yes, madam.'

Mike struggled his way through a second cup of coffee and paid the bill. He imagined himself a proper explorer and kind of macho, which he was enjoying a lot. When he mentioned this to Gloria, she laughed and smiled at him, the way a mother smiles at a small boy who has announced his ambition to be an astronaut. It didn't put him off. Here he was, Mike Morton, a plump, middle-aged man, in the jungle on a rescue mission.

Edward would love this. He lived a fantasy life through the tales Mike told him of where his money was being spent. He would be sure to keep financing Mike now, and his wife would be furious, given their reduced funds. How could life get any better? Mike let out a contented sigh and sat back in his chair.

***

The mood in Arenas was also subdued, mirroring that of Alfredo whose deep dejection was catching. He sipped his coffee in silence and refused all offers of food. His face was grey with tiredness. Sam secreted several bananas in her satchel in case he changed his mind on the journey back to Riccuarte.

They readied themselves for the trip, checking that the equipment was packed and wrapped in plastic. Alfredo poked in all the bags, turning them out on the floor and stuffing their contents back in, higgledy-piggledy.

'Oh no!' he said, 'I can't believe it. I've left my compass at the site.'

'Are you sure? Couldn't it be in one of your bags?' said Sam.

'No, it's not there. I've gone through all my things.'

'When did you last use it?' said Sam.

'The last time I remember seeing it was when you took measurements on the platform. You gave it back to me, didn't you?'

'Yes, I did,' said Sam.

'Can you buy another?' said Don Moises.

'No. This one was special.'

'Was it expensive?' said Sam.

'I doubt it was worth five dollars to sell, but it was priceless to me. My old friend, and fellow treasure hunter, Jorge Vasquez gave it to me on his deathbed. I can't lose it. I can't.'

'We are going past the site on our way home,'' said Sam. 'Can't we stop and look for it?'

'You'll never find it,' said Moises.

'But we have to try. I'll never forgive myself if I leave it there without searching,' said Alfredo. 'Also, there is one measurement that got rubbed out of my notebook in the rain. I would like to take it again. Just in case.'

'I'll help you look,' said Sam.

'Okay, we can stop,' said Moises, 'but not for long. I don't want to get caught in the rain on our way to Riccuarte.'

'Excellent. Thank you,' said Alfredo.

The dry night had reduced the current in the river, which although still full of debris, flowed at a normal rate. They beached the canoe at the site of the serpent ciphers and set out for the plateau. They had already agreed that the whole team would mount a search for the compass, but only for an hour. The platform was not large and if the compass had become buried by mud, there was little hope of finding it.

They set off into the jungle through the sticky mud. Upon reaching the steps, Alfredo took the lead up to the plateau followed by a panting Sam. She fell behind after dropping her hat and emerged to find them pacing the plateau with their heads bent.

The search for the compass was a thankless task.

They started from the outside and worked in, the earth
churning to mud as they walked back and forth.

'This is pointless,' said Moises. 'We need to
leave.'

Then, out of the corner of her eye, Sam saw one of
the crew bend down and pick something up. He did not
shout out, or draw attention to himself. He crossed the
square to Moises and whispered in his ear. Moises put
out his hand and the man passed something to him,
which he slipped into his pocket.

Sam straightened and looked Moises in the face,
daring him to react. He did not blink. What was going
on? Moises had made it obvious wanted them to leave
as soon as possible. If they found the compass, they
might stay longer. She recalled his anxiety when
Wilson wanted to see the steps on their first visit to the
area. Moises knew more than he had let on, but what
was he hiding?

The hour was up. Alfredo bent double and ran his
hands through his hair, muttering. Don Moises looked
at his watch. Despite her natural reluctance to rock the
boat, and her respect for Moises, Sam couldn't let the
incident go by without saying anything.

'Um, Moises, what did you put in your pocket?'

'I don't understand,' said Moises.

'But I saw him find something and hand it to you,'
she said, pointing at the man.

Alfredo had come over and was looking from one
to the other in bemusement.

'What are you accusing me of?' said Moises.

Sam got hot with embarrassment. 'Nothing. I...'

'What did you see?' said Alfredo, suddenly alert.

'That man found something. He gave it to Moises,'
said Sam.

She hadn't learned his name. She gesticulated at

him, flushing. Alfredo stepped towards him. The man stepped backwards. To Sam's surprise, he sank into the ground and almost disappeared, getting buried up to the waist in wet soil. Panic appeared on his face.

The other men ran forward to pull him out. Alfredo gasped and put his hands to his mouth. There was a discernible shallow depression in the plateau that had not been obvious the previous afternoon. Alfredo knelt down beside the depression and excavated it with his hands, flinging the earth behind him like a dog looking for a bone. He made a sharp intake of breath as his fingers found stone edges. He worked his way around it, joined by Sam.

They dug down about fifty centimetres before stopping, soil flying behind them onto the feet of Don Moises, who stood like a statue, his face white with shock.

'I knew it,' said Alfredo. 'It's here.'

She didn't remind him that half an hour before he had been ready to go home. The stone opening was rectangular, about four metres long and one metre wide. They uncovered two descending steps without help as the rest of the crew stood back from them observing their progress.

Don Moises had still not moved. He stood rooted to the spot, staring at the depression. He appeared to be in a quandary, but he finally recovered and beckoned the men forward, indicating that they should go back to the village and retrieve their spades. He reached into his pocket and pulled out Alfredo's compass. Handing it to him, he said, 'Take your measurements. We will wait here until they come back.'

He did not apologise or make any further comment. He didn't excuse his behaviour. Alfredo had stopped digging was having some sort of panic attack.

He gasped with excitement and sat down with a bewildered expression on his face, hugging his knees to his chest and rocking back and forth like a lunatic.

'Are you okay?' said Sam.

'I never believed I could find the treasure. I'm wrestling with amazement. It's like a strange dream,' said Alfredo

'It is a little surreal. I had to pinch myself to check if I was dreaming too,' said Sam. She had felt the pinch, but she wondered why this proved that she was awake. *If you pinched yourself in a dream, wouldn't it be the same?* She sat down beside Alfredo and held an imaginary microphone to his lips.

'So, treasure hunter, what is your reaction to being on the brink of a great discovery after all these years?'

'So far it's only a hole in the ground. Let's not get ahead of ourselves,' said Alfredo, but he beamed.

*****

Carlos woke at midday, his head aching in the hot sun. He looked around in confusion. Then he remembered. Wilson! The bastard had taken his canoe. He was stranded, and like many local people, was not a strong swimmer. There was nothing he could do but wait until another local passed by in a canoe and picked him up. He rubbed his head ruefully. Doña Elodea was going to kill him.

*****

Wilson looked out from a clump of trees, rubbing his wrists where they had chaffed as he had struggled to release the cords that bound them. Wilson's longing for the treasure had triumphed over his exhaustion, and he had made it to the plateau. His legs were like jelly after his ordeal in Arenas and being tied up for so long.

He had not expected this extra obstacle. Moises had stabbed him in the back, but he blamed himself for trusting a half-breed.

He watched the workers dig the earth out from the centre of the platform with increasing excitement. His best option was to remain hidden and wait for the team to discover something before holding them at gunpoint. That gringa bitch would get hers too. He wasn't finished with Sam Harris, not by a long shot. They would pay for this.

Bit by bit, the team exposed steps that led down to a stone door with a large and elaborate serpent cipher on it. There was a solemnity to the work which surprised him. It was more like an exhumation than the excavation of a treasure. Don Moises was subdued and could not be persuaded into conversation. Excitement had drugged Alfredo who could not communicate either. It was not at all what Wilson had imagined.

The horseplay amongst the workforce had ceased, and they cleared the steps with a certain reverence, like people cleaning a church. They worked slowly as if preserving their strength for a great effort. Wilson's excitement drained away as the mood affected him too. He watched as Sam went to sit with Alfredo, apart from the group, eating the last of her precious chocolate supplies and taking photographs of the digging.

By early afternoon, the steps and the door were clear of earth.

'I think we should go back to Arenas until morning,' said Don Moises, 'it is too late to continue tonight.'

Alfredo looked like he was going to disagree. He stood up and walked over to the cleared steps and peered into the hole.

'The clouds are gathering again,' said Sam.

Wilson watched them go. He made a small clearing in the trees on the opposite side of the plateau from the Inca steps and lined it with leaves. His effort had exhausted him and soon he was fast asleep.

Sam and Alfredo returned to the village where they left most of their goods in the canoe and only took the bare essentials to the house. Nobody looked pleased to see them. Their hostile stares bored into her back as she walked through the village. The women prepared their evening meal as before but there were no attempts to communicate and they melted into their houses.

'They thought they were rid of us,' she said to Alfredo.

'I think they did.'

After a frugal supper, Alfredo and Sam sat on the steps deep in thought.

'How are you now?' said Sam.

'Earlier I was elated but I'm having a moment of horrible clarity. I'm not sure if I'm more worried about finding the treasure or not finding it.'

'What do you mean?'

'What happens if we discover it? It's a national treasure. Mike is a great guy, but he has no interest in history. I'm sure that most, if not all, of the treasure will head out of the country.'

'I guess that's correct. I don't know Edward. But if he's like Mike, he'll sell it to the highest bidder,' said Sam.

'The problem for me is that as a historian and a patriot, I've been struck by the thought that I have agreed to plunder the history of my country for money. I'm no better than a grave robber.'

'It might go to the Sierramar national museum.'

'Unlikely. They're broke and can't pay for any exhibits. I'm desperate to see the treasure after all these years of searching but what if that leads to it being plundered by Edward and taken away from Sierramar?'

Sam didn't have an answer. Alfredo stood up and walked into the night.

'Where are you going?' she said.

'I need to speak to Don Moises,' said Alfredo, over his shoulder.

'Can I come?'

'No. I'm sorry, but this is something I need to do alone.'

He headed into the darkness.
Moises was on his balcony making good headway with a bottle of unadulterated chicha. He looked unsurprised to see Alfredo.

'I need to talk to you. Is that okay?' said Alfredo.

Moises nodded. 'I've been expecting you.'

***

Gloria had organised a lift on a pickup delivering a load of groceries to Riccuarte. Chickens squawked and flapped in wooden crates on top of sacks of rice and sugar. Boxes of cooking oil glistened in the morning sunshine where some had spilt out onto the cardboard. They sat up front in the truck with Gloria in the middle and Mike squashed against the door.

Gloria had to deal with the driver's inability to keep his hand on the gearstick. She soon noticed that it kept slipping off onto her knee at the slightest bump in the road. She had picked up some of Sam's indignation at the casual sexism of men in Sierramar, and she pretended to mistakenly burned the back of his hand with her cigarette when he got more daring and put his hand on her thigh.

He got the hint and drove the rest of the way in a

huff. She had become a proper liberated woman. What would Sam say? Mike, being Mike, did not notice this drama, leaning out of the window, until a large insect hit him in the mouth and was nearly shocked as he was. He withdrew inside the cabin and tried to wind up the window, but the handle revolved without catching, so it stayed down.

As they drew into the main square of Riccuarte, Gloria spotted Segundo walking beside a plump black woman. They were laughing and she had her arm slipped through his. Gloria and Mike got down from the car and caught up with the pair.

'Segundo?' she said, tapping his shoulder. 'What's going on? Where's Sam? Who's this?'

He spun around, looked guilty for a second but soon recovered.

'Miss Gloria, what are you doing here? This is Doña Elodea.'

Gloria nodded at Elodea, but turned her attention back to Segundo.

'We came to see if we could help, but it looks like you have everything under control.'

Her sarcasm left its mark. Segundo looked at the ground, uncertain.

'The villagers will not let me leave,' he said. 'Carlos has gone to Arenas to alert Don Moises that Wilson Ortega must not be allowed to go to the plateau. Don Moises is the chief of the Indian tribe who live at Arenas so Wilson will not be able to escape them. Carlos will bring him back here.'

'Don Moises will not let us down,' said Doña Elodea.

'Who is Don Moises?' said Mike.

He suddenly felt sick and faint. A horrible pain coursed up his arm. He reached out to Gloria but fell before he could grab her arm.

Gloria screamed.

Segundo knelt on the ground beside Mike and checked his pulse.

'Is he dead?' asked Gloria. She was white with shock.

'I don't think so.'

'Take him to my house,' said Doña Elodea. 'I'm the village healer.'

Segundo bent down and levered Mike over his shoulder. He placed him into the front seat of the truck. The driver was happy to drive to Doña Elodea's house with Segundo balanced on the tailgate of the truck shouting instructions.

Gloria followed behind the truck with Doña Elodea. They were showered in muddy water as the truck dropped into a large pothole.

The driver had helped Segundo carry Mike into the house and was emerging from the front door, munching on an empanada.

'Driver, can you take us to San Lorenzo tonight?' asked Segundo.

'Sure. Let me unload all the groceries first, and I'll come back after lunch to collect anyone who wants to go.'

Gloria went into the house and was relieved to see that Mike was lying down, but he had his eyes open. Doña Elodea had put some sort of poultice on his chest. She looked around when Gloria entered and said, 'Angina attack.' Then, she continued fussing around Mike and mixing odd-looking ingredients in bowls. Gloria suspected that she was a witch, but she said nothing in case she was right. Mike had regained colour and was chirpier.

'What happened?' he said.

'You had an angina attack. Have you ever had one before?' said Gloria.

'Um, yes, I told you I've got a heart problem.'

'I thought you were exaggerating. Why didn't you tell us how bad it is?'

'You wouldn't have let me come.'

'No, I wouldn't. Anyway, you must go to the hospital for a check-up with your history.'

'What about Alfredo and Sam?'

'Don Moises will make sure Wilson can't hurt them. They'll be okay, and who knows? What if they find the treasure and bring it home?'

'But, I'm fine now.'

'How do you know that? Do you think I'm going to let the source of my salary go into the jungle to have another heart attack? Forget it. We're going home.'

Mike smiled.

'You can't fool me. You love me more than a bank. Okay, I'll go. I lost consciousness for a moment that can't be right. Sam and Alfredo are safe and might be about to make an astonishing discovery. Shouldn't we leave Segundo here?'

'He refuses to stay until he knows I am safely back in Calderon, so I'm taking you back to the hospital with him. We can wait for news there. We should phone my father from San Lorenzo to let him know we're safe. I'll get him to send a car to Riccuarte to wait until Alfredo and Sam come out of the jungle,' said Gloria. 'Get some rest. The driver will be back at about three o'clock, and you must be ready to travel.'

'Go and smoke and leave me in peace.'

Gloria left, grabbing one of Doña Elodea's empanadas on her way.

The driver returned for Gloria, Mike and Segundo in the late afternoon. Mike and Gloria sat in the front.

The driver did not touch Gloria's knee on the return trip. Segundo had a talk with him about respect for the daughter of Señor Hernan Sanchez, which almost made him faint in fright. Mike was subdued but had recovered from his turn.

They stayed in the filthy hotel in San Lorenzo again. Gloria bought a mosquito net on their way through the market and took it into her room like contraband. They ate in a nearby cantina, but no one was in the mood for food. Gloria went to the local shop where they had the only telephone line in the village and called her father to tell him they were safe.

'Papi? It's me, Gloria. Can you hear me?'

'Yes, chickpea, I can hear you. Are you okay?'

'It's been an adventure. Mike had an angina attack, but he's fine now. I'm taking him to the hospital in Calderon.'

'Did you find Wilson Ortega?'

'Not exactly but the locals are looking for him and he won't get far.'

'Excellent news! Where are Sam and Alfredo?'

'They're still in the jungle. Could you please send your driver to Riccuarte to wait for them. I expect they'll be exhausted when they come out. We have no news of their progress, but they're safe now that the locals know about Wilson.'

'That would be my pleasure, sweetheart. Can you ask Segundo to speak to me, please?'

'He's right here. Oh, and can you send the driver to collect us tomorrow morning so that we can catch the afternoon flight to Calderon? He can then return to Riccuarte to wait for Sam and Alfredo.'

'I'll call him after I speak to Segundo. Take care, and I'll see you soon.'

Gloria put the receiver down on the shelf and went

to get Segundo. He walked over and lifted the telephone to his ear.

'Good evening, boss,' he said.

'Good evening, Segundo. Get my daughter out of there before she gets into trouble.'

'No problem, boss.'

'You're a good man in a crisis. You know where to pick up your money.'

'I do, boss. Thank you.'

Segundo replaced the telephone with a smile, and they went back to their rustling rooms.

Chapter XXIII

Sam and Alfredo travelled to site early. The nightly rain had washed the entrance clean and the steps descending to the stone entrance looked new. A massive stone door sealed the entrance. How on earth were they going to get in through solid rock? Sam took out her camera but Don Moises asked her to put it away again.

'You may not take any photographs,' he said.

'But I have to,' said Sam and she turned to Alfredo for support. He shook his head.

'You'll understand shortly,' he said.

It had to be something to do with his chat last night but he wouldn't talk about it. 'You'll see,' is all he would say. The elevation of his mood since the night before was obvious. He seemed like a different man.

Alfredo and Sam descended the steps to the stone door. Alfredo walked like a man entranced, his feet hardly touched the ground. Sam had never seen anyone so happy. When they reached the door, they checked it from corner to corner.

'I can't find any catch or hinge,' said Sam. 'How are we going to open this? It must weigh over a ton.'

Alfredo muttered to himself and reached into his rucksack for his notebook. After leafing through the pages for a few minutes, he found the one he was looking for.

'I can do it,' he announced, dazed.

'We can't open it without first getting permission from the gods,' said Don Moises, who had grown in stature. 'We must perform the blessing ceremony first.'

Alfredo nodded and whispered to Sam, 'There's a short ritual that will take place now. This is important to them. You must take part, or they will not let you into the chamber.'

Sam nodded back, but it confused her. *How did Alfredo know this?* She couldn't believe that they would open the door and see the treasure. *Was it really still there?* She couldn't comprehend it. She was most definitely awake, as she had pinched herself black and blue, and she couldn't remember ever getting a bruise in a dream.

'You knew this was going to happen, didn't you? What do we have to do?' she asked Alfredo.

'I knew. Moises told me last night. Shush now. Do what I do.'

Don Moises beckoned one worker forward. He was carrying a large hessian sack, which he gave to Moises with reverential gestures. Moises pulled out an embroidered robe with a serpent cipher on the back and front. He pushed his head through a hole in the middle. Struck dumb with amazement, a shiver ran down Sam's spine. Alfredo showed no surprise at this development. He had been expecting it.

Moises took a golden beaker out of the sack and raised it to the sky. Another worker offered two bottles of opaque liquid, which he gave to the now priestly looking Don Moises. Moises opened one bottle and poured it into the beaker. He drank from it and passed it around the workers. Alfredo tried to take it, but they handed it back to Moises. He poured it on the steps, muttering an incantation in a strange language.

Moises opened the other bottle and offered the liquid in a beaker to Sam and Alfredo. It was bitter and grainy, but Sam did not complain. It was as if she had gone back five hundred years to the time of Atahualpa. She didn't understand how calm everyone was, as if they had known this was going to happen. Alfredo held the beaker up and drank with something approaching ecstasy.

'You may open the door,' said Don Moises.

'I'll do it,' said Alfredo.

Two of the strongest workers descended the stairs with Alfredo who, using the instructions in his book, showed them where to place their hands on the door. They pushed the door hard on its left side. To Sam's astonishment, after a couple of meaty shoves, it rotated, swinging open to leave a narrow entrance. It was pitch black inside. Alfredo reached into his rucksack and pulled out a torch. He beckoned Sam down the stairs.

'Are you ready to be astounded?' he asked.

She nodded and crept her way into the chamber using the walls as a guide. Alfredo switched on the torch and pointed it inside. The reflections from a thousand precious objects flashed back at them. There were life-size human figures made of beaten gold and silver, birds and animals, gold and silver flowers. There were goblets, ewers, salvers and pots full of the most incredible jewellery and golden vases full of green stones that looked like emeralds. Exquisite.

The sight of the treasure blew Sam away. Her mouth dropped open with astonishment. This had to be the find of the century. This was how Howard Carter felt when he discovered Tutankhamun's tomb.

They moved into the chamber followed by Don

Moises, who handed Sam another torch. With her heart in her throat, she walked forward into the chamber being careful not to tread on any of the artefacts. She squatted down on her haunches to inspect one object on the floor—a cornstalk with a golden ear and silver leaves and tassels. The delicacy of the workmanship and the ingenious designs attested to the rare talent of the artisans. There were no words to describe her elation. It was like Aladdin's cave.

'Bloody hell!' she managed.

All around them in random piles, were wonders from the Inca age. Alfredo moved from piece to piece, purring like a cat. He put on a stunning ceremonial necklace with a ferocious face as its centrepiece. He stroked the embroidered gowns, running the material through his fingertips and marvelling at the designs of swirling suns with faces and strange creatures. Like a small boy in Santa's grotto, he couldn't see enough, pouncing on one new object after another. Time passed with no expectation of seeing all that the crypt contained. The treasure appeared infinite.

'Sweat of the sun, tears of the moon. Gold and silver had no monetary value for the Incas. They valued it for its properties that allowed them to make such beautiful things,' said Alfredo.

There was so much to see. Alfredo clutched at objects with a religious fervour. Dizziness overcame her as she watched him. Was she in shock? It was like being drunk. After an hour, they entered a second chamber at the back of the first. There was a row of many mummies on a stone slab along the back wall of the chamber, covered in fine materials and wearing funerary masks.

Alfredo rushed forward to examine them. He turned in question.

'The keepers of the treasure?' he asked Don Moises, who stood at the entrance to the second chamber.

Moises nodded, and Sam wondered how he knew.

'Yes, they're all here. I'll be next.'

It had surprised neither Alfredo nor Don Moises to find the treasure or the mummies. Sam opened her mouth to ask why but there was a loud retort outside.

'What was that?' she said.

'It sounded like a gunshot,' said Alfredo.

Don Moises went pale and headed for the entrance. He started up the stairs but soon returned backing away from Wilson, who held a gun pointed at him and the rest of the Indians who also descended into the crypt.

'So you thought you'd get rid of me so easily? You must think I'm an idiot.'

He sneered.

'But how--' said Alfredo.

'You stupid drunk. Who do you think told me?'

Alfredo blanched.

'Okay everyone into the other room. Not you,' he said pointing the gun at Sam. 'I haven't finished with you yet.'

He grabbed her arm and pulled her roughly towards him, thrusting a hessian sack into her hands.

'Fill it,' he hissed. 'Chose the most valuable pieces.'

Sam was about to say that she had no idea which pieces were most valuable but one look from him stopped her from speaking. She picked up the golden chalice and various other pieces of tableware lying on the floor in front of her. Wilson kept his gun trained on the others who were standing in the doorway of the mummies' room. There was the sound of someone coming down the stairs.

One of the workers had returned from the shore to collect a packet of cigarettes and seeing no one outside descended the stairs. Wilson whipped around at the sound. Sam hit him over the head with a golden wheatsheaf baton and he staggered around waving the pistol. He placed his foot on a second baton and it shot across the floor throwing him backwards into the treasure still holding the gun. It went off firing a bullet into the ceiling which ricocheted harmlessly into the floor.

You'll pay for that, you bitch,' he said, trying to stand up. 'You'll wish you'd never been born.'

Suddenly blood started to trickle from his mouth and a bewildered expression crossed his face. He pitched forward and didn't move again. A jewel-encrusted Inca dagger protruded from his back. Sam touched his shoulder but there was no reaction.

'Holy crap,' said Alfredo, running to pull her backwards. 'He's dead.'

'I killed him,' said Sam, shocked.

'No, you didn't. He killed himself,' said Moises.

Sam's stomach flipped, and nausea overcame her. She sat down on a golden throne in the corner of the chamber, and the room swam before her eyes. She couldn't control her limbs. *What on earth was happening to her? Was this just a bad dream?* Then, she remembered.

'The drink,' she said, falling to the floor.

'Not yet,' she heard Alfredo say. 'Please, not yet.'

Sam slumped on the ground where she was joined by Alfredo, still pleading for more time. Her world went black.

***

They carried Sam and Alfredo out of the vault and up

onto the surface. Their slumber was so deep that they appeared lifeless.

'Take the foreigners back to the village,' said Don Moises. 'My granddaughter will take care of them when they wake. We have a great deal of work to do here.'

The men carried Sam and Alfredo down to the riverbank and loaded them into canoes for the short ride to Arenas. They passed other inhabitants of the village on their way who arrived at the plateau as they left. Filing into the chamber, they emptied it of its riches, piece by piece, enveloping them in hessian sacking. They wrapped the mummies in many layers of plastic and then strapped them to stretchers.

Some villagers cut a narrow path north into the jungle, the sort of path lost to regrowth in weeks. They followed ancient signs cut into the trees and rocks, which only they could distinguish. Moises directed the work with a quiet gravitas.

As the day turned into night, the work continued until the chamber echoed in its emptiness. They re-sealed the vault by shutting the entrance and covering it once more with earth. The vines that trailed over the surface of the platform would soon obscure it from human eyes until it might be needed again. They put a sharp piece of bamboo into the hole made by the knife and loaded Wilson's body into a small canoe which they pushed into the stream.

'The local police will think it's an accident. They won't come into the jungle to investigate,' said Don Moises.

They loaded the golden cargo onto mules and sleds and backs, and the villagers moved away into the jungle, which closed over them.

'Where are we going, sir?' asked one child.

'Far away,' answered Don Moises. A lifetime away.'

Chapter XXIV

Sam opened her eyes but she shut them again on the assumption that she was hallucinating. She opened them to find that she was looking into the anxious eyes of Tati, who hovered over her.

'Alfredo?' Sam asked.

'Here, *chica*,' she heard him say.

'Where are we?'

'Arenas, I guess.'

Tati nodded and smiled.

'But what are we doing here, Alfredo? What happened to the treasure? Did I dream the whole thing?'

'No, you didn't, but I think you should know the whole truth as told to me by Don Moises. Let's have something to eat. Tati has cooked us a tasty meal.'

'What is Tati doing here? I don't understand. What's she got to do with anything?'

'Tati has got everything to do with this. She is the granddaughter of Don Moises.'

'Sam sat up quickly and then lay down assailed by waves of dizziness. She tried again, this time slowly, and swung her legs over the edge of the bed, raising her head with caution. She saw that Alfredo had also sat up and was smiling at her, a beatific sort of smile, like a cat who had not only got the cream but had gone for a swim in it.

'Wasn't it marvellous?' he said. 'I never thought I'd live to see the day.'

'But what happened to the treasure? Did Wilson really try to kill us? What's Tati doing here? You must explain.'

'Let's have a cup of coffee, and I'll tell you the whole story.'

Sam got up and tottered outside to pee behind the house. She had a nasty taste in her mouth and felt as if she had the worst hangover in the world. She wavered over her bent legs and almost fell into the rubbish on the ground at the back of the building. After she had finished, she mounted the stairs into the house with her eyes screwed up against the bright sunlight, which poked through the fluffy clouds, assaulting her eyeballs.

Once they were seated at the crude wooden table, drinking cheap Nescafe, which was bitter and sticky with age, Tati gestured for Alfredo to speak. Alfredo nodded.

'Do you remember what I told you about Valverde, the Spanish soldier who married an Inca princess who led him to the treasure?'

'Yes, I do.'

'The Incas realised that the only way to keep the treasure's location a secret from the Spanish was to move it regularly. However, moving such a great amount of treasure was impractical, so they selected only the best and most precious objects for removal from the hoard. They chose a family of servants most loyal to the Inca to be the keepers of the treasure. He gave them the task of guarding it for posterity and of moving it any time it was in danger. You've met the descendants of this extended family.'

'The inhabitants of Arenas? I thought it was odd that there was an Indian village in the jungle. I know they prefer to live in the Andes.'

'Yes, you're right, but they moved the treasure here one hundred years ago when one of the treasure hunters got too close to the last hiding place before this one. The present leader of the family who guards the treasure is Don Moises. He'll end up with the other mummies in the vault where the treasure is hidden.

'He told me about this when he realised that he would have to move the treasure again. He'd heard about my work, and he knew that for me, the history was more important than the money. He offered me the chance of seeing the treasure if I promised never to look for it again. It's our heritage. Moises made me understand that we should let no one take it out of Sierramar. Not even Mike.'

'So, you let Moises drug us on condition that we got to see it? But how did he know what we were after when we came back? No one told anyone what we were doing...' Sam's voice trailed off, and she looked across the table at Tati.

'It was you, wasn't it, Tati? I saw you at the station at San Martin.'

Tati got the gist of what Sam was saying and nodded, laughing.

'I knew I had seen her. I knew it,' said Sam. 'But who told Tati? Oh, Marta, I guess.'

'Yes, she's not the most discrete person on the planet and couldn't keep the secret of our trip.'

Sam turned to Tati. 'Was it you?' she said. 'Did you get someone to steal my wallet?'

Tati laughed again.

'Now I understand,' said Alfredo. 'I should have

known that the police wouldn't give you your money back. Tati wanted to get to Riccuarte ahead of us so she arranged a delay.'

'But how did Wilson know about the treasure?' said Sam.

'I'm afraid that Wilson found out about the treasure from me. He already suspected something was going on. Marta is not good at keeping a secret. I drank too much and I put us all in danger. I'm so sorry.'

'Don't apologise. I'm not convinced he didn't know already.'

'Wilson thought that I would agree to kill you and split the treasure, but he must have decided to kill me too. When Don Moises heard from Tati that we were coming back to Arenas, he decided to move the treasure. Then Wilson asked him for help in disposing of us. Moises talked to me when he found out about Wilson, because he didn't want a man like that getting his hands on our Sierramarian heritage. A man called Segundo turned up in Riccuarte looking for Wilson. Segundo claimed that Wilson paid for the car crash that almost killed us in Calderon. Segundo told Doña Elodea that Wilson planned to kill us. Doña Elodea sent Carlos to warn Don Moises and to capture Wilson. I think Segundo works for Gloria's father who is no angel himself.'

Sam had an inkling. Her head swam.

'How did he escape?'

'I have no idea.'

'But I killed him,' she said.

'No, you didn't. He fell on a knife. It was suicide. You must forget it.'

'I don't know how, but I don't think we have a choice.'

'They pushed his body downstream in a canoe. He

will be found and buried. We owe you, Sam. You saved the treasure.'

'It was my fault we found it in the first place, but I'm glad,' she said, not knowing whether to laugh or cry. 'Where is the treasure now?'

'The villagers have taken it and are transporting it to one of the hiding places designated by the original Incas. They'll build a new village and guard it there. It's their sacred duty. They bury alive anyone who betrays them. Wilson is lucky. Although I suspect that whoever is looking for him may have a similar punishment in mind.'

'I think I'd better lie down for a minute,' said Sam.

'You do that. You'll be queasy today until the effect of the sleeping draught wears off. We'll leave tomorrow. Carlos is coming to pick us up in a canoe with Rijer.'

Sam lay back down on her bed. She was dog tired but there was something sharp sticking in her back. She was lying on her rucksack so she rolled sideways and pulled it out from under her. Throwing it to one side, she pulled the rough wool blanket over her body. Wilson was dead, but, somehow, she couldn't bring herself to care.

***

Alfredo, who had been watching her, lay down, too. Unlike her, he was still wide-eyed with wonder. He replayed the video he had recorded in his head of the treasure they had seen. He sighed a great big contented sigh.

***

Tati smiled and cleared away the coffee cups. She would have to get a new job after what had happened, but she had fulfilled her destiny as a descendant of the keepers of the treasure, and she was proud of her role in the drama. What a pity she couldn't tell Marta about it this time. Marta would have loved this story.

***

The driver arrived at San Lorenzo and picked up Gloria and Mike, who were waiting at the cantina to be rescued from their adventure. Mike felt an ache in his chest, and he knew that he had been lucky to survive his fright. Maybe it was time to go home to his long-suffering wife and stay there. He didn't have the money for the lifestyle he craved, but he had enough to make her happy. She wanted a quiet life.

He wouldn't decide while there was still the chance that Sam and Alfredo would find the treasure. *Would he be able to get it out of the country? How much would his share be? Maybe they could buy a house in the countryside and have some racehorses?*

***

Alone with her thoughts on the way to the airport, Gloria realised she was in love with Alfredo. He might be flawed, but he was loyal and honest. Something about him had appealed to her and she found it habit forming. He had a special charisma and sense of humour. Her mother would have called him a keeper. She was determined to make a go of it. She crossed her fingers and prayed that he and Sam got home in one piece.

***

Sam woke up early the next day and went down to the river to wash. She remembered what Alfredo had said about the crayfish, and to her horror, she found that it was true. No amount of rationalisation about molecules being recycled made her feel any better about it. She was now ready to go home. Living in the jungle for a while was exciting, but she was desperate for a hot shower and some tasty food that didn't have tuna or rice in it.

Tati cooked them a late breakfast, and Carlos arrived to finish the leftovers, hoovering them up in double-quick time. The rains had relented, and the river was less swollen and easier to navigate. They set off for Riccuarte through the muddy waters and made good time.

When they arrived, Doña Elodea was waiting at the riverbank with a basket full of empanadas. She was sitting on a log with the driver sent by Sanchez, who was helping himself to the delicious crunchy envelopes until she slapped his hand to show that he had eaten more than his share.

Sam and Alfredo said goodbye to Tati, who was staying on at Riccuarte for a few days, and set off for a final night in San Lorenzo. The pickup bucked and bounced along the road, making Sam feel sick after her ration of empanadas. They stayed in the hotel with the rustling beds. Sam was woken up by the occupants feasting on her blood again, but she couldn't offer any resistance and fell back into a heavy sleep.

Sam and Alfredo arrived at the airport in Calderon to be enveloped in kisses and hugs from an ecstatic Gloria. Sam was tempted to tell her to 'get a room' when her welcome of Alfredo went over the top. Gloria did not take them home, but instead, they went straight to the hospital where Mike had been installed in a private room hooked up to a drip.

Mike was under observation while the doctors decided what had caused the attack of angina, although

Sam had heard from Gloria that it was an attack of heroics, making her giggle in complicity. Sam let Alfredo tell Mike the story of the still lost treasure of the Incas and its amazing history. The result would satisfy Mike, but not Edward. There was no proof of their amazing story. Mike would lose Edward as an investor if he didn't believe the incredible story.

Mike sat up in bed when they arrived. His face was animated.

'Did you find it? Are we rich?' he said

'We found it but we aren't rich. Alfredo will tell you all about it.'

Sam hugged him gingerly, trying not to get tangled up with the tubes. She and Gloria left Alfredo to fill Mike in on their adventure and went back to the Avenida Miranda where Marta was waiting to be updated on the gossip. They would not tell her about Tati, who had disappeared into the jungle with the treasure keepers and would not be back to Calderon.

Later that evening Sam emptied her rucksack, separating the notebook, camera, penknife and other bric-à-brac from the sweet papers and other unidentifiable rubbish at the bottom of her bag. She searched all the pockets and shook them out. There was something stuck in one pocket. It was small and heavy, and made of metal with several sharp spikey bits sticking out, which had caught in the rucksack's material.

She fiddled around loosening the fabric around it and the object came out. It was a small gold brooch in the shape of a serpent. The fine detail and exquisite craftsmanship indicated that it was from the Inca treasure. How had it got into her rucksack? Who had put it there and why? Someone had done this with a purpose, perhaps as a gift, perhaps as a reminder to keep the secret.

Sam ran her fingers over the brooch. It was so beautiful it brought a lump to her throat. Astonished and sad at the same time, she knew she couldn't keep it. Someone needed it more than she did.

The next morning, they allowed Mike to leave the hospital and came back to the flat a chastened man.

'Oh God, what am I going to tell Edward? He'll never believe the truth. It's too far-fetched. I need him on my side if I ever want to have funding for another project. If only I had some sort of evidence.'

'I think I can help you with that,' said Sam, 'if you keep me in mind as a possible employee.'

'Don't fuck with me, Sam. I'm a broken man.'

'What makes you think that I'm messing you about? Shut your eyes and open your hand.'

Mike stretched out his hand. Sam made him wait for a few seconds and then dropped the brooch into his palm. Mike gasped in amazement as he opened his eyes.

'What the fuck? It's the serpent cipher, right? Where did you get it?'

'I don't know. I discovered it in my rucksack. Maybe Don Moises put it there?'

'It's from the treasure? I can't believe it. This will be worth the world to Edward.'

'You want to keep it, then?'

'Is that a real question? What do you want for it?'

'Well, if you're going home, I wondered if I could stay on in the flat until the lease runs out?'

'I suppose you need some money, too?'

'I was getting to that. Some extra money would be nice. My bank account hasn't received any money from you yet.'

Mike's face was a picture.

'Jesus, I forgot. I'll ring them now. You've learned something since you came to work for me, Sam,' he said. 'You drive a hard bargain.'

'I learned from the best,' she said.

***

Sam looked out at the view over Calderon in a pensive mood. What had she gained from her adventure? They would never take the treasure from its caretakers. Alfredo had convinced her that it was where it belonged. And she was one of the few people who had seen it. The sight of the treasure would always stay with her and give her joy.

Wilson's body, along with his rucksack, gun and identification card washed up in San Lorenzo causing a momentary ripple in the news media. The police looked up from their game of poker long enough to declare his death unexplained and probably accidental. His wife made a brief show of grief, and married her lover after a short period of mourning.

Sam had no idea what she would do next, but she could wait. Perhaps she would stay in Sierramar longer and do some real geology. The country was full of mineral deposits especially gold ones. As Mike didn't want to continue, there were plenty of other companies sniffing around for exploration opportunities, and a cheap English-speaking geologist who could also communicate in reasonable Spanish might be what they were looking for.

She had also learned to appreciate another culture and what it took to work in one. Her survival in the jungle convinced her about her ability to cope with adversity and to rise above it with the help of others. Gloria had demonstrated that it was possible to contain courage behind a facade of organised chaos. Sam still hid behind the wall around her heart but Alfredo and Gloria were proof that love conquered all. And then there was Simon. Not an easy subject. Not one she wanted to dwell on yet.

The intercom buzzed, echoing in the half-empty flat. She went to pick it up.

'Hey *gringa*, just because Mike has gone home doesn't mean you have to be a hermit. *Vamos*.'

'Where are we going?'

'Who cares?'

Thank you for reading my book. If you enjoyed it, please take a moment to leave me a review at your favourite retailer.

The Next Book in the Series is Hitler's Finger.

You can stay up to date with new releases and offers

by signing up to my Facebook page: PJSkinnerAuthor

Other Books by PJ Skinner

Hitler's Finger - Book 2
The second book in the Sam Harris Series sees the return of our heroine Sam Harris to Sierramar to help her friend Gloria track down her boyfriend, the historian, Alfredo Vargas.

A missing historian, a vengeful journalist, some unhinged Nazis and a possible pregnancy. Has Sam gone too far on her return to Sierramar? Historian, Alfredo Vargas, and journalist, Saul Rosen, have disappeared while searching for a group of fugitive Nazi war criminals. Sam and her friend Gloria join forces to find them and are soon caught up in a dangerous mystery. A man is murdered, and a sinister stranger follows their every move. Even the government is involved. Can they find Alfredo before he disappears for good?

The background to the book is the presence of Nazi war criminals in South America which was often ignored by locals who had fascist sympathies during World War II. Themes such as tacit acceptance of fascism, and local collaboration with fugitives from justice are examined and developed in the context of Sam's constant ability to find herself in the middle of an adventure or mystery. Sam's home life provides a contrast to her adventures and feeds her need to escape. Her continuing attachment to an unsuitable boyfriend is about to be tested to the limit

The Star of Simbako - Book 3
The third book in the Sam Harris Series sees Sam Harris on her first contract to West Africa to Simbako, a land of tribal kingdoms and voodoo.

A fabled diamond, a jealous voodoo priestess, disturbing cultural practices. What could possibly go wrong?

Nursing a broken heart, Sam Harris goes to Simbako to work in the diamond fields of Fona. She is soon involved with a cast of characters who are starring in their own soap opera, a dangerous mix of superstition, cultural practices and ignorance (mostly her own). Add a love triangle and a jealous woman who wants her dead and Sam is in trouble again. Where is the Star of Simbako? Is Sam going to survive the chaos?

This book is based on visits made to the Paramount Chiefdoms of West Africa. Despite being nominally Christian communities, Voodoo practices are still part of daily life out there. This often leads to conflicts of interest. Combine this with the horrific ritual of FGM and it makes for a potent cocktail of conflicting loyalties. Sam is pulled into this life by her friend, Adanna, and soon finds herself involved in goings on that she doesn't understand.

The Pink Elephants

The fourth book in the Sam Harris Series presents Sam with her sternest test yet as she goes to Africa to fix a failing project. A failing project, beleaguered pygmies and endangered elephants. Can Sam save them all or will she have to choose?

Sam gets a call in the middle of the night that takes her to the Masaibu project in eastern Lumbono. The project is collapsing under the weight of corruption and chicanery engendered by management, both in country and back on the main company board. Sam has to navigate murky waters to get it back on course, not helped by interference from people who want her to fail. When poachers invade the elephant sanctuary next door, her problems multiply. Can Sam protect the elephants and save the project or will she have to choose? The day to day problems encountered by Sam in her work are typical of any project manager in the Congo which has been rent apart by warring factions, leaving the local population frightened and rootless. Elephants with pink tusks do exist, but not in the area where the project is based. They are being slaughtered by poachers in Gabon for the Chinese market and will soon be extinct, so I have put the guns in the hands of those responsible for the massacre of these defenceless animals. The themes of this novel are impossible choices and brave decisions.

The Bonita Protocol - Book 5
An erratic boss. Suspicious results. Stock market shenanigans. Can Sam Harris expose the scam before they silence her? It's 1996. Geologist Sam Harris has been around the block, but she's prone to nostalgia, so she snatches the chance to work in Sierramar, her old stomping ground. But she never expected to be working for a company that is breaking all the rules.

When the analysis results from drill samples are suspiciously high, Sam makes a decision that puts her life in peril. Can she blow the lid on the conspiracy before they shut her up for good?

The Bonita Protocol is the fifth book in the Sam Harris Adventure series. If you like gutsy heroines, complex twists and turns, and heart pounding action, then you'll love PJ Skinner's thrilling novel.

Digging Deeper - Book 6
A feisty geologist working in the diamond fields of West Africa is kidnapped by rebels. Can she survive

the ordeal or will this adventure be her last? It's 1998. Geologist Sam Harris is desperate for money so she takes a job in a tinpot mining company working in war-torn Tamazia. But she never expected to be kidnapped by blood thirsty rebels.

Working in Gemsite was never going to be easy with its culture of misogyny and corruption. Her boss, the notorious Adrian Black is engaged in a game of cat and mouse with the government over taxation. Just when Sam makes a breakthrough, the camp is overrun by rebels and Sam is taken captive.
Will anyone bother to rescue her, and will she still be alive if they do?

Concrete Jungle - Book 7 (series end)
Armed with an MBA, Sam Harris is storming the City But has she swapped one jungle for another?
Forging a new career was never going to be easy, and Sam Harris soon discovers she has not escaped from the culture of misogyny and corruption that blighted her field career.
Her heroic past is revealed at a mining drinks party, and she finally achieves the acceptance she has always craved. But being one of the boys is not the panacea she expected. When her due diligence uncovers a scam, she is presented with the stark choice of compromising her principles to keep her new position, or exposing the truth behind the façade.
Will she finally get what she wants or was it all a mirage?

The Green Family Saga
Rebel Green – Book 1
Relationships fracture when two families find
themselves caught up in the Irish Troubles.
The Green family move to Kilkenny from England in
1969, at the beginning of the conflict in Northern
Ireland. They rent a farmhouse on the outskirts of
town, and make friends with the O'Connor family
next door. Not every member of the family adapts
easily to their new life, and their differing approaches
lead to misunderstandings and friction. Despite this,
the bonds between the family members deepen with
time.

Perturbed by the worsening violence in the North
threatening to invade their lives, the children make a
pact never to let the troubles come between them. But
promises can be broken, with tragic consequences for
everyone.

If you like family sagas in an authentic Irish
setting, Rebel Green will thrill and move you in equal
measure. Buy it now

Africa Green – Book 2
Will a white chimp save its rescuers or get them
killed?
Journalist Isabella Green travels to Sierra Leone, a
country emerging from civil war, to write an article
about a chimp sanctuary. Animals that need saving
are her obsession, and she can't resist getting
involved with the project, which is on the verge of
bankruptcy. She forms a bond with local boy, Ten,
and army veteran, Pete, to try and save it.

When they rescue a rare white chimp from a
village frequented by a dangerous rebel splinter
group, the resulting media interest could save the

sanctuary. But the rebel group have not signed the cease fire. They believe the voodoo power of the white chimp protects them from bullets, and they are determined to take it back so they can storm the capital.

When Pete and Ten go missing, only Isabella stands in the rebels' way. Her love for the chimps unlocks the fighting spirit within her. Can she save the sanctuary or will she die trying?

All of the books are available in paperback.

Please go to your favourite online retailer to order them.

About the Author

The author has spent 30 years working as an exploration geologist managing remote sites and doing due diligence of projects in more than thirty countries. During this time, she has been collecting tall tales and real-life experiences which inspired her to write the Sam Harris Series chronicling the adventures of a female geologist as a pioneer in a hitherto exclusively male world. PJ has worked in various countries in South America and Africa in remote, strange and often dangerous places and loved every minute of it despite encountering her fair share of misogyny and other perils. She is now writing these fact-based adventure books from the relative safety of London but still travels all over the world collecting data for her writing.

The Sam Harris Series is perfect for lovers of classic adventure, and has a unique viewpoint provided by Sam, a female interloper in a male world, as she struggles with alien cultures and failed relationships.

The author is also working on two other new books, one of which, Rebel Green, is based on her childhood in Ireland.

Connect with the Author
If you would like updates on the latest in the Sam Harris Series or to contact the author with your questions please go to the following link: www.pjskinner.com